A PRINCE'S CARESS

"That isn't a proper saddle," I declared. I had always ridden astride. But the horse master patiently explained how I should position myself, and helped me hook my leg around the off-center horn of the sidesaddle. I was sure I would fall off.

Verdant fields stretched before us. Gulls screeched as they circled overhead, and crisp salty air filled my lungs as the sea tossed endlessly against the rocks and cliffs. When Michael dismounted in a grassy meadow, he untied the wicker lunch hamper from his saddle and beckoned to me.

I sat on the mare like a frozen statue. *How did one dismount from this contraption?* Finally, I managed to unhook my leg, but still I could not move. Michael held up his arms to me, and I gratefully slid into them, my hands braced on his biceps.

His face was inches from mine. His grip on my waist tightened; his head turned slightly; his lips parted. One arm went around my waist, the other over my shoulder, so his hand could cradle my head. His lips moved over mine as he crushed me to the length of his hard body. Without reservation, I yielded to him. My hands moved up his arms and over his wide shoulders.

The world spun and twirled like a dizzy toy top in my head. I had found my prince, and he loved me . . .

A Memorable Collection of Regency Romances

BY ANTHEA MALCOLM AND VALERIE KING

THE COUNTERFEIT HEART   (3425, $3.95/$4.95)
by Anthea Malcolm
Nicola Crawford was hardly surprised when her cousin's betrothed disappeared on some mysterious quest. Anyone engaged to such an unromantic, but handsome man was bound to run off sooner or later. Nicola could never entrust her heart to such a conventional, but so deucedly handsome man. . . .

THE COURTING OF PHILIPPA   (2714, $3.95/$4.95)
by Anthea Malcolm
Miss Philippa was a very successful author of romantic novels. Thus she was chagrined to be snubbed by the handsome writer Henry Ashton whose own books she admired. And when she learned he considered love stories completely beneath his notice, she vowed to teach him a thing or two about the subject of love. . . .

THE WIDOW'S GAMBIT   (2357, $3.50/$4.50)
by Anthea Malcolm
The eldest of the orphaned Neville sisters needed a chaperone for a London season. So the ever-resourceful Livia added several years to her age, invented a deceased husband, and became the respectable Widow Royce. She was certain she'd never regret abandoning her girlhood until she met dashing Nicholas Warwick. . . .

A DARING WAGER   (2558, $3.95/$4.95)
by Valerie King
Ellie Dearborne's penchant for gaming had finally led her to ruin. It seemed like such a lark, wagering her devious cousin George that she would obtain the snuffboxes of three of society's most dashing peers in one month's time. She could easily succeed, too, were it not for that exasperating Lord Ravenworth. . . .

THE WILLFUL WIDOW   (3323, $3.95/$4.95)
by Valerie King
The lovely young widow, Mrs. Henrietta Harte, was not all inclined to pursue the sort of romantic folly the persistent King Brandish had in mind. She had to concentrate on marrying off her penniless sisters and managing her spendthrift mama. Surely Mr. Brandish could fit in with her plans somehow . . .

BEVERLY C. WARREN

THE HAUNTED HEIRESS OF WYNDCLIFFE MANOR

ZEBRA BOOKS
KENSINGTON PUBLISHING CORP.

ZEBRA BOOKS

are published by

Kensington Publishing Corp.
475 Park Avenue South
New York, NY 10016

First printing: September, 1992

Printed in the United States of America

One

Cream puffs with powdered sugar, eclairs, jam tarts, napoleons, and cream tarts with a dollop of raspberry jam in the middle. How could I ever forget those luscious cream tarts? Even though I had never had one, the cream tarts were the first to catch my eye as I gazed through the bakery window. I could have stood there for hours, imagining what each pastry might taste like. But the baker's wife came out with a broom and swatted me away from the front of the shop. I didn't like her. When I was well beyond the reach of the broom, I stuck my tongue out at her.

I soon forgot about the baker's wife, but not the delectable pastries in the window. Now I concentrated all my thoughts on them, as if the very sight of them could erase the agony of my body. I wished I had never turned fourteen.

Oh, how I longed for the time when I was a trapper. Though I sat in the dark for eight hours a day, all I had to do was keep the flaps fanning air into the coal mine shafts.

Now I was working in the mine shafts, pulling corves (or carts) of coal up the steep mine passages on all fours like a donkey. The tunnel was only three feet high, less in places. That was one reason for crouching down. The cart had to be pulled along the steep, rough ground, and I needed my hands to pull myself along. That was another reason. Sometimes my hands would sink in over my wrists, in the mire created by dampness and those who couldn't control their bladders.

A belt around my waist was connected to chains which passed between my legs and, in turn, hooked to the cart. I hated that most of all, for the chains would wear away the material of my trousers and expose my thighs. Bad enough I was half-naked, with my chest bare and my hair stuffed into a cap so I'd look like a boy, as were the rest of the girls down in the mine. The owners didn't want the authorities knowing they had young girls working the mines. Most of the girls hadn't started to develop yet, but I had. While down in the mines I didn't think too much about it, however when I came out of the mine, I was subjected to the teasing of the boys and the ridicule of the girls. And I didn't like the way some of the older men looked at me. I began to wear my older brother's tattered shirt. I slipped into it at lunchtime, and wore it to and from work at the colliery.

On top of everything, I now had to work twelve hours a day. But worst of all, I was lonely. I talked different from everyone else at work and at the row houses where we lived. I couldn't understand why I sounded so different. But then there were a lot of things I didn't understand.

I waited to walk home with my sisters. Though they seldom talked to me and ignored me for the most part, at least it was company.

Sarah was a strapping girl of nineteen and smoked a pipe. She loaded coal onto the railroad cars. Dressed in clogs, trousers, a short sacking apron, and pit bonnet, she was almost as filthy as I. I was practically black.

6

Coal dust settled everywhere, even seeping into one's pores.

Sarah and another sister, Alice, were in animated conversation as they walked toward home. Alice was tall and large-boned. She wore a cotton-padded bonnet, blue-striped shirt, patched corduroy trousers, and a ragged double-breasted waistcoat. Her feet were encased in leather-topped clogs, whose wooden soles were capped with iron around the edges, much like horseshoes.

"Come along, moppet," Sarah angrily called to me. Neither of them broke the stride of their long, powerful legs. I had to run to keep up with them.

I wondered how long it would be before I attained their height and size. All the Boothes were big-boned, tall, chunky people. Except my brother, Charlie. But he was only twelve. Henry, another brother, was fifteen and beginning to get the hefty muscles of our father, Frank Boothe. Even Maggie, another sister, was blossoming into a strapping girl of sixteen. I guess I was the runt of the litter. My bones were small, and I was not nearly as tall as the rest of them. Their heights hovered between five-ten and six feet. I was only five foot. I still had some growing to do though.

All the Boothes worked at the colliery, except Ma. She had all she could do at home, what with laundry, cooking, and trying to keep the tiny row house clean. Da was very particular about having a clean house. I don't know why. He was in a drunken stupor most of the time. With his blurred vision, I don't know how he could see if the place was clean or not.

After work we all went to the small backyard, where a pitcher of water, soap, and a basin sat on a crate. We had to wash our hands and face before going into the house for supper. By the time everyone was washed and seated at the supper table, it was almost eight o'clock.

"Where's the bloody meat in this hot pot?" Da fished the ladle around in the large bowl of potatoes, beef, and onions which had been boiled together for hours.

"There's some at the bottom of the bowl, Frank," Ma answered wearily.

He scooped the meat and potatoes onto his plate grudgingly, then passed the bowl to his oldest son, Henry. The bowl was then passed to Charlie, then Ma, then the older girls. I was the last to get the bowl, which now contained no meat and only one potato. I scooped it onto my plate along with a few ladles of the watery gravy, in which I soaked a hunk of stale bread. The same ritual was followed every night. Some nights even Da didn't get any meat. Bits of bones or fatty bacon were used to flavor the gravy.

I reached for another piece of bread. My hand felt the sting of the long birch rod Da kept by the side of his chair.

"You not be earning enough, girlie, to have two pieces of bread," Da boomed, then coughed.

I sometimes wondered if Da were deaf, for he always shouted. I got a sympathetic glance from Ma, but she said nothing. She never said anything that might hint she was crossing or defying Da. He had a mean temper, which constantly bubbled just below the surface. Once in a while, Henry would speak up. He'd feel the bite of the birch for it. Whenever he did get the birch rod across his backside, murderous hatred spewed from his eyes. Da certainly didn't endear himself to his children.

One room served as kitchen, dining room, and all purpose room. Ma and Da had their bedroom. The rest of us shared the other bedroom. We four girls were separated from the two boys by a thin blanket draped over twine. We were too tired at night to really care.

As a rule we went to bed shortly after supper, except for Ma and Da. I would lie there and listen to my sisters

8

gossip about other girls and men at the colliery. They never included me in their talks. Perhaps they thought I was still too much of a baby. My brothers taunted and teased me, which was better than being totally ignored.

Everyone was up at four in the morning. Ma was up even earlier to have breakfast ready and the lunches.

After a breakfast of bread fried in bacon grease or watery porridge, we trotted off to the colliery, lunch pails in hand. The girls were way ahead of me. Da took a different route. I lagged behind with Charlie and Henry. Henry was in a black mood. He got a switching at breakfast for not sitting straight enough to suit Da.

"I'm taking me to Newcastle soon," Henry grumbled his thoughts aloud.

"What will you do there?" I asked, half-skipping to keep up with them.

"Get me a job on the railroads."

"Why?" I asked.

"Da's starting to use that switch on me too much."

"You're too young, Henry," Charlie said.

"I'll lie about my age."

"Can I go with you?" Charlie pleaded.

"No."

"Why?"

" 'Cause I don't know where I'll be living, and I can't be taking care of you."

"Have you ever been to Newcastle, Henry?" I asked.

"Once." His face brightened. "A big city, it is. So many ships going up and down the River Tyne. And churches whose spires seem to touch the sky. An ancient donjon—a castlekeep to you two—still stands tall, square, and black as coal itself. But the buildings along the riverbank are dim and dingy."

"Did you see the trains?" Charlie asked, his eyes wide in boyish wonder.

"Tracks and tracks, all over the place. Trains from

everywhere . . . Scotland, and Wales. I never saw so many trains. Imagine me, Henry Boothe, steering one of those steam monsters and pulling the whistle. Or I might take meself on one of those big ships and see the world. I might even go to China," Henry declared.

"Where's that?" Charlie asked.

"I dunno. Heard one of the men at the colliery mention it."

"How will you live until you find work?" I asked.

"I'll find a way. You can count on it."

Reaching the colliery as the sun began to make its appearance in the sky, we separated, each going to our respective work areas. I took off my shirt and wrapped it around my lunch pail. When they started to load the railroad cars, fine, suffocating, black dust would fill the air, almost obscuring the sun. Wrapping the shirt around the lunch pail helped to keep some of the dust from filtering into it.

I got into my harness of chains and hooked the other end to the cart. At least down in the shafts I couldn't hear the din above me. The hissing and chugging of trains. The rattle of coal going down the chute to slam into the coal cars. Though it was dark, and the air was foul, I had peace and quiet. I crawled down the shaft into the belly of the coal mine.

Another twelve-hour workday had begun.

"Did you hear about Polly Nelson?" Maggie asked in a half-whisper, as the four of us settled down in bed.

"Who's Polly Nelson?" Sarah asked.

"She's a greaser like me. Anyway, she's getting married. She's sixteen, like me."

"Who's she marrying?" came Alice's voice.

"An old man. I think he's almost forty. Horrid old man with pockmarks all over his face. Always yelling at

10

people with his filthy mouth. I don't envy Polly one bit. She'll have a time of it, she will."

"Why is she marrying him then, Maggie?" Sarah asked.

"Dunno."

Oh, how I wished they'd shut up so I could go to sleep. The day had been a horrid one. I had started my monthlies, and pulling the cart filled with coal had aggravated my cramps to such a point, I felt like screaming. Then it started.

The wall (against which our bed rested) shook as a heavy object slammed against it. No one had to tell us what that object was. It was Ma. Da was in his let's-beat-someone-up mood. Ma was his favorite target. I prayed she wouldn't start crying. That seemed to enrage him further. But she did. And, between heavy coughing, he started his usual string of curses.

Between my fatigue and the horrid scene in the next room, I wanted to cry. But no tears came. My sisters and brothers were as still as cats hunting prey. Sleep was a long while in coming.

Maggie pushed me out of bed. I thumped down on the floor.

"You didn't have to be so rough, Maggie," Sarah said without much conviction, as she and Alice climbed out of bed. "Are you hurt, moppet?"

I shook my head weakly and scrambled to my feet. My sisters and brothers always called me moppet. Da called me girlie. Only Ma called me by my proper name—Jane.

"It's four o'clock. We only have a half hour to dress and eat. She'd sleep all day if you let her. It's the best way to get her up and awake," Maggie declared.

I didn't have much to put on, so I was dressed first and the first one in the kitchen.

"Can I help, Ma?"

11

"No, Jane. Thank you anyway."

When she turned to face me, I saw the purple bruises on her face and the red welts on her arms. I winced at the thought of the beating she must have received.

"Sit you down, Jane."

I obeyed in silence. Soon everyone was seated. Breakfast was the usual fried bread and hot tea. I liked it better than porridge. About halfway through breakfast, my head started to nod, my eyelids leaden with weariness. I sat up straight when the birch rod came down on the top of my head.

"What's the matter with you, girlie?" Da bellowed, then coughed and spat phlegm on the floor.

"I'm still sleepy," I answered softly.

"Well, you'd best be getting over it, girlie. Today's payday, and I'll be needing your share in me cup."

I hated that cup he kept on the mantel. We all dropped a share of our wages in it, while he took the rest of our money. That cup was his pub money. Periodically, he'd empty it and take himself to the pub. When he'd come home, he was drunker than usual and in a really foul mood.

"We're all tired. You kept us up half the night with your screaming and hollering," Henry spewed at Da.

Da's pallid, fleshy face turned livid with rage. His watery blue eyes narrowed as he reached down for his birch rod. For a big man, he was around the table with lightning speed. He pulled Henry's collar and yanked him from his seat. Henry was soundly thrashed across his back and the backs of his legs.

"Defy me, will you? You're a little piece of snot. I'll be teaching you not to give me your lip." Da raised and lowered the switch with such speed and force, it whistled through the air.

"Please stop, Frank. His back is starting to bleed," Ma pleaded, on the verge of tears.

12

"Stay out of this, Mary, or you'll be getting what's for," he shouted at her.

"The lad won't be able to go to work if you keep at it," Ma claimed.

Ma had said the magic words. The switch stopped in midair, and Da let Henry go. When Da sat back down, he was breathing heavily, his barrel chest going up and down like bellows before he surrendered to a coughing fit.

Henry's expresson displayed no pain, no anger. Nothing. But there was something in his eyes that frightened me. The kind of emptiness that is fertile ground for growing evil.

An ominous silence hovered between the boys and me as we marched to work. Coming to the spot where we usually parted company, Charlie held back.

"At lunch time, meet me at the first coal car, moppet."

I nodded and he dashed off.

As I crawled back and forth with my cart, empty then full, I wondered what Charlie wanted to talk to me about. Never before had he requested a private conversation with me. Why now? And Henry concerned me. He was like a boiling kettle, whose lid would pop off at any minute. I had the feeling that he would like to take an axe to Da and chop him up in tiny bits. It scared me. With my thoughts bouncing between Charlie and Henry, the morning slid by.

I unwrapped my lunch pail and put the shirt on. Grabbing the lunch pail, I headed for the railroad cars. When I got there, Charlie was nowhere in sight. Was Charlie playing a prank on me? If so, I didn't like it one bit. I had used up five minutes of my lunch time walking over to the railroad car. I was about to stomp away when I heard Charlie's voice.

"Up here, moppet."

I looked up and saw Charlie sitting atop a coal car, his legs dangling over the edge. Clutching my lunch pail in one hand, I clambered to the top.

"What did you want to talk to me about, Charlie?" I plunked down next to him, letting my legs dangle over the edge.

"Henry."

"What about Henry?"

"He's really mad this time. I could hear his teeth grinding last night, while Da was giving Ma what for. He kept muttering 'I'll kill him. I'll kill him.' Do you think he'd really do Da in?"

"Da's still bigger and stronger than Henry. I don't think Henry would try anything like that."

"He could do it while Da's in his cups."

I shrugged and opened my lunch pail. Bread and butter. A jar of cold tea with no milk. Always the same. What I wouldn't give for a bit of jam on the bread. For some reason, I couldn't get used to eating with my hands coal black. Charlie took it as a matter of course. I looked around as I munched on the bread and butter. The day was humid, making the coal dust hang in the air to create a grayish veil in the atmosphere. Breathing was difficult on days like this.

With the rare exception of a yellow, green, or red scarf, the people and the surroundings were various shades of gray sinking into black. My world was bleak indeed. A hopeless mood seemed to come on me with more and more frequency.

"Do you think Henry will really go to Newcastle?"

"What?" I hadn't been listening. In fact, I had almost forgotten that Charlie was sitting next to me.

"Why don't you listen to me, moppet? You never listen to any of us. Always off in some fantasy world of your own. I wanted to know if you thought Henry really would go to Newcastle."

"I think he's more likely to go to Newcastle than kill Da."

"Do you think he'd take me with him if I pleaded?"

"No. He'll have enough trouble watching out for himself, without having to watch out for you, too."

"I'm going to ask him again anyway."

"It'll do you no good."

"I don't care. If he won't be taking me, maybe I'll be taking meself there."

"Do that and you'll probably be taken by a press gang. They'll make you a slave on some foul ship."

"How do you know that?"

"I hear things, Charlie. I hear things."

"At least they wouldn't be beating me on a ship."

"They'll probably beat you more."

Charlie stopped chewing and stared straight ahead. "Maybe I won't go to Newcastle. Maybe I'll go inland."

"Where?"

"I dunno."

My tea and bread and butter gone, I started to close my lunch pail, when I noticed a small object wrapped in a scrap of cloth. I took it out and unwrapped it. To my sheer delight, I found a piece of hardened treacle. Once I started down the shaft, I could pop it in my mouth. The taste of molasses would last for most of the afternoon.

"What you got there, moppet?" Charlie asked, as he peered down into my hand.

"Treacle. Don't you have one?"

He searched through his lunch pail. He turned it upside down and shook it. Nothing.

"I don't have any treacle. How come *you* got treacle?"

I shrugged. He snatched it from my hand and jumped off the coal car to the ground. He stumbled once, but was soon running off.

15

The distance to the ground was too far for me to jump. After tossing my lunch pail to the ground, I climbed down as swiftly as I could, then raced after Charlie. I was bound and determined to get my treacle back. It was the first treat I had had in a long time, and I wanted to be the one to savor it.

I was swifter than Charlie. He was still growing and a bit awkward on his gangly legs. I was closing the distance between us, when he darted behind the head man's shack.

Being wary of going anywhere near the head man, I came to a sudden halt. He might dock my wages for running around instead of being in my own work area. Besides, lunch time was just about over. If my pay was docked, I would surely get a sound thrashing from Da. I thought about the treacle, and my mouth watered. I weighed the treacle against a thrashing. The treacle won out. At top speed I ran toward the shack.

As I rounded the corner, I slammed into the hard body of a man. He grabbed my shoulders and held me tight at arm's length.

"Well, well. What do we have here?"

I looked up at the tall, broad-shouldered man. He was the handsomest man I had ever seen. Thick chestnut hair, eyes like chunks of coal. A wide mouth in a clean-shaven face. A partrician nose. The honed planes of his face were well proportioned. He smiled down at me, causing deep furrows to crease around his mouth. He was the prince I had seen in a picture book and always dreamed about. I wondered if he lived in a castle and rode a white horse.

"Cat got your tongue, lad?" he asked in a deep baritone voice.

Suddenly I was ashamed of my filthy appearance, my patched and tattered clothes. I didn't speak. I didn't want him to know I was a girl. I stared at him blatantly.

I wanted to memorize every detail of his handsome face. The loss of the treacle meant nothing now. My prince was real, not just a picture in a book.

"Something wrong, Mr. Savage?" the head man asked, as he came out of the shack. His eyes then locked on me. "What are you doing here? I'll see your wages are docked for this. Now get back to work," he screamed at me.

"Don't be hard on the lad, Mr. Hardy. Sometimes the exuberance of youth is hard to contain, especially with boys."

He let go of my shoulders and I ran back to the coal car. My lunch pail was gone, along with my tea jar. The loss along with the docking of my wages would surely earn me more than a thrashing. I'll be getting a sound whipping. Somehow I didn't care. Mr. Savage. The name echoed in my head like a sweet love song. I wondered what his first name was. Something princely, I thought.

Down the shaft I went. As I crawled back and forth, the image of Mr. Savage's face glowed in the dark before me. Perhaps he was a new foreman at the colliery. The thought excited me. If I could catch a glimpse of him every day, my fantasies would be steadily fueled.

With thoughts of Mr. Savage crowding my mind, I never felt the strain on my legs nor the chains cutting into me.

As usual my sisters chatted among themselves, and ignored me as we walked home. This time I was glad, for I wanted to wallow in thoughts of Mr. Savage.

Sensing something was wrong, I frowned. A picture of a prince on a white horse in front of a castle? In a book? There were no books at home. No one in the family could read or write, which was true of most everyone in the row houses. How could I have seen a picture of a prince? Borrowed a book? From whom? No one in the neighborhood could read, much less afford to spend hard earned money on a book. I struggled to remember where I had seen the picture. But it was all a blank.

My dilemma vanished when we arrived at home. Da was standing outside, a fierce scowl on his face, his hands curled into fists.

"Me cup is empty! Which one of you bloody snots stole me pub money?"

Two

A terrible silence hovered in the house as we filed in. When it was apparent that Henry was not among us, Da allowed us to wash and sit at the supper table. All heads were bowed to stare at empty plates. Not Da's. His head swiveled to stare at the rear door, as he held his empty cup in his meaty hand. He had made it clear that no supper was to be served until Henry made an appearance.

If Henry did appear, which I doubted, the ensuing scene would make swallowing food impossible. Ma was struggling to keep her tears from trickling down. Her pasty face was ashen, her brown hair streaked with gray. I had once heard Sarah say that Ma, in her mid-thirties, looked like an old woman. I was determined never to marry. Of course, if Mr. Savage asked me, I'd say yes in a wink.

Fingers of darkness crept into the house. Ma unobtrusively rose to light a single oil lamp. She placed it on the table, then resumed her seat. Da's chilling voice cut through the stillness.

"All of you put your wages in me cup," he ordered, his voice frighteningly low.

One by one we rose and put our wages in his cup. I

19

hoped he was too agitated to notice the shortage in my wage. He said nothing when I dribbled my coins into the cup. When the last of the coins were in the cup, he upturned it into his hand and shoved the money into his pocket without counting it. He pushed his chair back so roughly, it made a scraping noise on the floor. He got up and left the house.

In the frenzy of the lost cup money and Henry's disappearance, coming home without my lunch pail and short wages went unnoticed by Da. I knew Ma would fix me another pail without mentioning the loss to Da. In a way I was thankful to Henry.

Ma quickly went to the stove and spooned out the cold porridge. Bad enough when it was hot. But cold? I kept telling myself that at least it was food. I hated the porridge even more thinking about Da taking our wages and going to the pub, where he'd probably feast on steak and kidney pie, then swill down gin until the money was gone.

"Where's Henry, Ma?" Alice asked.

"I wish I knew."

"Do you think he took Da's money?"

"I dunno. He might have come in the front way while I was in back doing laundry." Ma slowly shook her head in despair.

"He took it, all right. And I know where he went." A sunny smile formed on Charlie's youthful face. All eyes shifted to him.

"Where is he, Charlie?" Sarah asked.

"Newcastle."

"What makes you say that?"

"He told me he was going to Newcastle. He took the money to tide him over 'til he found himself a position. He's going to be a railroad man." Charlie straightened up in his chair, proud of his brother's independence and bravery.

"He'll be back," Maggie declared.

"No, he won't," Charlie almost shouted. I don't think he wanted his hero to show any sign of weakness. Silence.

I helped Ma clear the table.

"Jane, I found a scrap of corduroy you can use for a patch on your pants. I thought it might wear better than cotton."

"Thanks, Ma. I'll do it tomorrow while everyone's at church."

"That's a good girl, Jane."

I was sound asleep when it started. Slam! The thin wall shuddered.

"He's your rotten, bloody son!" Da's voice was thick with drink.

Slam.

"If he ever comes back here, I'll kill him."

Slam.

"Taking me money like the sneak thief he is."

Slam.

It seemed like hours before the ranting stopped. When it finally did, I could hear Charlie softly crying into his pillow. I went back to sleep.

Taking her frustrations out on me, Maggie pushed me out of bed. I waited until the three of them climbed out, then I crawled back in to sleep some more. Sunday morning everyone except me went to church. I didn't have a proper frock to wear to church like my older sisters did.

The house was empty when I finally got up and dressed. A frying pan with bacon grease—Da always ate the bacon—was on the stove. On the table two slices of bread rested on a cracked plate. Two slices! If Da had seen that, Ma would have paid dearly for her

21

extravagance. For some reason, Ma seemed to favor me. Perhaps it was because the other girls paid little attention to her, and treated her like a slave. Ma paid little attention to the boys, as though she knew they would soon leave, and so she didn't want to become too attached to them.

After I cleaned up the kitchen, I took my trousers off and set about patching them. That done, I peeled potatoes and onions for our Sunday dinner, then prepared the carrots. Ma always took care of the meat. The beef shanks were already cooking on the back of the stove.

With dinner over, the girls went to the village to socialize and flirt. Charlie skipped off with his chums. Da went to play lawn ball with his mates. Ma usually caught up with her patching of clothes, after I helped her clean the dishes and pans.

I thought about going to the colliery to see if Mr. Savage was there, but quickly dismissed that notion. The colliery was closed and locked up on Sundays. No one would be there. Besides, I wanted one day a week where I wouldn't have to look at that drab and bleak place.

Instead I headed for the other side of the row houses and village. The walk to the old cemetery was a long one, but to me the rewards were infinite. It was the only place in the vicinity that boasted some color. The cemetery was an old one and not used anymore. Pretty and colorful wildflowers poked up from tufts of green grass. When I got tired of contemplating the marvelous colors, I let myself daydream about all sorts of things.

Reaching the cemetery, I sat down under a rowan tree. The sun was hot, and the shade offered some degree of comfort. I leaned back against the trunk and watched the wildflowers sway when an occasional breeze wafted over.

A large tombstone loomed to my right. I had seen it before, but never really looked at it. Usually I was too beguiled by the flowers. When that fascination wore off, I quickly slipped into daydreaming with my eyes closed.

But today the tombstone caught my attention as the sun brought the lettering into a sharp focus.

MARY WICKES
1742-1756
May she soar with angels

Learning she was born exactly a hundred years ago, and that she was my age when she died, filled me with a strange sadness. I wondered if she was now soaring with the angels. I hoped so. I closed my eyes and rested my head on the trunk of the tree.

I was in the process of conjuring up an image of Mr. Savage, when my eyelids flew open. I sprang to my feet and scooted from tombstone to tombstone, reading names, dates, and captions. I couldn't believe it. My heart beat rapidly in my chest. My throat went dry, and I had to keep swallowing. I could *read!* How? Why could I read? I didn't remember going to school. None of the Boothes went to school. No one in the family could read. Why me? How did this happen? Thinking it might have been an aberration, I flitted around more tombstones, reading each one easily. I remembered the book with the pictures of the prince and his horse.

Feeling lost and confused, I stumbled back to the tree and plunked down.

"Are you sick or something, boy?"

I spun my head to the source of the sound. A young girl stood staring at me, hands on hips. She wore a long dark blue skirt and a light blue, scooped-neck blouse. Her black hair hung down to her waist in one long

23

braid. Her dark eyes had a flash to them. One gold earring dangled from her earlobe. As her bare feet brought her closer, her hips swayed. Though as usual I was black from soot, she was filthy. She sat down beside me.

"Can't you talk, boy?" she asked, her dark eyes stabbing into mine.

"I'm not a boy." I swiped off my hat to let my long curly hair fall over my shoulders and almost down to my waist.

She took a handful of my hair and studied it. "What color is your hair? It looks gray."

"It's not," I said indignantly. I whipped my head to the side and pulled my hair from her hand. "When I wash my hair, I think it's red."

"Why are you wearing pants? Girls don't wear pants."

"They're my work clothes. They're all I have."

"Are you poor?"

"Maybe. Are you?"

"No. I'm rich."

"Then why are you so dirty? Why do you have holes in your skirt?"

"I'll have a whole new set of clothes when these are worn out. No sense getting new ones until these have served their full use. What's your name?"

"Jane. Jane Boothe. What's yours?"

"Carla. Carla Lee. What are you doing here?"

"Looking at the flowers. What are you doing here?"

"Just looking."

"Looking for what?"

"Coins. Sometimes they fall out of people's pockets when they come to visit the graves of their loved ones."

For the first time in ages, I laughed. "This cemetery has no visitors. The people here died centuries ago. I don't think anyone comes here to mourn." I paused for a minute. "If you're so rich, why are you looking for coins in a cemetery?"

"'Cause I had nothing else to do."

"Don't you work?"

"When I feel like it."

"What kind of job is that, Carla?"

She shrugged. "Let's play a game of tag."

"All right. How do you play it?"

"You try to catch me. When you do, then I try to catch you. And you're allowed to hide."

Carla was like a butterfly as she scampered through the cemetery. She'd dart behind a tombstone and when I came near her, she would flit away. When I caught her, it was her turn to catch me. Hours drifted away. I never felt freer or happier in my life. Childish games had never been part of my life. Tired, we tumbled to the ground with silly, childish laughter.

"What shall we do now, Carla?"

"Why don't you come and meet my mother?"

"How far is it?"

"Not too far. Down by the river."

"The Tyne?"

"Oh, no. A much smaller one."

"All right. But I do have to be back in a couple of hours."

"Oh, we'll be back in plenty of time. How old are you, Jane?" she asked as we started to walk.

"Fourteen. And you?"

"Twelve."

"You look much older than twelve," I commented.

Carla smiled and began to skip along rhythmically. I didn't know how to skip, but I soon learned. It might have seemed a short distance to Carla, but it was a long distance for me. I had never before ventured farther than the cemetery. I made a careful note of the surroundings, so I could find my way back.

25

As we crossed a rutted road, a clearing appeared. Beyond that, the small river Carla had spoken about. When we approached what seemed like some sort of camp, hordes of dogs came rushing at me, barking and howling, and making all kinds of threatening sounds and movements. I stopped.

"Don't be afraid of them, Jane. They won't hurt you, not while I'm with you." Carla took my hand and dragged me forward.

In the clearing stood ten covered wagons on high wheels. The wagons were of heavily varnished natural oak with whitish roofs. The double doors at the rear of the wagons opened onto a wide board, much like a miniature porch. The wagons boasted three small windows on either side.

When we were noticed, a host of children ran to greet Carla and study me. They were barefoot and half-clothed in tattered rags. The very young ones were naked. All of the children were dirty. They danced around us as though we were the main attraction at a circus. With a few of the children following, Carla led me to a group of women, squatting before a large cauldron suspended on a tripod over an open fire.

"Mama, I have a new friend," Carla announced to one of the women, causing the woman to stand.

She was a handsome woman with dark, smooth skin. Her long black hair hung in a plait down her back. Her multilayered skirt was dark brown and long, but not long enough to cover her bare feet. Hooped gold earrings dangled from her earlobes. Both her wrists were covered with gold bracelets that tinkled when she placed her hands on her hips. Her loose white blouse was cut so low, I could see the deep cleavage of her swelling bosom. She walked around me, her dark eyes narrowed in scrutiny.

"Carla, is this a boy or a girl? It has long hair like a

girl, but dressed in pants like a boy. I have never seen a creature such as this."

"Oh, Mama. She's a girl."

"In pants?"

"They are my work clothes, and the only clothes I have. When I turn sixteen, I'll be getting a frock, Mrs. Lee."

"Zorina. No one calls me Mrs. Lee. If you are my daughter's friend, then you are my friend. What is your name, child?"

"Jane."

"And what is this work you do?"

"I work down in the mines at the colliery."

"No wonder you are soot from head to toe."

"I had my tub bath last night. We all take baths on a Saturday night, to be clean for church on Sunday," I explained.

"You sit in a tub and bathe, Jane?" Zorina looked horrified.

"Yes, Mrs.—Zorina."

Carla laughed. "How barbaric! Sitting in your own dirty water, and trying to get clean!"

I never thought of it like that. I wondered what they would say if they knew my sisters had used the same water before me. "How do *you* wash, Carla?"

"In a flowing river. The water is always moving and washes our grime away. That way we always have clean water streaming over us. Mama, can I show Jane our wagon?"

"If you wish, but do not play in there," Zorina warned.

"No, Mama," Carla called as we skipped away.

The two doors were opened and Carla led me inside. My jaw sagged in awe. Bright red velvets, royal blue satins covered pillows and padded benches. Gold moiré material formed curtains at the windows. A

27

black potbellied stove stood in the center, its pipe going up through the roof of the wagon. I thought it looked like a palace compared to the dingy, dim interiors of our row house.

"It's beautiful!" I exclaimed. "Does your whole family sleep in here?"

"Oh, no. We have large feather-filled, quiltlike beds for sleeping outside," Carla informed me. "There's only Mama, my brother, and me. Father got kicked by a horse and died a long time ago. My brother, Rico, usually sleeps outside."

"I'm sorry about your father."

Carla shrugged. "It was a long time ago. My brother is head of the family now."

"How old is he?"

"I'm not sure. Somewhere around nineteen or twenty. Would you like to meet him?"

I nodded and we left the wagon. As she led me to the river, I asked, "Where do you sleep when it rains?"

"We all huddle in the wagon and do the best we can."

As we strolled toward the river, I could feel the eyes of the people in the camp watching us, me in particular. My cheeks turned crimson as I became acutely aware of my multipatched pants. I tried to ignore the stares by glancing around. Horses, tethered on long chains, seemed to be everywhere.

"Rico! Rico!" Carla cried.

A stocky man of average height came toward us. His white shirt was well worn, as were his gray trousers, which were tucked into dark brown riding boots. His swarthy complexion complemented his exotic good looks. His shiny black hair was straight and—from what I could see under the broad-brimmed hat he wore—badly in need of cutting. His eyes were dark like Carla's.

"Rico, I want you to meet my new friend, Jane."

28

"A girl?" His black eyes were expressive. There was no mistaking the amusement in them.

"Yes. I'm a girl." I stuck my chin out defiantly.

He put his hands on his hips, threw his head back, and laughed. His laughter slowly subsided. "Carla, you do find the oddest friends. Picking up strays will get you in trouble one day."

"I'm not a stray. I have a family and a home. I work for wages, so don't call me a stray." I liked Carla and her mother. I wasn't so sure about her brother, despite his good looks.

"At least she's a feisty one, Carla."

"Don't be making fun of my friends, Rico."

"What difference does it make, Carla? She's a Gorgio, no matter how she's dressed."

"What's a Gorgio?" I asked of Carla. I didn't want any more conversation with this rude man.

"Anyone who isn't a true Gypsy, Jane."

"Jane. What a horrid, lackluster name," Rico declared.

"Are you a real Gypsy, Carla?"

"Yes. Didn't you know?"

"What's a Gypsy?" I asked.

With a broad smile on his sensual lips, Rico shook his head.

"We live off the land, and go where we please when we please," Carla told me.

"When we please isn't always true, Jane. Sometimes the farmers or townspeople or police decided when we should move along."

"Why?"

He shrugged. "I guess some people don't like us."

"Are all these horses yours, Rico?" He seemed a little friendlier. I decided to give him a second chance for Carla's sake.

"Not all of them. I own about four. Want to see

them?" Rico asked.

"Could I?" I didn't remember ever having seen a horse close up. With Carla at my side, he led us from horse to horse.

No two of them were alike. Rico gave a running account of each one. A piebald pony, two draft horses, and a chestnut belonged to Rico. He was quite proud of them. I was bold enough to stroke their necks. I had absolutely no fear of them. Something about them struck a familiar chord. But it was so dim, I couldn't think of what it might be. Besides, dusk was settling in.

"I have to go home now, Carla. It'll soon be night."

"Oh, do stay and have supper with us," Carla pleaded.

"I can't. My Da—" I caught myself in time. There was no reason for anyone to know the circumstances at home. "They'll worry about me."

"Oh, do have supper with us, Jane," Carla insisted.

"I appreciate the offer, but I'd better not."

As we walked back toward camp, a tantalizing aroma wafted in the air. I knew what was waiting for me at home. Porridge. These delicious scents smelled of real food. I weighed the thought of a thrashing against a full stomach. The food was here and now. The thrashing was a distant thought.

Approaching Carla's mother, I looked down into the cauldron. Onions, tomatoes, red peppers, garlic, and meat simmered in the black cauldron. I watched Zorina add pepper and salt. My mouth watered. Food won the day.

"Perhaps I will stay," I said to Carla.

She clapped her hands and whirled about. "Marvelous. Mama, Jane is going to stay and eat with us."

Zorina smiled. When she saw Rico coming toward her, her smile widened. Her love for her son was obvious. I furtively looked at him. His wide-brimmed, black felt hat made him appear fiercely handsome.

Food was plentiful and delicious beyond my expectations. Along with the meat stew were pickled cucumbers, bread, and strong black coffee. I felt like a princess at a king's banquet. No one seemed to mind when I took a second helping of the stew. When the meal was over, night had brought down its curtain of darkness.

"I really must leave now. Thank you for inviting me to have supper with you, Carla."

"You must come again."

"I have to go to to work tomorrow."

"Next Sunday then."

"All right."

"I'll meet you at the cemetery."

I nodded, then asked, "Is there a path through the woods?"

"Rico and I will walk you back to the cemetery. We know the way."

"Please don't go to any trouble on my account." Secretly I was glad of the offer. I wasn't sure if I could find my way through the woods at night. It was one thing to come home late, quite another if I didn't get to work on time. A thrashing would become an all-out beating. I didn't relish the thought of that.

"No trouble, Jane." She turned and cried, "Rico!"

He came in a loping gait. "What is it, Carla?"

"I told Jane we'd walk her back to the cemetery."

"Zoe is going to tell a story, and I want to hear it."

"Please, Rico," Carla implored.

"I can manage by myself, Carla. I don't want anyone putting themself out for me."

"I'll go with you. Rico can listen to his old story."

Rico's chivalry asserted itself. "I can't be letting my sister wander about in the dead of night. One never

31

knows who's out there. Let's go right now and hurry along."

Carla smiled triumphantly. We trotted behind Rico, whose stride was long, quick, and sure.

Once at the cemetery, Rico gathered his sister's arm and started back toward the Gypsy camp. He said nothing. Carla managed to call, "See you next Sunday," before she disappeared into the night.

I ran all the way back to my house. To my disappointment and dread, the lights were still on. I went to the back door, took a deep breath, then opened it.

Three

"Ssh." Ma's index finger was over her lips. "He's asleep. Been in his cups all night, he has. Where have you been, Jane?"

"I met a new friend and had supper with her. It was a feast." To show the full range of my enthusiasm was difficult when whispering.

"Well, get yourself straight to bed."

"Don't you want to hear about my new friend, Ma?"

"Not now. Himself will be waking soon. I'll hear about it tomorrow. Now scoot."

I was anxious to tell someone about Carla. But I did as I was told. Better to contain my exuberance than to wake Da.

I crawled into bed, hoping one of my sisters was awake so I could relate my wondrous tale of the Gypsies. They'd look at me with a keener eye, if they knew about the sumptuous supper I had had. I wiggled around in the bed, but no one woke up. Maggie, who was next to me, only groaned and rolled over. Knowing I would have to wait until tomorrow, I sighed and promptly fell asleep.

To my surprise and delight, nothing was said at breakfast about my being absent for supper. It seemed

33

I wouldn't get a thrashing after all.

Da didn't look good. His eyes were a watery red. His bulbous nose was mottled purple. He seemed to be having difficulty breathing. All in all, he seemed to be ailing. But whatever it was, it didn't impede his appetite.

My sisters were as quiet as birds expecting a storm. Though I wanted to tell them and Ma about Carla, I wasn't about to remind Da that I was absent last night. I decided to save my narrative for Charlie as we walked to the colliery.

"And the food!" After telling him about Carla, I went on to describe the plentiful and delicious supper I had.

"They must be very rich," Charlie said.

"They didn't look it. Their clothes were in worse shape than ours. The real young ones were naked."

"Who are they?"

"Carla said they were Gypsies."

"Gypsies! If Da hears you were with the Gypsies, you'll be getting more than the birch switch. Don't you know they're thieves and steal children? And they can put a curse on you! They probably have already."

"Don't be silly, Charlie. They're people just like us. They certainly were good to me."

"Well, if Da knows they're around here, he'll be telling the constables. He'll make the police bugger them off."

"Don't talk like that, Charlie. You won't tell Da, will you?"

"Nay. I have me own thinking to do. I can't be bothered with you and your Gypsies."

"What are you thinking about?"

"I'm thinking of Henry, and how I might be going off to find him."

34

"You'll never find him now. Besides, you're too young."

"I'll be thirteen soon."

"And what will you do for money? Da isn't going to keep his money in the cup anymore. He's going to hide it."

"I'm thinking on it."

I had plenty of time to think, once I got hitched to my cart and began the trek back and forth in the dark, narrow passages of the mine.

I thought about the food at the Gypsy camp and the good time I had had with Carla. Though two years younger than I, Carla seemed much older. I could hardly wait until Sunday, when I would meet her at the cemetery. What if she didn't come? I refused to let myself think such a horrid thought. I had to believe she would come. It offered the only ray of sunshine in my gloomy life.

Thinking about the cemetery, I remembered my ability to read the tombstones. I promised myself I would ask Ma about it tonight.

I gobbled down my lunch, then carried the pail with me as I wandered about the colliery, in hopes of getting a glimpse of Mr. Savage. I didn't see him anywhere.

While I helped Ma clear the supper table, I told her about my ability to read the tombstones. Her expression altered. I couldn't tell if it was amazement or fear.

"Why can I read and the others can't, Ma?"

"You've spent too many hours sitting in that old cemetery. Maybe you think you can read the tombstones by now," she offered as an explanation.

"But I can read the sayings, too," I argued.

"Your mind is playing tricks on you, Jane. Let's not talk about it anymore. Tell me about this new friend of yours."

The fact that I could read slipped from my mind as I told her about Carla and the Gypsy camp.

"Don't be telling your Da about this, Jane. He doesn't hold with having Gypsies around."

"Why?"

"He doesn't trust them. Says they're always sneaking about stealing things."

"They seemed like nice and friendly people to me."

"Da says they are an evil people, Jane. They put curses on us plain folk. Mark my words and stay away from them. They might decide to steal you, and give you to one of their men as his bride."

When Ma said that, I thought about Rico. Knowing I would probably never see my prince, Mr. Savage, again, Rico had possibilities. I said no more about the gypsies.

In the middle of the week, my life started to fall apart.

I came home from work and as usual went directly to the backyard to wash up. Da was there waiting for me. His face was livid with rage as he swished the birch rod through the air. A glimmer of utter cruelty sparkled in his eyes as he stalked toward me. The nearer he came, the stronger the smell of gin.

"Whoring around with Gypsy men, are you now, girlie? I'll be teaching you to stay away from those camps with their evil doings. Get down on your hands and knees, girlie," he bellowed at me.

My eyes widened in sheer terror. I had once seen him beat Henry that way, and the force of his blows nearly broke Henry's back. Henry was in pain for weeks. I knew if he beat *me* like that, I would never be able to pull the coal cart. If I did, the pain would be excruciating. I stood and stared at him in horror.

"Don't tell me you're going deaf, girlie. I said get down on all fours!"

"No. I won't."

"What did you say?" His hand holding the switch began to quiver. His eyes shot rays of hate at me.

"I won't get down on all fours."

"I'll teach you to defy me."

Just then Maggie and Sarah came into the backyard and diverted my attention. I never should have taken my eyes off Da. His meaty hand whizzed through the air, catching me on the side of the head. I went sprawling, face down on the ground. Though stunned, I was able to scramble to my feet when he next struck.

I heard the squeal of the rod cutting through the air, a second before I felt the stinging blow across my back. Again I tried to get to my feet, but the flailing of the birch rod was too swift. I bit down on my lower lip to prevent the screams caught in my throat from issuing forth. I didn't want Da to know the shame and misery I was experiencing, especially with my two sisters standing there watching. As my back began to feel numb, Da brought the switch down on my buttocks, as if he knew he had inflicted all the pain my back could tolerate.

I started to wish I was built more like my sisters. They had fleshy rumps which would have helped cushion the blows. Each blow that rained down on me seemed to cut straight to the bone. When the switch whistled down on the backs of my legs, I could no longer stem the screams. Screams of agony, despair, and pain shattered the air like peals of crackling lightning. I prayed for the mercy of unconsciousness. But oblivion did not come to my rescue.

"Frank! That's enough!" Ma's voice screamed. "You'll be killing her."

"So what? She's not of my flesh."

Two more blows. Two more screams. Then nothing. A coughing spasm had taken hold of him, and the blows ceased while he spat dark phlegm on the ground. The next thing I knew, Ma was pushing my sooty hair from my face.

"Come along, Jane, and have some supper."

"She's to have no supper," Da roared, then stalked into the house.

Ma helped me to stand. My legs pained so I could barely stand and walk.

"Maggie, Sarah . . . come help me with her," Ma ordered.

"I'll not be helping the likes of her. She got what she deserved." Maggie turned on her heel and went into the house.

Sarah helped me walk, but I could sense it was with reluctance. They helped me to bed, where I instantly fell asleep from fatigue.

The next morning my body was stiff and sore. Not having washed the night before and being put to bed with soot covering me, I presented a sorry sight at the breakfast table. An ominous silence hovered in the room. Finally Ma spoke, her voice sounding weak and tenuous.

"I think Jane should stay home from work today, Frank. She's not fit for work."

"She'll go to work like the rest of us," he grumbled.

"But Frank . . ."

"No more, woman, or I'll deal with you tonight."

I left the table and got my lunch pail. I didn't want to be the cause of any trouble for Ma. Besides, my gait was slow because of my stiff legs, and I had to leave a little earlier than usual. I walked alone to the colliery, wondering who had told Da about my visit to the Gypsy camp.

Ma never would have told him. And the only other person I had told was Charlie. I had never known Charlie to be one to carry tales to Da. But he might have told our sisters. Sarah and Alice only spoke to Da when spoken to. Maggie. For some reason known only to her, Maggie hated me. If anyone had told Da, it had to be Maggie. I sighed. What did it matter now? I received my thrashing. I didn't think I'd get another one for at least a few days.

I was grateful the chains ran under my legs and not across my back. I don't think I could have stood the pain of them pressing on the welts across my back. Once I started pulling the coal cart up to the surface, I had to do most of the pulling with my hands. My legs weren't capable of pushing too hard.

Like a mindless animal, I went back and forth in the limited space of the dark tunnel. But I wasn't mindless. My brain was active with thoughts I couldn't shut off. Though shrouded in a vague mist, hazy words sprung into my mind. What did Da mean when he said "not of my flesh"?

Then all the questions came tumbling in on me. Why was I the only one able to read? Why was my build so much smaller than my brothers and sisters? Why was I the only one Ma seemed to like? And why did Da beat me with far more ferocity than usual? When he beat Henry, it didn't appear to be as hateful and vicious.

Thinking of Henry, I began to wonder if *I* shouldn't run away. I didn't think I could survive another beating like that. In fact, I didn't think Da would stop next time until I was dead. But where could I go? Besides, I couldn't leave Ma. I cared about her. I didn't give a fig for the rest of them.

Perhaps Carla could help me to answer some of the questions gnawing at me. She seemed wise in the ways of the world. Her mother, Zorina, would certainly know the answers. But first I would try to get Ma to answer them, no matter how reluctant she was.

If she couldn't—or wouldn't—explain things to me,

I would certainly go to Zorina. If Gypsies could tell the future, they must know how to delve into the past. I could hardly wait until Sunday.

Saturday was unusually hot and humid. Da took himself off to the pub after supper. After Sarah, Alice, and Maggie had their baths, they went to a village dance. I let Charlie have his bath before me, as this was the first opportunity I had to be alone with Ma. I knew Charlie would leave right after his bath to play with his chums.

I stripped and lowered myself into the large washtub, which was kept outside and only brought in for Saturday night baths. I thought of Carla as I looked at the sooty, greasy water which was now cool. I was never *really* clean. The murky water did nothing to clean my coal dust-ridden pores, nor did it ever really clean my hair.

"You poor child," Ma remarked as she gingerly dried my back. "Does your back still hurt?"

"A little. The backs of my legs feel worse."

"I wish I had something to put on those welts. But you know how your Da is about spending money on medicine. I do wish Sarah and Alice would get married. They're old enough."

"I think they have beaux."

"I wouldn't be surprised. I know they're flirtatious, but they're good girls at heart. I have a clean shirt and pants for you. They might be a little too big, but I'm sure you'll grow into them. Henry left them behind."

"Do you miss him, Ma?"

"Sometimes I do. But I'm glad he's out of it. The older he became, the more fights he'd have with Da. I don't think it would have ended until one of them killed the other."

"Ma, what did Da mean when he said I was not of his flesh?"

"He was out of his head and didn't know what he was saying."

"Before he starts drinking real heavy, he always knows what he is saying. Please tell me."

"Forget about it, Jane. What you don't know can't hurt you."

"I have to know, Ma. It's troubling me something fierce. If you don't tell me, I'll ask Da."

Her face turned a ghostly white. "No, Jane. You must never ask him that. Do you hear me?"

"I will if you don't tell me. I don't care if he beats me again. I have to know why I can read and the others can't. I'll die if I don't have some answers. Please, Ma."

She gazed at me with enormous sorrow in her eyes. Her eyes glazed over, as though she was about to cry. Her bosom heaved in a tremulous sigh. "Sit down, Jane. I'll make us a cup of tea and we can talk about it."

I did as I was told. I watched her get the mugs and place them on the table. She filled the teapots with tea leaves, her motions slow, as though in a dream. A pan of boiling water was always kept on the back of the stove. She poured some into the teapot, which she placed on the table to steep. After sitting down, Ma stared at the teapot as though it had the magical ability to say the words she wanted to speak. I waited patiently, knowing this time I would get some answers. Ma didn't speak until the tea was brewed and she poured.

"About three or four years ago, a horrible and devastating train accident occurred outside of New-castle, not too far from the colliery. The men from the mines went to help, including Frank. He found you wandering around in a daze. Somehow you must have been thrown clear, as most of the passengers were killed. Those who came out of it alive had no idea who you were." Ma's expression hinted at a smile.

41

"Oh, I remember the day he brought you home. You must have been around eleven at the time. You wore a bright green wool coat with a white fur collar and cuffs. Your little hands were tucked into a white fur muff, and you had a green silk bonnet all trimmed with the same white fur. Your little black boots were all shiny and new against your long white stockings. You were so adorable. Like a little princess, you were. I fell in love with you on sight. Your frock was an emerald green moiré with fine frilly lace. I'll never forget the looks on my girls' faces. They had never seen anything like you. Such a little princess, with a real gold locket about your neck."

"Where are those things now?" I interrupted.

"Da sold everything, including the gold locket. Brought a pretty penny, they did. We had roast of pork, potatoes, and vegetables the next day. I haven't seen the likes of that feast since."

"Why did he sell them?"

"For the money, of course. Besides, he wanted to get the cash for them right away, in case your memory came back. When it didn't, he sent you to work in the mines, so you'd earn your keep."

"Why didn't he just take my things, then bring me to a constable? Surely someone was looking for me?"

"He was afraid you'd tell the authorities he stole your things. I think he might have had it in the back of his mind that someday someone would come searching for you, and then he might get a reward or be able to ransom you. When no one came, I could see his hatred of you growing in his eyes day by day."

"Then you're not my real Ma and Da?" To my amazement I was stunned and relieved at the same time.

"No, we're not, Jane. Anymore than Sarah, Alice, Maggie, Henry, and Charlie are your sisters and brothers."

"Why do you treat me kinder than you do your own children?"

"Not only did I feel sorry for you, but I was filled with guilt. From the way you were dressed, it was obvious you were of a genteel and wealthy family. Perhaps if Frank had taken you to the authorities, you might have been reunited with your real family and not have to drudge in the mines. Besides, you were a sweet little thing, not at all like my strapping, selfish girls. They resented you the minute you stepped into the house."

"They don't resent me, they hate me," I said, voicing my thoughts aloud.

"Perhaps they do, Jane. And envy you. You are getting prettier each day. They are rugged with coarse looks. Aye. They have every reason to be jealous of you."

"Is Jane my real name?"

"I don't think so. The initials on your locket were *J.H.* I tried to keep the locket for you, but Frank was having none of that, claiming the locket would fetch more than the clothes."

"Were there pictures of my real mother and father in the locket?"

"No, Jane. The locket was empty. If there had been pictures, I certainly would have tried to save them for you."

I was having a hard time trying to digest the surprising information. But it did help to answer some of the questions plaguing me. "Is that why I can read?"

"Probably. Most wealthy children have tutors, and begin to read at an early age."

"Do you think if I went to the constable now, they could find my real parents?"

"My poor Jane. Too many years have passed. Being on a train going to Newcastle, it would be hard for anyone to know if you lived in Newcastle or were going there for a visit. I fear the authorities would put you in an orphanage, and that might be worse than living here and working in the mines."

Nothing could be worse than living here, with the constant threat of a beating and the hauling chains cutting into my flesh, I thought. I didn't say it aloud, as I didn't want to hurt Ma's feelings. She tried to do her best for me, and even if she wasn't my real mother, I still had feelings of warmth toward her. I stood.

"I'm tired, Ma. I think I'll go to bed." I really wanted to be alone. I needed time to think.

Ma left her chair and came to me. She kissed my forehead tenderly. "We've done you a great wrong, Jane. I hope you'll find it in your heart to forgive us someday."

"I forgive you, Ma. I'll always forgive you."

"Promise me you won't tell Da that I told you the truth."

"I won't. I know what he'd do to you if I did. I won't say anything to the girls or Charlie either. I have the feeling they'd love to see me get another beating. Good night, Ma."

"Good night, Jane." A wan smile formed on her lips as she gently patted my shoulder.

I lay in bed, my eyes open and staring into the darkness. A few hours ago I had a family, a home, and a name. Now I had nothing. A nameless creature with only initials—*J.H.* Who was *J.H.?* Where had I come from? Where did I belong? I couldn't remember anything.

If I did go to the authorities, would they really put me in an orphanage? Would it be worse than living here? Now that I had some answers to my earlier questions, a whole new set of questions tormented me.

With this new knowledge, I was certain I could no

44

longer stay under this roof. I could no longer let this man beat me. But an orphanage? That seemed just as dire. Perhaps I should run away like Henry. But there wasn't a cup with money in it in plain sight anymore. Without a farthing to my name, I wouldn't get very far. I would be considered an indigent and put in the workhouse, where I would probably be cruelly used.

Then it came to me. I would ask Carla or Zorina what I should do. Certainly they would know. With that settled in my mind, I fell asleep.

Next morning, though awake, I purposely stayed in bed until I was sure all of them had left for church. I dressed, ate the breakfast of watery porridge Ma had left for me, cleaned up the kitchen, then left for the cemetery to wait for Carla.

With a newfound pride, I darted among the tombstones and read each one aloud. When I heard the obscene laughter, I stopped and slowly turned around. Maggie!

"What are you doing here? Why aren't you in church?" I was angry and felt my privacy had been violated. Besides, I didn't like Maggie, standing there in her Sunday finery, a new bonnet on her head, her hands on her hips, her head thrown back in cackling laughter.

The laughter died and she eyed me suspiciously. "Dancing on people's graves, are you? What a horrid, vile thing to do on the Sabbath. You'll pay for it, moppet. Mark my words. You'll pay for it."

"Why aren't you in church, Maggie?"

"I wanted to see what you did of a Sunday."

"How did you know I'd be here?"

"I told them I didn't feel well and was going back to the house to lie down. I waited outside, then followed you here."

"Why?"

45

"I wanted to see the Gypsy man you're meeting here." A haughty smirk crossed her face.

"I'm not meeting any gypsy man here, so go home."

"I'll wait." She folded her arms across her chest just under her ample bosom.

"If you stay here, I'll have my Gypsy friend put a curse on you," I threatened.

Her jaw sagged and her arms fell to her sides. She stared at me in horror. "You wouldn't."

"Oh, yes, I would."

"Wait until I tell Da what you're about. He'll give you what for. You think the other day was bad. He'll flay your skin off this time. In fact, I think I'll go home right now and tell him the minute he comes in the house. I'll tell him where you are, so he'll come and fetch you right away. I might come myself, so I can have the pleasure of watching him drag you home."

"Go ahead. You've always been a spiteful witch, Maggie Boothe."

"And you're a rotten brat!"

With my hands on my hips and a mean scowl on my face, I started to walk toward her with purposeful strides. She took one look at me, lifted her skirts, and bolted toward home. My laughter echoed after her. Suddenly the reality of the situation struck me, and the laughter stopped.

Maggie would do exactly what she threatened. I wouldn't be surprised if she went directly to the church and dragged Da out I had to stop calling Frank Boothe Da. He wasn't my father. I would have liked to sit down and ponder about my real father. Who he was. What he looked like. But I wasn't about to be caught at the cemetery. I couldn't wait for Carla. I would have to find their camp on my own. I headed for the woods, hoping I could find the obscure path Carla had used.

I picked my way slowly through the trees and brush,

studying the ground. To my right the brush seemed to be trampled and the way slightly open. I made my way over to it, then trod a little more quickly. Elation filled me when I came to the road. I looked across to see that the clearing was empty. Perhaps I had come out of the woods at the wrong spot.

I crossed the road, deciding to skirt along the river until I found the Gypsy camp. As I made my way across the clearing toward the river, my heart sunk. Animal bones, ashes from fires, odd scraps, and horse manure were scattered about. This was the Gypsy camp. And they were gone!

Four

I stood there, panic welling up inside me. I couldn't go back to the Boothes now. I was sure Maggie had elaborated on our conversation at the cemetery. She might have added colorful lies to enrage her father. I had no doubt he would flail my skin until it was raw, and Ma wouldn't be able to stop him. I was still sore and tender from the last beating. I didn't think I could survive a more rigorous one. I had to find Carla.

I went out into the road and looked up and down. In the distance I could see a spot of white disappearing down a hill. The roofs of the Gypsy wagons were painted white, I recalled. Perhaps it was they. I had to take the chance. I had no choice.

I ran after the white spot as though my life depended on it. To my mind, it did.

I thought my lungs would burst in my chest. My heart was pulsating so fast, my head pounded with its thundering beat. But I was gaining.

One of the dogs saw me and started barking. Other dogs came to assist him. This time I was happy to hear them bark. Their din caused the last wagon to stop. Fate was with me. A young girl jumped down from the driver's seat. As she came toward me, I stopped running and put a splayed hand to my heaving chest. If I had any breath left, I would have laughed for sheer joy. The girl coming toward me was Carla. She quieted the dogs, then looked up at me. As recognition came over her, she smiled and ran to me shouting, "Jane . . . Jane!"

When she stood before me, we embraced. Tears trickled over my cheeks. As we walked back to the wagon, I told her of the events that had transpired since I had last seen her.

"He beat you?"

I nodded.

"How awful! Then you really don't have any brothers or sisters?"

"Not that I know of. I don't even know if I have a family. Ma—Mrs. Boothe—told me I was in a daze when they found me. I was dressed in fancy clothes trimmed with fur and a real gold locket about my neck. Mr. Boothe sold everything."

"Don't you remember anything, Jane?"

I shook my head. "All I remember is the Boothes and the mines. Nothing before that."

Carla looked pensive for a moment, then said brightly, "Perhaps you are a princess of royal blood."

I laughed. "If I was a princess, I'm sure a thorough search would have been instituted."

"Then at least a lord's daughter or the daughter of a very wealthy man. Only the very rich would have bought a child clothes with fur trimmings. Are you going to try and find out who you are?"

"I wouldn't know how to go about it. Besides, four or five years have passed. I look different now. My family, if I have a family, wouldn't recognize me."

"Carla! Come back here," her brother Rico bellowed, as he stuck his head around the wagon.

"Don't mind him, Jane. He's in a foul mood," Carla said as we approached the wagon.

"Why?"

"He might have to sell one of his best horses to help raise my bridal price."

"Bridal price? Are you going to be married?" I was more than astounded, I was shocked.

"Soon. Probably before winter."

"But you're only twelve, Carla!"

"Gypsy girls marry young." Carla nodded for me to climb onto the wooden seat of the wagon where Rico held the leather reins. She was soon beside me.

"What's she doing here?" Rico asked of his sister, as though I wasn't present.

"She's coming with us," Carla stated matter-of-factly.

"Does Mama know?"

"No. When she hears Jane's story, she'll be only too happy I made the decision for Jane to come with us." Carla proceeded to tell her brother everything I had told her.

I was busy watching the passing scenery, smelling the fresh, clean air. Green grass. Trees. An occasional whitewashed cottage with a thatched roof and a profusion of colorful flowers dancing around the cottage. What a marvelous place to live, I thought. Soon the air was no longer filled with miniscule particles of coal dust. The world was becoming brighter.

"Where are we going?" I asked.

"To the summer carnival at York," Carla answered. "We'll be there in two or three days. Maybe four. We take the days as they come. Somehow we manage to get there on time."

"What's a carnival?" I asked. A new excitement bubbled in me. I was off to a new life with wondrous adventures. I prayed Zorina would let me stay with them.

"Clowns, magicians, freaks, rides—all sorts of amusements. We usually do quite well at carnivals," Carla informed me. "Haven't you ever been to a carnival, Jane?"

"Not that I can remember. I don't remember ever being away from the colliery. It sounds like a great deal of fun. What do you do at these carnivals?"

"Dance, sing, read palms. The children beg. The men give pony rides. All sorts of things."

"Read palms? What's that?"

"Some of the older women tell fortunes by looking at the palms of people's hands."

"Do you think I can get my fortune told, Carla?"

"I don't see why not."

"What does your future hold?"

"We don't read palms among ourselves. It's only for the Gorgios," Rico interjected in a sullen voice.

His tone harbored a warning. I didn't pursue the topic.

I turned my attention back to the scenery. The pace of the wagon was neither slow nor fast. Moderate. All the wagons went at a moderate pace. My stomach grumbled, but noon came and went without a slowing of our pace. I thought it best not to ask any more questions, no matter how hungry I was.

The sun was lowering in the sky when we finally stopped. The wagons moved off the road to a large, secluded, grassy area. Again, a river was nearby. Rico was the first one down on the ground, then Carla, then me. Rico quickly unharnessed the horse and led the animal away.

51

Zorina came out of the wagon carrying long black rods and a black cauldron. Her dark eyebrows raised in mild surprise when she saw me. Carla rushed to help her mother and, I presumed, to explain my presence. Carla took the things from her mother and went about the task of setting up the tripod which would hold the cauldron. Zorina swished over to me, her hips swaying seductively with each step. Her expression was grim. My body tensed with the fear I was going to be cast out. With her hands on her hips, she circled around me. I stood quite still.

"If you're going to be with us for a while, we can't have you going around dressed in pants. And you need to wash." With a nod of her head, she went back into the wagon.

I rushed over to Carla, joy beating in my heart. "Your mother is going to let me stay."

"I know." Carla flashed me a wide smile, her teeth made whiter by her dusky skin. "If I know Mama, she'll make you wash first."

"She did say something about it," I admitted.

"She'll stand there and make you scrub until your skin is raw. And the soap is strong. Sometimes it stings."

I liked the thought of being really clean. I vaguely remembered a voice once telling me that cleanliness is next to godliness. Zorina came out of the wagon with a bundle under one arm and a large bar of yellow soap in her free hand.

"Come along, child." I followed her to the river, then downriver for quite a way. "Take off your clothes." When I did, she handed me the bar of soap and a rag and said, "Now get in the water and start scrubbing."

The water was cold, and I inched my way in until it was up to my hips. I began to scrub. I watched the dark

52

bubbles float away, my body constantly splashed with the clear water running over me. I noticed my arms and chest becoming whiter than I had ever seen them.

"Duck your head in the water, then come here," Zorina cried from the shore. She brought the hems of her skirt and petticoats from the back and pulled them through her legs. She tucked them into her waistband. From her knees downward, she was bare. She waded into the shallow water near the bank as I approached her. "Turn around. I'll clean your back."

I heard her gasp, but she said nothing. She took the soap and rag from me. I gathered my lower lip between my teeth in preparation for the scrubbing to come. The welts on my back were still sore. Zorina's washing of my back was so gentle, I soon released my lip. My hair was another story. She scrubbed it with the soap so vigorously, I thought my scalp would fall off.

When I was fully soaped, she ordered me to go back into the deeper water and thoroughly rinse my body and hair. By the time I came back to the shore, I was tingling from head to toe. Zorina took a rag and dried my body, then squeezed my hair until it no longer dripped.

"You have very pretty hair. So thick and long. Like polished copper, it is," Zorina exclaimed. She stooped and picked up the bundle. "Here. Put these on. I made them for Carla. But you need them more than she does. Carla's clothes will do her for a while longer."

"I can't be taking Carla's clothes." I put my hands up, palms facing Zorina as I backed away.

"Don't worry about Carla. I'll be making her new ones for her wedding. She told me to give you these. She didn't like the color of the skirt anyway." Zorina thrust the bundle at me.

Suddenly conscious of my nakedness, I quickly

53

slipped into the chemise, three petticoats, a low-cut, loose, white blouse, and a dark green merino skirt with large, deep pockets. The warm breeze had almost dried my hair. Zorina pulled a rough comb from her pocket and started on my tangled hair. I winced several times, but the discomfort was nowhere near as painful as the birch rod of Frank Boothe.

When all the snarls were out, Zorina plaited my hair until it hung in a low braid down my back. She picked up my old clothes, and we headed back to camp. The experience of walking with a skirt on was new to me. At first the sensation was peculiar, but I soon began to delight in the feel of it.

"Why did we walk so far down the riverbank, Zorina, when we could have used the river directly next to the camp?" I asked, basking in the glory of my clean body, hair, and clothes.

"We get our drinking water and catch fish upstream. We certainly don't want to be drinking water or eating fish that has been fouled by soapy water," Zorina explained, as we veered inland, away from the river.

Entering camp, Carla came running up to us. "Oh, Jane, you look ever so much better. Real pretty, you are. And your hair! Like the flames of a fire. I didn't recognize you at first. But when I saw that green skirt, I knew it had to be my Jane."

"Don't call her Jane anymore, Carla. We must find another name for her. A Gypsy name. Now run along and find some food for supper."

"I know where there are tomatoes, peppers, and squash." Carla took my hand and we scampered off, the dogs giving us lazy glances.

We crossed the road and walked along the hedgerow lining the road. Carla halted, looked around, then pushed her way through the hedgerow and motioned

54

for me to follow. We came to a low stone wall, some stones lay at the base, as though tired of being part of the wall.

Carla put her hand on my shoulder and signaled for me to crouch down beside her. Every now and then she would peer over the wall.

"Come on," she whispered, then hopped over the stone wall and sprinted to bushes in the field. "Do as I do."

She waddled in a low crouch. Her mode of moving like that must have taken much practice. When I tried it, I had a tendency to fall on my rump. We squatted down behind a full grown squash plant. Carla's hands moved swiftly as she plucked the ripe, yellow squash from the vines and stuffed them into her skirt's pockets. I managed to get a few before she moved down several rows to the tomato plants. Ripe tomatoes became red flashes before disappearing into her pockets. The peppers were next.

"Oh, look." Carla's voice was low as she pointed to some bushes. "String beans. Let's get some of those."

"We'd better go back, Carla. We have enough."

She paid no heed to my words. Soon she was busy yanking beans from their stalks. With a shrug of resignation, I started picking. Then a dog began to bark ferociously. My hand flew out and I grabbed Carla's arm. She had heard it, too. We headed for the wall and dove over it. I felt something wet against my leg. A tomato had been squashed. We pushed through the hedgerow, crossed the road, and dashed back to camp through the trees. My pockets were full. Carla's were bulging.

"Carla, we shouldn't have taken the vegetables. It's stealing. The constable could put us in jail for what we just did."

"We don't steal. We only take what we need to live. The farmer won't miss these few vegetables. He has rows of them. If we hadn't taken them, coons or hedgehogs would have eaten them. Stealing is when you go into someone's house and take what they think is valuable. We don't do that."

I shook my head. I realized that if I was going to stay with the gypsies, I would have to get use to their ways.

Rico was stacking wood under the cauldron when we got back to camp. He looked up at me and stared. A strange glimmer came into his dark eyes as they traveled over me. At Zorina's approach, he turned back to his chore, finished it, then walked away.

Zorina had a large pail out on the ground. We filled the pail with the contents of our pockets.

"You did very well, girls." Zorina smiled. Out of her pockets came two big onions, garlic, and some knives. She handed one to Carla and one to me. We went to work on the food.

With the fire lighted and the cauldron three-quarters full, the aromas began to tantalize my palate. I was famished.

Fires glowed throughout the camp. Noisy children and barking dogs began to quiet down, as the time to eat drew nearer.

Rico swaggered to our fire. The flickering light of the flames emphasized his dark good looks. The dark yellow kerchief around his neck danced with different colors as the firelight hit it. He kept his hat on throughout the meal, which I thought was quite rude. But I kept my thoughts to myself. Zorina pulled off chunks of bread when the meal was over. She handed a chunk to each of us. The Lees promptly began to clean the inside of the cauldron with the bread. Carla nodded for me to do the same. I was stuffed, but I followed suit. No one spoke until Zorina had poured each of us a mug of hot, black coffee.

"Now we must decide on a name for Jane. Have you thought about it, Carla?" Zorina asked.

"I think Dolores is nice. What do you think, Mama?"

"I thought of Lottie. But perhaps Jane has chosen a name for herself. Have you, Jane?"

"No. I don't know any Gypsy names."

"Well, which do you like, Lottie or Dolores?" Zorina took a deep swallow of her coffee.

"Esmeralda." Rico's deep voice caused me to turn and look at him. His dark eyes pierced mine. "Her green eyes sparkle and shine like emeralds. Esmeralda is the only fit name for a green-eyed beauty."

"What do you think, Jane?" Zorina asked.

Rico had called me a beauty. No one had ever called me that. And he was smiling at me. I would have agreed to any name he wanted to bestow on me. "Esmeralda is fine," I finally said, returning Rico's smile.

"Esmeralda . . ." the name rolled off Carla's tongue as though it was a savory morsel. "Esmeralda. I like it. It's musical. Oh, Rico, you're so clever."

With fists on his hips, he lifted his chin and peered down at us. His expression was a mixture of haughtiness and pride. "I must see to the horses."

"Esmeralda, it is," Zorina confirmed.

Carla and I wandered about the camp. She introduced me as Esmeralda. With my new name and new clothes, I felt like a butterfly emerging from its chrysalis. Young and old Gypsy men eyed me with gleams in their eyes.

I was struck by the similarity of their dress. All the men wore hats, mostly dark and broad-brimmed, along with kerchiefs around their necks. Brown or black boots shod their feet with either twilled or corduroy pants tucked in them. Shirts, fitted or blousy. Coats, short or three-quarters. Some men were clean-shaven, some sported thick, long mustaches.

The women wore dark skirts and white or pale-colored blouses which were invariably cut low. The older they were, the more gold jewelry they displayed in their ears, on their fingers, around their necks and wrists. All were barefoot.

They were most friendly to me and appeared to be fascinated by the mixture of orange, yellow, and red in my hair. Though they genuinely seemed to like me, I sensed there was an invisible barrier between me and the Gypsies. I shrugged the feeling off, thinking time would bring any barrier down.

"Did you notice how the men looked at you, Esmeralda?" Carla asked.

"I'll admit they seemed interested, but I think that it's nothing but curiosity. I suspect anyone new in camp would get the same kind of scrutiny."

"They were more than curious. They looked at you with a hunger." Carla paused thoughtfully. "You talk funny, Esmeralda."

"Funny? How?"

"Maybe funny isn't the right word. Different. Aye. That's it. Different from all the other people in the northern part of England. You sound like someone from the south of England."

"How do you know, Carla?"

"We travel back and forth the length of England. Soon we'll be heading south again. Horse fairs. County fairs. More carnivals."

"Will I be going with you?"

"Of course. But you will have to learn our ways and earn your keep. You don't mind, do you?"

"I've always earned my keep, Carla. At least ever

58

since I can remember."

"Well, we do things a little differently."

"What do you mean?"

"You'll see tomorrow, when we pass near a small village." Carla's head swiveled around, as though she were searching for a particular person. Her expression brightened when her eyes fastened on an old woman. She grabbed my hand. "Do you still want your fortune told?"

"Yes." My reply was enthusiastic. The name Esmeralda was still alien to me. I suppose I would get use to it.

Carla led me to a bony woman who seemed positively ancient. Her once-dark hair, now heavily streaked with gray, hung in a braid down her back. Her dusky, leathery skin had long white and black hairs sprouting out in odd places, mostly on her long chin. Her nose arched high between two of the most peculiar eyes I had ever seen. The centers of her eyes were like ink spots. Red veins shattered across what once had been the whites of her eyes. A drop of ink in a pool of blood was all I could think of. They glimmered with an eerie glow as she stared at me, puffing away on her pipe.

"Zoe, this is my new friend, Esmeralda. She would like her fortune told."

"So this is the Gorgio that has come to live among us. Come closer, child."

I took a few steps forward. She reached out and lightly touched my hair.

"Esmeralda, is it?" Zoe asked, her eyes narrowing.

I nodded. I was too awed to speak.

"At fairs, carnivals, and entering villages, you must cover your hair, Esmeralda. And keep your eyes downcast. Your flaming hair and green eyes mark you

59

as a non-Gypsy. People will notice and think we stole you. Then the constable will come and take you away, probably to an orphanage," Zoe advised me.

"My . . . Frank Boothe told me you steal babies." Though I had found my voice, I had to keep reminding myself that the Boothes were no kin of mine.

The old woman threw her head back and cackled what might have been laughter. She slapped her knee with her bony hand, long talons sprouting from her fingertips. The cackle waned to raspy grunts.

"Steal babies? Look around you, Esmeralda. We have no need to steal babies. We have enough of our own. Now, what is it you want of me?" Zoe asked.

"She wants her fortune told," Carla repeated.

"Let the child speak for herself, Carla," Zoe admonished. "Is that what you want, Esmeralda?"

"Please. I would like to know my future very much."

"Give me your hands."

She took the pipe out of her mouth and put it aside, then held out her hands. I placed my hands in hers. My hands felt as though they were being clutched by spidery branches of a wintry bush. Her eyes closed tight. At first her hands were ice cold. They gradually warmed, until her flesh seemed to burn into mine.

"I see darkness. Great mists swirl out of this darkness. Water. Large, pulsing waves of water. Strange, disembodied voices. I can't hear what they are saying. The water is too loud. A great house. The darkness makes everything unclear. I can't quite see. Ah! It's clearing now. The darkness is fading. I see . . . I see . . ."

Zoe squeezed my hands, then dropped them as though they burned her. Her eyes flew open and glowed with terror and fear.

"What did you see, Zoe?" I asked, anxiety and

curiosity mixing within me.

"Nothing, child. Go now. Go."

"Please. I must know. You can't leave me wondering what you saw," I pleaded.

She looked at me and slowly shook her head. "You don't want to know, Esmeralda."

"I do. I really do. Please tell me, Zoe."

"You know the rules, Zoe. You must tell the whole fortune," Carla insisted.

Those black and red eyes pierced mine with an intensity that frightened me. With a solemn expression, Zoe said one word. "Death."

"Whose death?"

"Much death." She stood and walked away.

Five

While Rico slept outside in an eiderdown quilt, Zorina, Carla, and I retired to the wagon. Carla and Zorina went to sleep instantly. I laid there thinking about the fortune Zoe had read in my palm. Mists, water, and death. I had no idea what it all meant, much less if it might be true. A great house. Was I born in that great house? Did I live there? By death, did Zoe mean my parents were dead? These thoughts and many more kept pricking my brain until I fell asleep.

Breakfast consisted of floured nettles browned in goose fat, along with potatoes and dark bread, all washed down with strong, black coffee. I marveled at the fact that I could eat all I wanted. At the Boothes you were given a certain portion—a small one at that—and that was it.

Though I had to be told what to do, I felt I was of some help in the breaking up of camp, as I washed the spoons and pans in the river. The caravan and the horses were on the move again. Zorina sat beside Rico as the big wheels slowly turned on the road. Carla and I walked alongside the wagon with the dogs.

"What do you think Zoe meant when she told my

fortune?" I asked Carla.

Carla shrugged.

"Death, mist, and water. Voices. Does it make any sense to you?"

"Nay. I suspect she was being dramatic. Trying to impress you, she was. Zoe likes people to be in awe of her. Wait 'til you see her at the carnival. She uses tarot cards or reads their palms. The looks on their faces show they believe every word she utters."

"You mean she makes up their fortunes?"

"As a rule. But she is a keen observer of people. Just by looking at them, she can tell how rich or poor they are, where they stand in society, their personalities, and whether they are in good health or ill," Carla said.

"She can tell all that just by looking at them?"

"Aye."

"Do you think she made up my fortune?"

"Probably. I wouldn't give it a second thought if I was you."

"I suppose you're right, Carla. When will we get to the carnival?"

"Soon. We're almost at the village, we'll camp at a distance from it for the night. We'll probably get to the carnival the next day. Have you ever begged, Esmeralda?"

"Begged? No. Why should I do that?"

"Whenever we're near a village or town, we go in and beg for money," Carla explained.

"Why?"

"For fun, and to see who can get the most money. You'd be surprised how much we get."

"What do you do? What do you say?" I couldn't dream of asking people for money. I didn't see any fun in doing that. It sounded degrading.

63

"I can see I'll have to teach you a few things, Esmeralda."

Carla gave me a running account of what to do, what to say, and how to act. I listened to her with growing amazement as we strolled along. Every once in a while I'd wince, as my bare foot came down on a stone or pebble. Carla plodded on heedless of anything on the road.

The sun had passed its zenith when the caravan drew into a pasture, where a fast-running brook could be heard gurgling over rocks.

As usual Rico unharnassed the horses, gathered up his horses, and led the animals to a lush section of the pasture where he tethered them on long chains.

Zorina disappeared inside the covered wagons. She came out with a bright green cotton kerchief and handed it to me. She pulled large, bone hairpins from the pocket of her skirt. She twisted my long braid around and around the back of my head, then secured it with the hairpins. Taking the kerchief back, she wrapped it around my head so that not a tendril of my hair showed.

"That should do it," Zorina said, as she stepped back and surveyed her handiwork. "Remember not to look at anyone directly, Esmeralda. Don't let them see the color of your eyes."

"I won't." I smiled. I was beginning to develop a deep affection for Zorina. Her dusky skin made her teeth so white when she smiled at me. Her features were ordinary on the whole. Black eyes. Sharp, thin nose. Full lips. High cheekbones. But all together, they created an exotic beauty.

With a group of other children of varying ages, Carla and I headed for the village. An air of jovial mischief infected the group as some skipped, some ran, and

64

some walked along the road. Reaching the village, everyone scattered.

"Do you remember what I told you, Esmeralda?" Carla asked.

"I think so." With that, Carla scampered off.

The village was a large one. Like most northern villages and towns, it exuded a gray aura. Buildings were of gray stone, as were the cobblestoned streets. I was reminded of the colliery and all the horrors I had left behind. I was so preoccupied with these thoughts, I bumped into an older man coming out of the butcher shop. The accident jolted me back to my reason for being there.

"I'm so sorry, sir. I should have watched where I was going."

"I should think so, lass. You'd best be keeping your mind on walking."

"I was thinking of my sick mother, and wondering how I could get a farthing or two to buy her some bread."

He laughed. "You'll never be buying much of anything with a couple of farthings."

This wasn't what I expected. Carla told me they'd either shoo me away, or give me the farthings. She never said they would laugh. I was in a muddle and didn't know what to do or say next, especially when the man remained standing there in front of me. I felt like a fool and wanted to run. I hung my head in shame for having failed my first test as a Gypsy. The thought of disappointing Carla and Zorina caused tears to flow from my eyes. I felt a crooked forefinger under my chin, lifting my face. I quickly closed my eyes.

"There, there, lass. No need for tears. I shouldn't have laughed at your plight." After removing his finger, he thrust his hand into his pants pocket. "Here, lass. Here's half a crown. Buy your mum the bread or whatever else she might need."

I lowered my head, took the proferred half crown, and dropped it in my roomy pocket. "Bless you, sir. I'll never forget your kindness. May all the angels in heaven bless you."

He patted me on the shoulder and walked away with a spring in his step.

I fingered the coin in my pocket with a strange sense of elation. Could one feel joy and guilt at the same time? It was so easy. A half crown for a few words! I didn't make that much working twelve hours a day, six days a week, down in the dank, dark mines. I felt triumphant. I wanted to run and find Carla to show her what I had. I quickly surpassed that impulse when I spied a middle-aged woman leaving the bakery shop. I repeated the routine. I was let down when the woman gave me a threepenny bit.

After a couple of hours, I noticed some of the children heading back to camp. I went to look for Carla.

She was several blocks down and around a corner. She was doing her act before a blacksmith. I stayed where I was, half-hidden in a dark doorway as night was coming on. I didn't want to spoil Carla's begging performance.

"Git out of 'ere, you Gypsy brat. I'll not be having the likes of you around 'ere. Be off before I fetch the constable." He gave Carla a rude shove that sent her to the ground.

She scrambled to her feet and brushed her skirt off with an indignant wave of her hand. She put her hands on her hips, leaned forward from the waist, and glared at the man.

"May all your children grow warts on their noses,"

she bellowed at him, then began to stalk away in my direction.

I looked at the man for a moment. Fear registered on his face and in his eyes. As Carla came alongside the doorway, I joined her, matching my stride to hers. We quickly turned the corner, then ran. By the time we reached the camp, we were laughing.

Seeing that Zorina wasn't outside, Carla and I climbed into the wagon. Zorina was sitting on her bed. Wide-eyed, I stared, then swallowed hard. Scattered over the purple velvet coverlet were gold sovereigns. She made no attempt to hide them.

"Look, my girls." Zorina waved her hand over the golden coins. "We still have the fairs and carnivals before us. We shall have a fine winter this year. When we reach Leeds, I shall buy the finest material for your wedding gown, Carla." She put the coins in a tin box, shoved it through a small door under her bed, and snapped the door shut. Then she turned to us. "How did your begging go?"

"Esmeralda did far better than me, Mama." Carla dug into her pockets and tossed the coins on the coverlet.

Zorina counted them. She handed half of them back to Carla, who promptly went to her own bed and sought out her tin box. Instinctively, I knew it was my turn. I took all the coins from my pockets and placed them on the coverlet.

"Oh, my. Half a crown." Zorina smiled up at me. "You did very well indeed, Esmeralda, especially for your first time out. I shall have to find you a tin box."

She stood and poked through some shelves over the top of her bed. She handed me a blue tin box that had held tobacco at one time. I took it and put the coins she handed back to me in it.

"Where should I put the box, Zorina?" I asked.

"There are little compartments under your bed. Put it there."

Carla and Zorina's beds were alongside the wagon. Mine was like a cot behind the small, cast iron stove, the driver's seat on the other side of the wall.

"What are you going to buy with your money, Esmeralda?" Carla asked when we were outside.

"I don't know. Maybe a cream puff with powdered sugar. And you?"

"I almost have enough for a gold bracelet. After the carnival, I might have enough for two gold bracelets!"

"Aren't you going to save any of it for your wedding day?"

"Nay." Her laughter was a light tinkle. "Gypsies judge your wealth by the amount of money you spend, not what you might have hidden away."

"Then perhaps I'll buy more than a cream puff."

"After the carnival, you might have enough for gold earrings."

I studied Carla's earlobes, then felt mine. "I don't have holes to put them through."

"Mama will take care of that. Oh, look. There's Rico with his whip. I wonder if he's going chicken whipping. Come. Let's go ask him."

I followed Carla. Rico was walking with a proud swagger. I still hadn't made up my mind whether I liked him or not. On the whole, he ignored me. But I was beginning to realize that there was a strict division between girls and boys. I never saw them mixing together. Neither did the men and women for that matter. I also noticed that the women waited until a man passed by. They avoided passing in front of a man.

"Are you going for chickens, Rico?" Carla asked her brother as we trailed behind him.

"Aye. That I am."

"Can we come?"

"I'll not be needing girls tagging about."

"Oh, please, Rico. Esmeralda has never seen you get chickens. I want her to see what a clever and skillful brother I have."

Carla knew how to get around her brother. His chin lifted with self-importance, and a smirk of confidence curled on his full lips.

"All right. But stay well behind me. I don't want anyone thinking you're with me."

After walking through fields and over stone walls, we came to a low stone wall that had been carefully reconstructed with cement. Rico looked all around, his whip in his hand. We peered over the stone wall to see a flock of chickens scratching in the dirt behind a large, fancy barn. No one else was in sight.

Rico unfurled his whip. He cast the whip back, then flung it forward with speed and accuracy. The tip of the whip curled tightly about the chicken's neck, killing the animal instantly. With a flick of his wrist, the dead chicken was at our feet. Again the whip went back. Another chicken was at our feet. He took one more, gathered them up, and headed back to camp as though we weren't present.

"Wasn't that something? It's the only real quiet way to nab chickens," Carla said, as we walked some distance behind Rico.

"I never saw anything like it. I must confess I was deeply impressed."

"Wait till you see him at the carnival."

"What does he do?"

"You'll see."

69

Water was boiling in the cauldron. Zorina dunked one chicken in. In seconds she pulled it out and handed it to Carla. I watched Carla yank the feathers out easily, then I did the same thing when Zorina handed me a chicken.

"Put the feathers in that bag, Esmeralda. They make nice pillows," Zorina said, as she defeathered her chicken.

Though I grimaced and pulled my nose up, I managed to disembowel the chicken. Unwanted parts were tossed to the dogs hovering around us.

The task was unpleasant, but worth the disagreeable chore. Supper was an exotic feast for me. The chicken had been cooked in the cauldron with onions, peppers, tomatoes, squash, garlic, and string beans, accompanied by hunks of bread. Although we only had two meals a day, I ate far more food than I ever did with the Boothes. I was beginning to fill out. All the clean, fresh air was making me more energetic, and put color in my cheeks and lips.

After supper the men of the camp started drinking. I didn't know what they were drinking, but I knew it wasn't gin. Being around Frank Boothe, I knew the smell of gin. I'd never forget it.

Groups of people were starting to form to tell stories. The younger people were drifting toward Zoe. Carla and I joined the younger group.

"Zoe must be of a mood to tell one of her stories. She makes everything sound so real. I know you'll enjoy it, Esmeralda," Carla said.

The moonless night made the stars appear brighter and closer. Fires, scattered through the camp, flickered red, orange, and yellow. The very young children sat cross-legged on the ground, while those our age sat on upturned pails or crates.

Zoe appeared majestic as she stood at the open doors of her wagon. She stared at everyone before sitting down on the ledge of her doorway. Like the others, the wagon was high off the ground. In the dark Zoe seemed to float in the air above us. When she spoke, her voice became a dramatic instrument.

"The woodsman was a big, burly man. He had brown hair and a long, brown beard, that spread over his huge chest. With a large axe slung over his shoulder, he left his house and marched into the woods. He searched for the largest, loveliest tree in the woods. When he found it, he put the head of his axe down between his booted feet, spit on his hands, then picked the axe up.

"Now the wee folk were watching this. The old tree was their favorite. They liked to cavort under it. Some of them even lived in and around that tree. They chatted among themselves, testing ideas that might stop the woodsman from chopping down their favorite tree. As he began to swing the axe back, they changed into a swarm of little bees. They stung his arms and then his legs above the tops of his boots. He put his axe down to brush them off and scratch where they had stung him. Satisfied with their work, they changed back, thinking the woodsman would leave that part of the forest.

"But the woodsman didn't leave. He was determined to chop down that particular tree. The wee folk realized they would have to use stronger magic on the woodsman. They picked one of the fairies and, using their considerable powers, changed her into a beautiful young woman, who would melt the hardest heart of any man.

"'Oh, please kind sir, do not chop down that tree," the lovely creature cried.

71

"The woodsman turned to face her. Her beauty wrenched his heart. Once more he put his axe down.

"'Who are ye?' the woodsman asked.

"'I've come to save the tree. I will give you any wish you desire if you spare that tree.'

"He stroked his beard for several minutes. 'Will ye come live with me? Cook and clean me house?'

"'If you will spare that tree, I will live with you and cook and clean your house.'

"So the woodsman put his axe over his shoulder, and led the beautiful girl back to his house.

"'Now ye clean the house and cook my supper. I must go and tend to the animals.' He closed and locked the door behind him.

"The beautiful creature sat down on a rough-hewn wooden chair. Her hearing was keen and she listened. She knew he was chopping down the tree of the wee folk. Each blow of the axe echoed in the forest, and pained her as though she was receiving the blows herself.

"The woodsman returned to fetch his oxen to drag the tree from the forest. But first he wanted to see the fair maiden. She stood when he entered the house, tears streaming down her face. The woodsman embraced her. As he did, she changed into a huge snake with many heads. The snake heads coiled back, fangs bared, as if to strike. The woodsman was so terrified, his hair turned white. He let go of the slimy body and dashed out of the house into the woods.

"He was so consumed by fear, he lost all his will, making it easy for the wee folk to cast a spell on him. They turned him into a tree, growing on the very spot where he chopped down their tree.

"They say in a wood somewhere, every time a woodpecker drills his holes or a deer peels bark off a

72

certain tree, a keening echoes in the woods, a mournful lament that stirs the heart. So ends my tale for tonight. But remember, never disturb anything in the woods, because the wee folk are watching you."

Zoe went into her wagon, shutting both sections of her Dutch door. The sound of those doors banging shut seemed to cast a finality to the night. Everyone remained silent, as though frightened to move or speak lest they disturb the wee folk. Whispering, Carla defied the silence.

"Isn't Zoe wonderful? She has so many different voices. You should hear her tell the story about the ghost that roams the castle with his head tucked under his arm."

"Why is his head tucked under his arm?" I asked.

"His new bride chopped it off." Glee coated Carla's voice. "He roams the castle looking for her."

"Does he find her?"

"You'll have to hear Zoe tell it."

"Oh, tell me, Carla."

"Nay. I'm not a storyteller. If I told the story, it would sound silly. When Zoe tells it, the fine hairs on your arms stand up."

We left the pails and slowly strolled toward our wagon. The fires were dying down. Occasionally a man's laughter could be heard. On the whole the camp was settling down for the night. No laughing or scrapping children. No barking dogs.

It was late and I was tired. I was glad to be climbing into the wagon. Zorina was sewing by candlelight. She looked quite beautiful in an exotic way, as the light flickered over her face.

Suddenly the still night was shattered by the furious barking of the dogs. It wasn't their normal bark of play or anger or curiosity. Their bark had a viciousness that frightened me. Zorina opened the upper part of the wagon's door and peered out.

"Esmeralda! Get out! Run to where we keep the horses," Zorina cried.

The urgency in Zorina's voice caused me not to question her but obey instantly, even though I had no idea why I was running away.

Six

I had no fear of the horses as I wandered among them. I liked them, and I think they sensed it. In the distance lights moved and voices bellowed. I had no idea what was going on back at the camp, and it frightened me. Seeking solace, I put my arms around a horse's mane.

I don't know how long I clung to that horse. It seemed like an eternity. I tightened my hold on the horse when I heard footsteps pounding on the ground and coming toward me.

"Esmeralda . . . you here?"

I released the horse and exhaled all the tension within me. "I'm here, Rico."

He came up to me. "Here, put this kerchief on your head, and go back to the wagon quietly."

"What happened?"

"The constable and his men. We're moving on," Rico informed me.

"Why?"

"Someone put a curse on the blacksmith. He told the constable that if we weren't out of here by morning, he'd get the villagers together and drive us out, even if they had to use guns. Get back to the wagon now,

Esmeralda. I have to get the horses ready to travel."

I knew Carla had hurled the curse, but didn't say anything. Without a word I went back to the wagon.

The next morning the camp was in a different place, a desolate spot next to a slow-moving river. The wagon was empty when I woke up. Outside, fires were already lighted, horses taken to pasture. Zorina handed me a cup of hot black coffee for which I was grateful.

"Where are we, Zorina?" I asked.

"Outside of York. We're within walking distance of the carnival."

"Where is Carla?"

"She went off to look for mushrooms, berries, or whatever else she could find."

"Is the carnival today?"

"Tomorrow." She handed me hunks of bread soaked in bacon grease. She also offered me some slices of melon.

Finishing breakfast, I asked, "I'd like to wash myself and my clothes. Can I use the soap, Zorina?"

With an amused smile on her face, she nodded her head, then went into the wagon. She came out with a blanket and her yellow bar of soap. "Go way down stream, Esmeralda. Use the blanket to cover yourself while your clothes dry."

"Thank you." I took the blanket and soap then walked to the river.

Reaching the water, I piled up some stones to mark the place where I should turn in to reach the camp. The entire area seemed to be devoid of human habitation. I walked a long way down along the river. When I came to a clump of trees and bushes, I stopped. I judged the distance from the camp to be adequate.

I took off all my clothes, then set about washing

76

them. When finished, I spread the clothes over the bushes in the sun. I unplaited my hair, took the soap, and inched my way into the water. I did my hair first, then my body. I noticed my skin was becoming whiter, my pores relinquishing residues of fine coal dust. I rinsed off and waded back to the bank, where I wrapped the blanket around me and sat down.

My first thoughts were of my prince, even though I knew I would never see him again. I closed my eyes and conjured up a vision of him and tried to burn it into my brain. But my thoughts soon wandered to consider what my life might have been before I was eleven. I concentrated all my powers to try and form a picture of my parents, all to no avail. I couldn't imagine what my real name might have been like. I could read, so I must have had some schooling, or a tutor if I was as richly dressed as Ma Boothe claimed.

Loud lowering came from across the river. I looked over to see a herd of cows. The sight and sounds of the cows brought me back to reality. I don't know how long I had been sitting there, but my clothes were dry. I dressed quickly, then plaited my hair in one braid. As I did, I noticed my hair was becoming shinier. I so liked being clean, I decided to wash at every opportunity.

Carla had returned to camp with wild mushrooms, berries, and herbs. The sun was high in the sky when we decided to go and watch the workmen prepare for tomorrow's carnival. Carla knew exactly where it would be held. The walk was long, but not that difficult. The soles of my feet were beginning to toughen.

When we got close enough to hear the workmen, I put a staying hand on Carla's arm. I coiled my braid around my head, secured it with a large whalebone pin, then swished the kerchief over my head. I tied it at the nape of my neck, tucking the triangular piece of cloth under the knot. My vibrant hair hidden from view, we proceeded on our way.

We sat on a knoll and watched the activity on the flat meadow before us. Hammers rang out as wooden stalls were erected. Large and small tents were being roped into place. Animal pens, whose paint had long since faded, were being newly whitewashed. Just watching them made me tingle with excitement. I didn't recall ever having seen a carnival. Dusk was falling when we left.

After supper the men, and some women, began drinking spirits. One man began singing and all gathered around him, including me. He didn't have a very good voice, but the poetry of his words and the meaning of the song held everyone rapt.

When he finished, a chant curled in the night. "Zorina! Zorina!"

Zorina walked into a circle ringed by fires. To the clapping of hands, stomping of feet, rapping of fists on any piece of wood, the clicking of tongues, Zorina began to dance.

With eyes wide, mouth agape, I stared at her. With speed and grace, she twirled, twisted, snapped her fingers, and gyrated her entire torso to the beat engendered by the people. She danced with great elegance, her head held high with pride. The flickering flames of the fires cast her in various lights, making her simple clothes shimmer with different hues. When she twirled, her braid stood straight out. She exuded an aura that put a spell on everyone, especially me.

"I wish I could dance like that," I whispered to Carla.

"Tell Mama. Maybe she'll teach you."

"Do you think she would?" Hope swelled in my heart.

Carla shrugged indifferently.

"Can you dance like that?" I asked Carla.

"I never tried. I really have no interest in dancing. I want to tell stories and fortunes like Zoe."

"Have you asked her to teach you?"

"I know most of her stories by heart. But I have to get her to tell me her secrets when judging people."

"Do you think she will?"

"I'll wear her down eventually. She's very old and won't live forever. I hope to convince her someone has to carry on her tradition."

That night as we prepared for bed, I asked Zorina if she would teach me how to dance. My prayers were answered when she said yes.

Carnival day had arrived. Some wagons rolled onto the carnival grounds, including Zoe's. Rico led one of his ponies toward the festivities, while Zorina, Carla, and I trailed behind.

"Remember, don't buy anything here. We will do our shopping in York. I know a jeweler there," Zorina said.

"What do Carla and I do at the carnival?" I asked.

"Beg. I'm sure you'll do well."

By the time we reached the carnival grounds, Zoe had her wagon positioned between two tents, her rear doors facing a dirt path whose grass had given up its life to the onslaught of a multitude of feet. The grounds had been used for carnivals and fairs for centuries.

As the grounds began to fill with people, I could hear old Zoe's voice crying, "Charms for warts here. Have your fortune told."

Other barkers began to hawk their special talents, games, wares, or assorted shows inside tents. The largest tent housed tables and benches, where food and all types of liquid refreshment could be served.

Children ran about screaming with delight at the

animals, games, and sweet treats offered by vendors. Even I was awed by all the sights, especially the camel whose sole purpose was to give rides to any adventure-some soul.

Once acclimated to my surroundings, the novelty wore off, and I set about my reason for being at the carnival.

I spied a man standing in front of the refreshment tent with a pint in his hand. He was middle-aged and prosperous-looking. Those were the best kind, as I learned from my first foray into begging. Unob-trusively, I sidled near him. I started to sob, just loud enough for him to hear me. Tears rolled over my cheeks, a feat which surprised me.

"There, there, lass. This is a day to laugh, not to cry," he said, patting my shoulder. I cried a little harder. "Now what is having you in all those tears, lass?"

"Someone pinched me half crown me mum gave me. Now I'll have to be going home without having enjoyed the carnival." I effectively managed to say this through choking sobs. From lowered eyes I could see his free hand reach into his pocket. I was able to keep a dour face, even though a triumphant joy was coursing through me.

"Take this, lass, and enjoy yourself." A half crown lay in the palm of his open hand, extended toward me.

"Oh, I couldn't, sir. Me mum told me never to accept money from strangers."

"I'm John Nichols. There. Now I'm not a stranger. Take it, lass. Please let me play knight errant to a lady in distress."

"Well . . . if you insist, sir."

"I do."

"Oh, thank you ever so much." I snatched the coin from his palm and happily skipped away.

I ignored the girls and young women. I knew their pity would only extend to "I'm sorry for you," not hard cash. I tried several matrons, but was lucky to get a shilling from them. Most of the time it was a pence or two. I decided to perform my act solely for the benefit of older men who were exceptionally welldressed.

Emboldened, I raised my pity plea to a crown with some success. I spotted another potential donor and started edging my way toward him. I abruptly halted. The man I had first approached had walked up to my new quarry as though greeting an old friend. I walked the other way. Coins were jingling in my skirt's deep pockets. I decided to spend the rest of the morning looking about. Carla had told me a different crowd usually came in the afternoon.

The hawker outside one tent proclaimed to have the smallest person in the world along with the biggest, a rubber man, and a tattoed lady—a veritable menagerie of human oddities. I would have liked to go in, but I heeded Zorina's admonition not to spend money at the carnival.

A line was forming at Zoe's wagon. I wondered what kind of fortunes she was telling. Rico also had a line of young children waiting for their ride on his piebald pony.

I heard music. Violins, a horn, and tambourines. I wandered toward the rapid, yet melodious sounds. They were Gypsies playing as Zorina danced. A small black pot with some coins in it was on the ground. On the whole, men formed the greater part of the audience. One or two women peered through the crowd out of curiosity. I watched her in utter fascination. When she finished, coins rained into the pot while shouts of *Again* echoed in the air. One of the Gypsy men emptied the pot of its coins, then put them in his pocket. The music and dance resumed. I left to stroll among the game stalls. I watched for a while then meandered along.

Rico's only competition was the camel ride. A tall, ugly animal. I think it frightened most of the children, as the line wasn't very long. Then, too, the camel ride cost twice as much as Rico's pony ride. I was studying the beast when Carla poked my arm. We walked to a less crowded area.

"How are you doing, Esmeralda?"

"Pretty good, I think. I haven't counted the money yet, but I do know I have two guineas."

"A whole guinea from one person?" She looked stunned.

"Yes."

"I don't know how you did that. I think they're a cheap crowd. If I was getting guineas, I'd still be at it. You look like you're resting," Carla said.

"I am. I've approached most of them here. I'm waiting for some new faces to appear this afternoon."

"I'm not doing any begging this afternoon. I've got better things to do." Carla's head lifted with an air of smug importance.

I knew she was dying for me to ask her what she was going to do. I complied. "Doing what?"

"I'm going to help Zoe." Pride coated her words.

"You're going to tell fortunes?" I found that hard to believe.

"No, silly. Zoe is so busy telling fortunes, she said I could sell her charms outside her wagon. I get a third of the money for each charm I sell."

"What are the charms for?"

"Warts and other infirmities. I'll also be selling vials of love potion. I think I'll make more money than begging. Too many Gypsy children are begging. After a while the Gorgios get tired of it and pay no attention."

"I saw Zorina dance. The music is wild and melodic

82

at the same time. It made the dance much more exciting. Why don't the musicians play at night around the camp fires when Zorina dances?"

"The musicians save their instruments for entertaining the Gorgios."

I shook my head. I wondered if I would ever understand the Gypsies or Gypsy life. The sun was high in the sky. I was hot and my throat was parched.

"I'm going to get some lemonade," I declared.

"You really shouldn't spend any money here, Esmeralda. Everything costs twice as much. You could probably get some water for free."

"I'm going to have lemonade. Don't worry, Carla. I'll take it from my share of today's earnings."

"Maybe I'll have some with you." She snaked her arm through mine, and we headed for the refreshment tent.

The afternoon went splendidly. I dropped my request for a guinea to a half crown. The afternoon gentlemen didn't look as prosperous. I was learning to judge which men would part with their money and how much. I was getting quite good at it. Against Zorina's advice, I let them see my green eyes. They never took me for one of the Gypsies, and it made my tale of woe more believable.

With my pockets fairly full and prospective clients waning, I wandered about the grounds. When I heard a lot of people oohing and aahing, I strolled over to see what was going on. I elbowed my way through a throng of people.

Zorina, with her hands on hips, stood with a cheroot in her mouth, her chin thrust forward. Rico stood several feet from her, whip in hand. His arm went back. The whip sounded a sharp crack as it flew forward. The cheroot in Zorina's mouth was cleanly severed. The crowd applauded and threw coins into the

83

same black pot used at Zorina's dance.

Rico wielded his whip in other feats of daring and skill with Zorina assisting. I watched for a considerable amount of time, as my opinion of Rico inched toward the better.

As day slipped into night, most of the Gypsies left, including Zorina, Carla, Rico, and me. The night crowd was mostly young people who weren't interested in pony rides, Gypsy dancing, or beggars. Zoe stayed, as fortune telling and the selling of love potions were popular with the younger folks.

Zorina was astounded at the amount of money I had acquired, and divided it equally. "After you make your purchases in York, Esmeralda, if you have any left, give it to me and I'll have it turned into gold sovereigns for you."

"How do you do that?" I asked.

"There is a man in a pub on our way to Leeds, who will convert shillings and half crowns into gold pieces."

As we approached the walled city of York on foot, I looked up at the castlelike north entrance to the city. Carla informed me it was called Bootham Bar. I could see the towering York Minster soaring above Bootham Bar. We went through the curved arch, and it was like entering a fantasy land.

We stopped for a bit when the great York Minster loomed before us. The imposing medieval cathedral overwhelmed me. I stood there, mouth agape, as though something had weighted my feet to the ground.

"Come along, Esmeralda," Carla urged, tugging at my arm.

I let myself be pulled along, and soon had other sights to replace the wonder of the cathedral. We had turned into a narrow street named Stonegate, where shops displayed their wares behind large glass windows. Both sides of the street were lined with shops. Above the shops were orieled windows decorated by half-timbered structures, the whitewashed sections emphasizing the dark timbers.

I declined going into the draper's shop with Carla and Zorina. I had seen a sundry shop I wanted to explore.

Inside the sundry shop were porcelain figurines, brasses, stationery items, and a multitude of wares which I had no idea of their use. A table caught my eye where, among other things, there were boxes of perfumed soap. I couldn't resist. I purchased three boxes. On my way out I noticed a bookshop across the street. I felt in an indulgent mood.

A distinctive odor assailed my nostrils when I entered. I had experienced that scent before. Like a stream coming to a precipice, my memory was about to fall down into the depths of total recall. I remembered great walls of books and a fire crackling in a large marble hearth. I tried to put people before that fire, but failed. The image faded when the shopkeeper approached and asked if he could help me.

"I would like a book about princes and princesses," I informed him, wondering if he had a book with a picture of my fondly remembered prince.

He lifted his wired-rimmed glasses and pinched the bridge of his nose. He put his glasses back on, as though he couldn't speak without them.

"I have Malory's *Morte D'Arthur*. That's about kings, queens, and knights. I also have the *Arabian Nights Entertainments,* translated from the French. A very popular book."

"What's it about?"

"All different stories. Princes and princesses. A boy with a magic lamp. A sailor who has all sorts of

85

adventures. Many stories in the book."

"I'll take both of them."

"Don't you want to know what they cost first?"

"I trust you won't cheat me. You look like an honest vendor."

He beamed with pride. "I have another book you might enjoy. It was translated last year from the Norwegian by George Dasent. I'll give you a good price on all three."

"Then I'll take all three. How much?" He told me as he went behind the counter to wrap the books. I dug in my pocket and put the correct amount of coins on the counter.

"Thank you, Miss. Do come by again."

I grabbed my parcel, smiled and nodded to him, then left. I looked through the window of the draper's. Carla and Zorina were still inside. I stayed outside and waited, one hand fingering the boxes of soap in one pocket, the other hand fingering the books in my other pocket. I was overjoyed with my purchases.

My complacency began to fade, as I wondered if my reading the tombstones was a happenstance. Perhaps I wasn't capable of reading a book? My face fell in despair.

"My poor child."

I looked up to see a well-dressed, portly woman. She was looking directly at me, pity in her eyes. She opened her reticule and pulled out a small change purse. She removed a number of coins and handed them to me.

"Now take these coins and buy yourself some stockings and a pair of shoes."

"Thank you ever so much, ma'am." I took the money and gave her my best smile. She walked away with a smile and a tilt to her head. I counted the money, to learn it was two shillings more than I had spent. When Carla and Zorina came out of the draper's, their arms

86

ladened with parcels, I told them what had transpired. We laughed until we reached our next destination, a jeweler's shop.

The short, pudgy, bald-headed shopkeeper rubbed his hands together and grinned when he saw Zorina. Clearly, they knew each other. After initial greetings the shopkeeper went into the back room, while a clerk kept an eagle eye on us. Though our business was prized, we were not trusted.

The pudgy man came out carrying a tray which he placed on the counter for our perusal. Gold earrings, neck chains, bracelets, rings, and a single gold locket glinted, as they rested on a bed of black velvet. While Zorina and Carla studied the pieces, I immediately picked up the gold locket, wondering if it resembled the one Frank Boothe had sold. I purchased it out of what one might call sentimentality. Once paid for, I put it on.

"What did you buy that for?" Carla asked me.

"I wanted it."

"You really should have bought earrings, Esmeralda," Zorina said, as she fingered a heavy gold neck chain.

"I have enough money to buy the earrings, too," I declared. My gaze returned to the velvet-lined tray. I spied a pair of earrings exactly like Zorina's. Heavy, wide hoops of gold. While I purchased them, Carla and Zorina settled on bracelets, Zorina's wider and thicker than Carla's.

We headed back toward Bootham Bar. As we came near the cathedral, I insisted on going in.

"Go ahead, Esmeralda." Zorina was eyeing some street vendors. "Don't be too long."

"I won't."

My pace brisk, I entered the magnificent York Minster. A shudder ran through me. Waves of familiarity washed over me. I had been here before.

Perhaps not this particular cathedral, but one extremely similar. I closed my eyes. The grandeur of size, an unbroken stretch of medieval vaulting. Sun streaming through stained glass windows of astounding geometrical tracery. Stone carved like a lace veil. I could almost hear and smell the sea. My recollections were so vivid, so real, they frightened me. I had to get out of the Minster, as what might be locked deep in my memory filled me with terror. An inexplicable concept overpowered me, telling me it might be best not to remember. I spun around and ran out of the cathedral before my memory could return.

Seven

I bit down on my lower lip and clenched my fists, vowing not to cry out in pain, especially with Rico standing nearby. Fortunately, Zorina was quick. The long, hot needle pierced each lobe in seconds. The earrings were immersed in a cup half-full of brandy. Zorina dipped a rag into the brandy, washed off my lobes, then put the earrings through the newly made holes in my earlobes. She promptly drained the cup of its contents. Between my gold locket and gold earrings, I felt quite regal. I went into the wagon and peered in the mirror. I moved my head from side to side, making the earrings sway and glint golden sparks. I dug into my pocket, took the remaining coins out, and put them into my tin box. Though the Gypsy creed was to spend money, I tended to hoard mine. Perhaps it was because I had never had any money of my own when I was at the Boothes'.

As summer began to wane, the caravan moved ever southward. We camped near a river south of Derby, where a horse fair was to be held just outside the city.

As we ate a supper of hedgehog, potatoes, cabbage, squash, onions, and garlic, I questioned Rico about the fair.

"Will you be selling any of your horses?"

A low rumble in his throat passed for a chuckle. "Aye. Probably to the same Gorgio farmer I bought them from."

Zorina smiled. Carla giggled.

"Won't the farmer know his own horse?"

"They never have. These farmers keep their horses in dank stables. They feed them musty oats and old, dusty hay. The horses soon get the heaves and lose weight. I buy them cheap, and the farmer thinks he has duped me. Through spring and summer I rest the horses, and let them feed on green pastures. Soon they are healthy and fat. Their coats have a sheen. The Gorgios never recognize them, and I get a very good price for them without spending a farthing. After a year or two, the horses are back in terrible condition. I buy them and the cycle starts again."

"Doesn't the farmer recognize you?"

"If I think they might, I send another Gypsy to buy the animal."

"Isn't the horse too old by now?"

"If the horse has any gray hairs, I cover them with ink, and hope it doesn't rain until the farmer takes the beast home. We are usually gone by then." He wiped the cauldron with bread, then licked his fingers and stood. "I'd better see to the horses now."

"Is the horse fair like the carnival?" I asked.

"Not this one," Carla answered me. "Just horse-trading. There might be a few vendors around. Zoe usually takes her wagon in hopes of selling some charms, herbs, or vials. The big horse fairs don't start until later. We'll be down in Somerset for the big one. That one is almost like a carnival."

"Will we be begging at this fair?"

"It doesn't pay," Zorina said. "The horse traders are

90

a miserly lot. We could start your dancing lessons, Esmeralda."

"But first we'll go and see what there is for food. Melons and corn are in season, along with everything else," Carla said.

As Rico gathered his horses the next morning, I headed downriver with my perfumed soap. I knew the Gypsies, including Carla and Zorina, thought my penchant for bathing peculiar, if not altogether demented. It also caused the first argument between Carla and me.

"You smell," she declared when I returned, her thumb and forefinger pinching her nostrils together.

"I'm clean. That's a smell you're not use to."

"At least I smell human. You reek like a whore."

"I do not. I smell like flowers."

"You stink like weeds. The whole camp is talking about your bathing all the time. They think you're bewitched by evil fairies."

"Don't be silly. No one has bewitched me."

"Everyone thinks you're trying to lure their men like some siren."

"You don't believe that, do you, Carla?"

"I see the way the men look at you, and the way you sashay around, swinging your hips."

I was shocked. I was only trying to imitate Zorina. I admired her so much. "Believe what you want, Carla. I don't care."

"Besides, you're fouling the water with all your washing and bathing."

"I go downriver where no one uses the water," I said defensively. "It's better than wiping my greasy hands on my hair, like some people I know."

91

"It makes my hair shine."

"It would shine better if you washed it."

"I wish old Jane was back. As Esmeralda you've taken on airs, as though you were a lord's lady. You hoard your money like a miser. You'll never be a Gypsy."

"If it means being dirty all the time, I don't want to be a Gypsy."

"Wait till winter comes. You won't be running to the river to scrub yourself with fancy soap."

"We'll see about that."

Carla laughed. "What are you going to do, milady? Rub yourself with chunks of ice? Roll naked in the snow?"

"I'll do what I have to. Snow and ice can be melted and warmed."

"I don't know who'll build the fire for you. Or are you planning to enchant Rico to do your bidding?"

"You're talking nonsense, Carla."

"Am I? I saw the way my intended gives you the eye. Stay away from him, Esmeralda, or I'll tear your eyes out."

"I don't even know who he is, Carla. And you're not strong enough to best me," I bragged. Our voices were raised in anger. "I'm beginning to think you're jealous of me."

"I could never be jealous of you. You have nothing I want."

"What is going on here? The two of you can be heard all over the camp." Zorina hovered over us.

"Nothing is going on," I said meekly. The last thing I wanted was to upset Zorina.

"Then be off with you, or there'll be no supper tonight." Zorina was definitely angry. She turned on her heel and talked off, hips swaying.

"Are you coming with me?" Carla's chin was thrust

forward, her hands on her hips.

"Yes."

We trudged toward the farms in silence, the tension growing. I hated it. I had been saturated with tension and strain when I lived with the Boothes. I didn't want to have that same painful relationship with Carla or her mother.

"I'm sorry, Carla. Ever since I can remember I was in the filth and slime of the coal mines. I had to bathe in water that had been used by other people before I got to use it. Dirty, sooty water. I was never really clean for years. When I bathed in the river and your mother washed my hair, I watched the dirt flow away. I never knew my skin was so white, I never knew the real color of my hair. Please indulge me, Carla."

"Oh, that's all right. I was upset. You had nothing to do with it really."

"What's bothering you?"

"Getting married. I'm scared. Mama keeps reassuring me everything is going to be all right, but I don't know Nicolo all that well. I've seen him when he drinks, and he looks mean."

"Which one is Nicolo?"

"I'll point him out in camp tonight. He'll be at the horse trading for most of the day."

"Is he an old man?" I asked, glad we were friends again.

"He's around twenty-five, I think."

"If you don't like him, why are you marrying him?"

"Well, he is handsome and spends his money freely. I'll have lots of gold bracelets, and he's a good horse trader. Mama thinks he will make a fine husband for me. Besides, he's the only one who has asked for my hand."

Our pockets were bulging when we returned to camp. We gave our gleanings to Zorina. While Carla

93

went to show her new bracelet to the other girls, I went into the wagon, got one of my newly purchased books, then went to search for a secluded spot by the river. If I couldn't read, I didn't want anyone to witness my embarrassment.

I had chosen the *Arabian Nights' Entertainments*. I sat down under a tree, my back against the stout trunk. I flipped through the pages, putting off the inevitable moment of truth. To my delight the book had black and white illustrations. I looked at all the pictures slowly. Finally I turned to the first page of the text. My eyes scanned the words with ease. I really could read!

I was soon lost in the marvelous tales of the Scheherazade. I didn't hear Carla calling me until she was almost upon me.

"What are you doing?" Carla asked, eyeing the book as though it was an alien and evil object.

"Reading. The stories are wonderful, Carla. I'll read some of them to you if you'd like."

"We don't have time now. We're going to eat, then move on. Hurry up. Everyone wants to be on the road by dusk."

By candlelight, Zorina sewed and I read a story as the wagon jostled along. Carla was rapt as I read aloud. Though feigning not to, I knew Zorina was listening with the same fascination.

The days went by swiftly. We helped ourselves to whatever food was available. We had to buy whatever food we couldn't find. Rico bought more horses. I became used to the clamor of the little children and the barking of dogs. Eight to ten wagons comprised our caravan.

All the families donated a certain sum, and a pig was bought to celebrate All Soul's Day. Each family purchased bottles of brandy to accompany the feast.

The men gutted the pig, throwing the entrails to the dogs. Then the roasting began. Dusk was falling when the feasting started. We ate for what seemed like hours. The brandy flowed freely. Zorina danced. Carla pointed out her husband-to-be. I wasn't impressed. I thought him coarse. His visage—what I could see of it under his broad-brimmed, black felt hat—appeared rough and pockmarked.

When we finished our strong, black coffee, Carla and I wandered over to Zoe's wagon, where she was telling one of her ghost stories, a fitting monologue for All Soul's Day when ghosts and goblins roamed the night. At every crucial point in the story, Zoe would pause to puff on her long-stemmed pipe. She knew how to hold her audience. The dark night and the flickering flames of various fires enhanced her eerie tales.

The next day all slept late. I was the only one stirring. With my precious soap, I padded down the stream we had camped beside. The water was becoming icy. My bath was quick and short. I was grateful for the hot coffee Zorina had brewed. Carla came out of the wagon as though the aroma of coffee had pierced the veil of sleep.

I learned we were camped on a barren stretch of land outside Salisbury. Late in the morning, Carla insisted I go with her.

"Where are we going?" I asked.

"I'm not going to tell you. I want you to see it."

At first the vast Salisbury Plain overwhelmed the stone monoliths in the distance. As we moved closer, the stones dominated the plain.

The giant, rough-hewn stones formed a circle, some were capped lintel-style by equally huge stones. Carla dashed into the circle and romped with carefree glee.

My head was thrown back as I stood and stared up at

the stones. I was reluctant to join Carla in the circle, but I didn't know why.

"Esmeralda! Come join me," Carla called.

With a sense of dread mingled with curiosity, I entered the somber circle. The minute I stepped in, I was embued with a feeling of timelessness, of a power beyond my ken. It was the same sensation I had felt in York Minster. I sat down on an overturned stone near the center.

"Don't you want to dance around the old stones?" Carla asked.

"No. I just want to sit here for a while." I didn't tell her I thought it was almost sacriligous to dance in what felt to be hallowed ground.

Though I stared at Carla while she cavorted, I didn't see her. I saw a young girl of six, dressed in pale green organdy, her orange-red hair dangling in vertical curls. A handsome, well-dressed man sat on a fallen monolith with a beautiful woman by his side. He had his arm around her shoulders. They talked in whispers, then laughed merrily. Every now and then they would look at the cavorting young girl, and smile fondly at her.

Instinctively I knew I was that young girl. This man and woman sitting on the stone were my parents. But I couldn't make out their faces. The clothes they wore were clear and distinct in my mind. But the faces were blurred. I almost cried. I desperately wanted to remember them, but I couldn't. Carla interrupted my introspection.

"Want to play hide-and-seek among the stones, Esmeralda?" she asked.

"Not really."

"You're no fun today." Her lips pursed in a pout. "We may as well go back to camp."

I agreed.

Outside of Dorchester, November was crisping the air as we prepared to walk to the horse fair. Rico had carefully groomed three of his horses for the fair, covering any gray with ink. Zoe's wagon rolled along at a steady pace. Carla and I were faster than Zoe's wagon. Zorina trailed behind with a group of other women. The men with horses and musical instruments had gone ahead. Children were scattered about, some running, some skipping, and some dallying as they played games with each other. We moved together like a disorganized invading army.

The horse fair was much more than I expected. The area of activity must have covered a couple of acres. The food tent was separated from the liquid refreshment tent. A special tent for food and libation was erected for the wealthy gentry. One had to have a special ticket to enter.

An air more reminiscent of a carnival prevailed. Vendors of every ilk had stalls, crates, or cloths spread on the ground, displaying their wares.

A crowd was gathering rapidly. Carla went to assist Zoe, as business promised to be brisk. I had not made friends with any of the other Gypsy girls. I tried several times, but was rebuffed quite rudely. I ceased any attempts in that direction.

Being on my own, I removed the kerchief, my bright red hair falling down my back in a single braid. In the past I noticed people had a tendency to be wary of Gypsies, and the men flirted outrageously with the Gypsy girls, some more bold and insistent than others.

I started my little act immediately. When I thought I had a reasonable amount of coins, I stopped the ruse and enjoyed the fair. People were in a festive and more than generous mood. My pockets jingled an hour before noon.

Monkeys and exotic birds were on display for pet fanciers. A dancing bear performed to the music of a hand-cranked organ. The organ-grinder had his cap on the ground to receive coins. Silks, linens, wines, and spices from the Orient were hawked, filling the air with the tumultuous din of diverse voices, not to mention the drone of adult voices and the squealing of children.

Resting on a large canvas square were books of every size. I squatted to peruse the titles. A very old book caught my eye. I picked it up and turned the now brown pages very carefully. The book contained a collection of stories by Charles Perrault. Two in particular interested me. *Sleeping Beauty* and *Cinderella*.

"How much?" I asked the vendor.

"A guinea."

"I don't believe it. The book is so old it's almost falling apart." I thought Zoe charged a lot for reading palms, but this man's prices bordered on usury.

"It's the first English edition published in 1729 of Perrault's French stories. It's a treasure that can't be replaced." The man was tall and lean, with a dark goatee that he kept stroking. His dark, beady eyes were barely separated by a large hooked nose. I placed the book back down on the canvas and started to walk away. "Miss! Miss! Do come back. Perhaps we can come to some agreement on price."

I turned and walked back to face him. "Six pence."

"Never." He feigned shock. "Four half crowns."

"Too much. The book will probably fall apart before I get home. Two shillings, and that's as high as I will go."

He looked around as though seeking a savior. But the crowds kept passing by his display, more interested in silks and the finer objects for sale. "Two shillings it is. But you have robbed me, Miss."

I handed him the money, picked up the book, and put it in my pocket. Feeling smug, I decided to treat myself. On my way to the food tent, tumblers and acrobats performed with enthusiasm for all who would watch. Charlatans at cards and cutpurses also plied the crowd.

Inside the food tent was a harried woman trying to keep up with her increasing customers. As my turn came at the long table, the stout woman serving eyed me curiously.

"Dearie, how would ye be liking to make yerself a couple of bob?" she asked me.

"Doing what?"

"Giving me a hand back 'ere. Me girl didn't show up."

"But I'm hungry. I came in for a meat pie," I told her. If she knew the amount of money I had in my pocket, she'd realize I had no need of a couple of shillings.

"After the rush of lunch, ye can have whatever ye want to eat for free."

"And a couple of shillings, too?"

"Aye."

I went behind the cloth-covered table. She quickly gave me instructions on how to ladle the soup, which meat pies were which, which were ham sandwiches and which were cheese, along with the cost of the items.

The work wasn't hard and I was enjoying myself. It felt good to be working, rather than begging or lifting food from various farms. I realized lazing around wasn't for me. I liked to be kept busy and being useful.

When the crowd subsided, I had a bowl of soup and a rabbit pie. The woman was kind enough to give me a glass of lemonade, which she made for herself and the girl who was supposed to help her.

"Do ye think ye can stay for the supper crowd, girlie?"

"I can't. I'm sorry. I have to go home."

"I'll be giving ye three bob and a free supper."

I shook my head. "But I'll stay the afternoon and help you clean up."

"How much?"

"For what we agreed upon. Two shillings and the lunch I just ate."

She gave me a sidelong glance, as though I were the village idiot. She shrugged. "All right. Get about it then, girlie. There are bowls to be washed and tins to be cleaned. Water and towels are in back."

I found a tray and loaded it with used dishes, tins, and utensils I had gathered off the long wooden tables. I took them out back and cleaned them. I brought everything back to the tent and put them in their proper place on the serving table. Every now and then a straggler would come in for a hot bowl of soup, to ward off the chill of a November breeze.

The afternoon was slipping by. I was about to tell the woman I was leaving, when in *he* walked! My prince, Mr. Savage, from the colliery. He was more handsome than I remembered. A tall, well-muscled man smartly dressed in black riding boots, dark breeches, and a dark frock coat. Hatless, his thick chestnut hair curled down in back to cover less than an inch of his coat's collar. I stared, a smile frozen on my face. He was approaching my end of the table.

"A bowl of soup, please," he said without looking at me.

My hand shook as I ladled the soup into the bowl. I handed him the bowl, and our fingers touched. I experienced a sensation that confounded me. The thrill it generated along my spine startled me.

"How much?" his deep voice asked.

I couldn't speak. I pointed to the stout woman at the other end of the table. He nodded and left. He still hadn't looked directly at me. He appeared to be preoccupied. He paid the woman and took a seat on the bench by one of the eating tables and began to eat his soup. I gazed at him fondly, as though in a stupor. I had to quell the urge to go and sit next to him.

Several men and a family came in for soup. By the time I had finished filling the bowls for them, my prince was gone. I wondered if he lived nearby, or was on a visit from Newcastle. I told the woman I was leaving. The minute the two shillings were in my hand, I scooted out of the tent and began to search for the prince of my dreams.

I didn't find him.

It was late when everyone returned to camp. After supper I went to Zoe's wagon.

After describing the man in the food tent, I asked Zoe, "Do you see someone like that playing a role in my life?"

She took a puff on her pipe, then put it aside. "Give me your hands, Esmeralda."

I placed my hands in hers. She closed her eyes. She stayed like that for several seconds, then her eyes flew open.

"I see you. I see him. He is reaching out for you. He is wearing a mask of death."

"What does that mean?"

"Wherever he is, death awaits you."

Eight

After a dreary winter, spring hovered in the air like the song of a beckoning siren. Rico decorated the wagon horse with bright red, yellow, and green pompoms. Soon reins snapped, wheels rolled, and harnesses jingled, as the ten-wagon caravan began its trek northward for the summer.

We were somewhere in the Midlands between Leicester and Nottingham, when Carla's bride price was paid in gold pieces. Her hair was symbolically unbraided, and she screamed and carried on while her new husband carried out a feigned abduction. From now on she would wear an orange silken scarf, knotted in a certain way. She now had her own wagon and I took over her old bed, careful to take my tin box of gold pieces with me.

I soon learned that the Gypsies revered family, and the highest feminine ideal was motherhood. I also learned never to bring cut flowers to Zorina. Gypsies thought them a sign of premature death.

I saw less and less of Carla, as she spent most of her time with Zoe learning the tricks of palmistry, the reading of the tarot cards, the use of different herbs, and how to formulate Zoe's elixirs.

Being with them for a year, I still remained on the fringe of being a true Gypsy. I couldn't understand the strict division of women and men, boys and girls. For them heaven and hell did not exist. The young girls would steal candles from any church. All of this and more went against my ingrained nature, especially the endless flow of Gypsy life without the concepts of good or evil, without form or goal.

I devoted a good deal of time to reading stories from my books to the young children of the camp. They seemed to find them as delightful as Zoe's ghost and horror stories. They especially like the one about Snow White and the seven dwarfs. Whatever spare time I had, I devoted to Zorina's dancing lessons.

My pulse quickened as we set up camp near Newcastle, where I had first met the Gypsies.

For several days I walked the outskirts of the colliery, hoping for a glimpse of my prince. I never saw him and soon gave up the quest. I reached the conclusion that he was only visiting here and that his real home was in the south of England.

One day curiosity got the better of me, and I ventured near the row house where the Boothes lived. I patiently waited for some time, and was rewarded when Charlie Boothe came out of the house alone. He didn't look much different than when I had left. Perhaps taller and leaner.

"Charlie! Charlie!" I called in a loud whisper. He turned, hesitated, gave me a puzzled look, then finally came over to me.

"Jane?" He studied me, his eyebrows clashing together in a questioning frown.

"Yes. It's me, Charlie."

"Where ye been? Ye look funny."

"I've been with the Gypsies. We've been traveling all over England."

103

"What ye doing here?"

"In winter we move south. In summer north. Tell me, how is everyone? Did Henry ever come back? Have you heard from him?"

"Nay. Nary a word."

"And the girls?"

"Sarah and Alice have married. Colliery men."

"And Maggie?"

"No man will be having her, with her mean disposition."

"And Ma. How is Ma?"

"Died."

"How?" I was shocked and saddened. She did try to be a good mother to me.

"When you disappeared, Da blamed it on her. Gave her a good thrashing he did. After that, I don't think she had the will to keep living. She got poorer and poorer, then died."

"I'm so sorry, Charlie. How are you doing?"

He shrugged. "All right, I guess. I'll be leaving here in another year or so. Going to Newcastle, I am, to look for Henry."

"And your Da? Has he taken to beating you, now that's there's no one left?"

"Nay. After Ma died, his cough became worse. Now his coughing spells leave him too weak to punish anyone. He justs sits and drinks 'til he's asleep. Maggie and me do as we want. Where did ye get the gold earrings? Do the Gypsies make ye wear them?"

"No. I bought them."

"Where did ye get the money?"

"At fairs and carnivals."

"Stealing?"

"No. I worked for my money." I wasn't about to tell him the kind of work I did. He would never understand how much work there was in begging.

He shrugged again as if he didn't care what kind of work I did. "I must go. Being Sunday, I'm meeting some of the lads in the village." Without so much as a wave goodbye, Charlie Boothe stalked off.

I stared after him for a few minutes, then went back to camp, knowing the Boothes would never be part of my life again.

As the seasons waxed and waned, the routine of horse fairs and carnivals was continued as we wended southward. Once again my hopes of seeing my prince became predominant. I was sharply disappointed when we turned southeast toward Kent, instead of southwest. We remained in Kent for the winter. In the spring Carla gave birth to a baby boy.

My life took on a different aspect when I was about eighteen. I was never sure of my exact age, but I judged eighteen to be about correct. A number of the Gypsy men took more than a casual interest in me, especially Rico. By this time I could dance as well as Zorina, and I noticed the lascivious glances he cast my way after I danced. Most of the men did. Now Rico smiled at me more often. On rainy days when we huddled in the wagon, he always sat next to me, one knee moving so it would touch mine.

"Would you like to ride one of my horses, Esmeralda?" he asked one day.

"I'd love it."

"Let's go."

He took my hand, and led me to the pasture where his horses were tethered. He put a bridle on a mare, then untethered her. I pulled the back of my skirt through my legs and tucked it in my waistband, as I had seen Zorina do many times. He made a foothold with his hands. After placing my foot in it, he heaved, and I was astride the horse. Rico handed me the reins and smiled.

"Don't go too far," he warned.

"I won't. I'll stay in this pasture."

At first I was apprehensive about my abilities to ride a horse, but didn't want Rico to think I was a coward. I gently urged the horse forward. As the mare plodded along, I felt completely at ease. In my mind's eye I could see a little girl with red curls, dressed in a green velvet riding habit on a chestnut mare. A handsome man on a stallion was riding next to her. I could hear the little girl saying, "Let's race, Poppa."

"In another year. Your skills aren't perfected yet," the man replied. Again his face was blurred. But I knew I was that little girl. The vision quickly faded and I couldn't bring it back.

Out of frustration I pressed my ankles into the mare's flanks. She took off at a lively trot. Riding seemed to come naturally to me. I quickened the mare's pace and loved the sensation. I rode from one end of the pasture to the other, then back to where Rico was standing.

"You ride well, Esmeralda." He held up his arms for me to dismount.

I lifted my leg over the horse's head and slid down, his hands curling about my small waist. His eyes hooded as he stared at my lips. Taking a firm grip on my waist, he pulled me against him, his mouth coming down on mine hard. When I started to pull away, one arm swept around me, the other cradled my head. I decided it was rather nice to be held and kissed. I relaxed. When the kiss was over, he dropped his hands, and stood back with a smug smile on his face.

"You have become a very beautiful woman, Esmeralda," he stated with a gleam in his eyes.

"I'm flattered that you think so, Rico."

106

"I think so. Very much. We'd better get back now."

He slipped his arm about my waist as we strolled back toward camp. The minute the camp came into view, Rico dropped his arm and walked off in a different direction.

With increasing frequency, Rico sought me out whenever I was alone. Over a period of time, his kisses became more intimate, more demanding. But he never came near me when others were around. I had a strong suspicion I was being courted and thoroughly enjoyed it, especially as I got to ride with a fair amount of constancy.

We were heading south again. We camped on a heath outside Falmouth in Cornwall, while waiting for the day of a large horse fair. Carla had given birth to another son and was too busy to accompany me and Zorina on a sojourn into Falmouth.

Falmouth was not only a popular seaside resort, but also hosted a shipbuilding industry and repair yards. More important to me and Zorina, was that the port had a busy coastal trade. We purchased silks and linens. Zorina couldn't resist some of the gold jewelry. My earrings and locket were enough for me. I preferred to see my gold coins increase.

With the horses well-groomed for the fair the next day, the men began their nightly ritual of drinking wine or brandy. I was pleased when the air echoed with my name, urging me to dance. To the clapping of hands and pounding of feet and hands, I began. I twirled, whirled, and undulated while snapping my fingers. Whenever I came near Rico, I would lift my skirt to reveal my well-turned ankles.

As I finished the dance, a young, seated Gypsy man grabbed my wrist and pulled me down into his lap. He kept trying to kiss me, but I avoided it by constantly turning my head. I also tried to get off his lap, but he had a firm arm around my waist.

Rico, clearly in a rage, stalked over, grabbed one of my flailing arms, then gave the man a shove so rough, he toppled off the crate he was sitting on. The man quickly scrambled to his feet and seized the whip curled at his side. Rico pushed me aside as he snatched his own whip. The two men moved to a clearer spot, and the stalking began.

They circled around each other, each judging their opponent. The man's whip whistled through the air as it reached for Rico. Rico neatly sidestepped the long, black weapon. In seconds his own whip snapped low, curling around the man's leg. Rico pulled his whip sharply, causing the man to tumble to the ground. With a flick of his wrist, Rico released his whip.

As Rico drew his whip back, the other gypsy man was hurling his whip back from a crouched position. He let it fly with amazing speed. The tip caught Rico at the side of his waist, tearing his white shirt and leaving a red welt on his flesh. Rico's eyes blazed with raw anger.

Furiously he flung his whip at the man over and over, first catching him on the arm, then on the shoulder. Trying for Rico's head, the man only succeeded in flicking Rico's hat off. With lips drawn in fury, Rico flexed his whip on the ground until it resembled a swiftly moving snake, as they circled each other once more. Suddenly Rico's whip crackled like a sharp clap of thunder, and his whip curled around the man's wrist, causing the other Gypsy to cry out in pain and drop his whip.

As Rico was about to wield his whip with deadly accuracy, an older Gypsy stepped between them.

"Enough! Honor has been served," the old man declared.

Rico picked up his hat and set it on his head. He coiled his whip, then refastened it at his hip. He stalked off toward the pasture where his horses were tethered.

Though thankful no one was seriously hurt, I felt a certain pride and satisfaction knowing that Rico had fought for me. I wondered how long it would be before he asked me to marry him. Even more curious, I pondered what my answer would be. Did I really want to marry Rico and be tied to the Gypsy way of life for the rest of my days?

This time I was to dance at the big fair while Zorina tended to Carla's babies, who were too young to go to the fair. I swooshed my skirts around, snapped my fingers, and danced to the accompaniment of gypsy music. To my elation I commanded the same admiring glances from men as did Zorina. I was quite pleased with myself, and the pot was filled and refilled with coins. When the coins were divided, I had a sizable amount.

The fair had gone well for the Gypsies. Much drinking and merriment ensued that night at the camp. Zorina danced. Zoe told ghostly tales. Men sang songs. I revelled in all of it, for I had the feeling that Rico was going to propose to me within the next few days.

The plan was for us to camp on the heath for the winter, or until we were told to move. Two days after the fair, Rico was watching me with unusual intensity. My heart pounded. He was going to ask me today, and I hadn't formulated a reply. I began to bite my lower lip as he came toward me.

"Would you like to ride one of my horses, Esmeralda?" he asked with a toothy, confident grin.

"Yes."

"I'm going to the pasture now. Wait a while before

109

you come down."

I nodded. I waited for what seemed an eternity, then padded toward the pasture, still not knowing what I would say if Rico did ask me. He had the horse untethered and the reins on. I managed a brisk gallop around the pasture, hoping to reach a decision. But my mind was numb. An image of Mr. Savage kept flashing before my eyes.

I brought the horse to a halt alongside Rico and slid down. After removing the halter and reins, he retethered the horse, then came to stand before me. He took me in his arms and hungrily kissed me. At the same time he brought me to the ground, his lips never leaving mine. His hand began to roam over my prone body. He fondled my breasts a little too roughly, I thought. When he reached down to grasp the hems of my skirt and petticoats and started to pull them up, I gave him a sharp rap on the shoulder, rolled away, and stood. He looked up at me, startled.

"What's the matter with you, Esmeralda?" His face was a dark cloud, his eyes narrowing and reflecting a cruelty born of frustration and anger.

"I don't want to do that."

"You don't even know what I was going to do."

"I do so." Inadvertently I had seen Frank Boothe having intercourse with his wife. It looked ugly. Frank Boothe was a brutish man who liked to hit while he performed the act.

"How do you know?"

"I just know."

His smile was more of a sneer. "All you female Gorgios like to have their men. How many men have you had, Esmeralda?"

"I've never had a man!" I cried.

"Then come here. I won't hurt you, I promise."

"I will not come to you, Rico. Never. Only husbands

110

and wives are intimate."

"You know better than that, Esmeralda." His face suddenly became lecherous. He got to his feet. The look in his eyes frightened me. He was a man bent on having his way, and he was much too strong for me. I knew I had to reach the safety of the camp before he did something I would regret for all my days. The pasture was much too isolated. I turned on my heel and ran for dear life.

"You're a bloody tease, Esmeralda. But you'll be mine before long," he called after me.

Zorina was preparing supper when I reached camp. I went over and haunched down beside her, letting the delicious aromas calm my rattled nerves.

"Did you have your pony ride?" Zorina asked.

"Yes." I paused thoughtfully. "When is Rico going to marry?"

"Soon." Zorina turned to gaze at me directly. "I hope you haven't fallen in love with my son. Have you, Esmeralda?"

I shook my head. "No." Too much cruelty was latent in Rico, but I didn't say that to Zorina.

"Well, don't. He will never marry a Gorgio girl. In fact, he has asked for Nicolo's sister as a wife. They will marry soon. She is a good girl and will make him a fine wife."

"She's only thirteen." I was stunned that he could try to make love to me after he had asked for another's hand in marriage. I was angry and hurt.

"Thirteen is not too young to become a Gypsy bride. It is time Rico married."

All through supper I felt like an utter fool. In the wagon that night, with Zorina gently snoring, I lay on my cot wide-awake. The foolish feeling left to be supplanted by the previous anger and hurt, but something new was added. Fear. If Rico had been engaged all along, I now realized that he had never intended to marry me. His advances were of a carnal nature, not a loving one. I became concerned for my well-being at the Gypsy camp. What if the other Gypsy men thought of me in that light? I would soon become the whore of the Gypsy men. There was nothing I could do but leave right away. I grabbed my shawl, carefully opened the cabinet under my bed, and took my tin of money. I shoved it into my pocket and silently left the wagon. I was thankful the dogs were used to me. Not one of them barked.

When I felt I had put enough distance between me and the Gypsy camp, I stretched out on the heath. I interlaced my fingers and put my hands under my head. While I stared at the stars, I knew I had to have a plan. Now I was glad I had saved my coins.

I plotted a course of action. I would buy a fashionable outfit, then study newspaper advertisements for a position as a ladies' companion or governess, even though my skills in that direction were probably not the highest. I had enough money to house and clothe myself for a considerable time. Surely I would find a position by then.

In the morning I longed for Zorina's hot, strong coffee. I decided to go into the town of Helston. Once I reached there, I would have a good breakfast, then book a room at the inn called Angel. I covered about two miles during the night. That would leave about six more miles of walking before I reached the bridge that crossed the River Cober. Then I'd be in Helston.

Entering the town, the first thing I looked for was a tea shop. My stomach was grumbling for food. Heads turned and eyed me warily as I walked down the main street. I spied a tea shop. With my head held high, I entered. Seeing the waitresses stop their work to stare at me, the owner looked my way. A stern frown settled

112

on her face. The tall, older woman bustled toward me. Hands on hips, she glared down at me.

"Git out of here. We don't be wanting the likes of your kind in here." She practically growled at me.

"I would like some breakfast. I have the money to pay for it," I declared.

"Out!" she screamed.

Not wanting to bring any further attention to myself, I left. Perhaps it would be better if I was properly dressed, I thought. I had passed a dress shop on my way to the tea shop. I turned around and retraced my steps. The people in the streets did more than keep an eye on me. They stopped and glared at me as though I was the head witch of a coven. I quickly entered the dress shop and closed the door behind me.

This time the woman was short, but hefty. I had no doubt she could lift me and throw me into the street bodily. Her lips were set in a thin, determined look as she marched toward me. She curled her pudgy fingers around my upper arm like an iron coil, then paraded me to the door. Without a word, she opened the door and shoved me out with such force, I went sprawling into the street.

As I got to my feet and brushed myself off, I was struck by a tomato.

"Git out of Helston! We don't want thieving Gypsies in our town, putting curses on our people." He hurled another tomato.

I tried Carla's old ploy. I put my fists on my hips, thrust my chin forward and yelled, "May all your children have warts on their noses." It was not the thing to do.

He was joined by several other men and a number of women. Vegetables began to pelt me until I thought it was best to make a hasty retreat.

I began to run, hoping I would soon be out of town.

To my amazement, they followed, gathering a group of children to run with them. Their aim was becoming more accurate. Ahead the buildings seemed to give way to trees and fields. I increased my speed. Unfortunately, so did my pursuers.

As I reached the road leading out of town, the impact of objects became brutally painful. I was stunned to see small rocks bouncing on the road. Their vegetables had given way to pebbles and stones.

I overcame my initial shock and became angry. I wasn't a man-eating beast to be warded off with lethal weapons. I stopped, turned around, and picked up some stones on the side of the road. I threw them at them with meticulous aim. One woman left crying. I was beginning to enjoy myself.

Suddenly the attack halted, some of the people taking backward steps.

"What's going on here?" asked a deep baritone voice behind me.

I turned. My mouth gaped. My eyes widened in disbelief. On the seat of a richly appointed trap, sat my Mr. Savage. I became immobile as I stood and stared at him. I was so enraptured, I never heard nor saw the stone that struck my temple. I crumpled to the ground as inky darkness drenched my brain.

Nine

I was lying on what felt like a leather couch. My head pounded as if a smithy was striking his anvil. Each hammering sent waves of pain coursing through me. Slowly, voices began to penetrate the veil of agony in my head.

"Are you sure, Tom?" the deep male voice asked.

"Positive. She is the only person I have ever seen with a star-shaped mole on her ankle. The old boy isn't in the best of health. You'd better get her to him right away."

"Can she be moved?"

"I don't think there has been any great damage. We'll know better when she comes around. She'll have quite a bump on the side of her head for at least a week. Perhaps less if cold compresses are used."

"Couldn't you give her some of the stuff that came out a few years ago to bring her around?"

"You mean smelling salts?"

"Yes. That's it."

"I'd rather not in this case. Head injuries are not the same as swooning. If she doesn't snap out of it soon, then it might be more serious than I thought."

I opened my eyes to see two men standing in the

middle of the room. One was my handsome prince. He was much taller than I remembered. He towered over the other man, who had a large paunch, a clean-shaven chin, with mutton chops of wiry gray and black hair stopping just short of his chin. His grizzled hair rose to a circle around his head, leaving his pate bald. Wire-rimmed glasses were perched just above the flare of his nostrils.

My eyes were magnetically drawn back to Mr. Savage. He still had that thick, wavy chestnut hair that curled below the collar of his frock coat. His shoulders seemed broader, his hips narrower. His tight, fawn-colored breeches and knee-high, black boots revealed well-muscled legs, especially his thighs. He still sported a clean-shaven face, which emphasized his wide mouth—a thin lip resting over a full lower lip. His eyes were still like chunks of coal, but now they had fine lines radiating from the corners.

I sat up. The minute I did, I had to cradle my head in my hands, lest it fall off my neck and roll across the floor.

"Ah! Our patient is awake," the stout man declared as he came over to me. "How do you feel, my dear?"

"My head hurts."

He chuckled. "I can well imagine. I'm Dr. Thomas Marsh. The man who brought you here is Mr. Michael Savage. And what is your name, my dear?"

Michael Savage. The name rolled in my head as though it would disperse the pain. "I'm called Esmeralda."

"And what is your last name?"

"I don't know." I looked over at Mr. Savage. He was gazing down at me, his arms folded across his chest.

"Don't you have a last name?" the doctor asked.

"Probably." As briefly as possible I related my circumstances from the age of eleven. I didn't mention

116

my reason for leaving the Gypsies. "So you see, prior to eleven years of age, I have no memory. I do know I can read and ride a horse."

Dr. Marsh turned his head and gave Mr. Savage a knowing glance before turning back to me. "Stand up for me, my dear, and walk around the room."

I did as requested, casting furtive glances at Mr. Savage. I even put a little swagger in my walk, as I had learned in the Gypsy camp. Though my head still hurt, everything else seemed to be all right.

"Do you feel dizzy?" Dr. Marsh asked.

"No."

"How is your vision? Any blurring or spots?"

"No."

Dr. Marsh turned to Mr. Savage. "I don't think any permanent or serious damage has been done, Michael. I'll have her take a small dose of laudanum. That should ease the pain as you travel to Wyndcliffe."

"Wyndcliffe? Where is that?" I asked.

"An estate on Cape Cornwall. About four miles from here," Mr. Savage informed me.

"Why are you taking me there?"

Mr. Savage's smile was enigmatic. "You'll soon find out, lass."

"Suppose I don't want to go?" I stuck my chin out defiantly, while my hands went automatically to my hips.

"Would you prefer I take you back to your Gypsy friends?" he asked, as the doctor left the room.

"I don't have to go back to any Gypsy camp. I'm perfectly capable of taking care of myself."

"I'll make a bargain with you. Let me take you to Wyndcliffe Manor. If you don't like it, you'll be free to leave. I'll even pay for your fare to whatever place you desire."

I frowned. "Why do you want me to go there?"

117

"There's someone there I want you to meet."

"Who?"

"I'd rather not say until you meet him."

I shrugged, thinking it wouldn't do any harm to see this person. I might even get a free meal. The doctor returned with a small glass in his hand.

"Drink this, my dear." He extended the glass to me. I took it and drank the liquid, then handed the glass back to him. "That should ease your distress for a while. If your head feels worse, or you have any dificulties as a result of the blow, do come back and see me." His smile was quite avuncular.

The fine hairs on my arms rippled when Mr. Savage took my hand and helped me onto the seat of the trap. No one had helped me clamber onto the Gypsy wagon. As he went around the trap to the driver's side, I stared out over Mount's Bay.

On a pyramidal hill gleamed a white castle, as the sun spread its rays on the crag surrounded by the sea. A fairy-tale aura clung to it. Perhaps that was a good omen.

"What is that?" I asked, pointing to the isle when he settled on the seat beside me.

"St. Michael's Mount. An old medieval monastary of the Benedictine Order. It boasts its own clear spring water."

"Do they run ferries to it?"

"No need. Low tide reveals a causeway, and one can walk to the Mount."

"Why do they call it St. Michael's Mount?"

"They claimed the archangel St. Michael appeared there in the fifth century. In the castle's chapel there is a beautiful stained glass window, depicting St. Michael spearing a devil."

"You've been there?"

"When I was very young." He turned and smiled at me.

118

"Are the monks still there?"

"It's privately owned now."

"What's it like inside?" Though the island was out of view, its memory lingered in my mind.

"Much lighter and airier than one would expect of those old medieval castles. As I said, I was young. All I remember is an armory, and an old vaulted hall with a plaster frieze of a hunt." He paused as we veered inland. "What was it like living with the Gypsies?"

I shrugged. "I was never really one of them. I was an outsider looking in. I guess my strongest impression was a sense of freedom. But I did get tired of always being on the road. Sometimes I longed to stay in one place."

He didn't question me further, and I offered no more information. I was more than content to furtively gaze at him when I thought he wasn't looking. Who was he? Would he turn out to be some sort of ogre? But I really wasn't worried. I knew how to handle myself, and how to ward off unwanted attentions from a man. He seemed kindly. After all, he did take me to a doctor when I was felled by that stone. He could have left me where I had fallen.

Soon I was distracted by a plethora of gulls stridently screeching overhead. Absorbed in their avian maneuvers, I didn't notice we had entered into a long, gravelled driveway until Mr. Savage said, "There she is. Wyndcliffe Manor."

The pride in his voice was pronounced, and caused me to look at my surroundings. The long driveway was lined with urns on raised pedestals. Behind the urns were shaped evergreens, tall, oblong ones with shorter, rounded ones in between. Though the driveway was impressive, the house dominated the landscape as it loomed before me.

Wyndcliffe Manor was a huge oblong block with

cross wings, much like a gigantic H. Tall windows shimmered and scintillated from the rays of the sun. They flickered in varying rainbow shades, as though each was being consumed by a ghostly fire. The prominent cornice was surmounted by a hipped roof from which windowed dormers protruded. Above the hipped roof of the main structure, the flat surface was encased by a balustrade. Chimneys were symetrically placed at intervals. Directly in the center of the flat roof, a decorative cupola soared above the chimneys. Flanking the first set of steps to the main entrance were statues of the human figure, with a Grecian flavor to them.

Mr. Savage brought the trap to a halt before the two sets of marble steps. As though by magic, a footman appeared to lead the trap away once we left it. Mr. Savage cupped my elbow and nodded for me to climb the steps to the immense front door.

Over the magnificent oak door, a protruding, semicircular canopy was supported by richly carved brackets. Under the hood of the canopy, a carved hawk was fiercely clutching a miniature figure of a man dressed in armor. To the right of the door was a long, brass chain with a large ring at the end of it. Mr. Savage pulled the ring.

An impressive butler opened the door. He was a tall, nicely proportioned man with a thin, sharp nose. But it was his eyes and his hair that struck me. His blue eyes bulged from their sockets, much like a frog's. His thick mane of white hair was heavily greased with pomade, as though it would fly about his head if not contained by the commercial product. He smiled at Mr. Savage, then looked at me. Though his facial expression didn't change, his eyes registered something akin to sheer horror. His gaze quickly reverted to Mr. Savage.

"Mr. Michael, the family is in the rear parlor," the

butler said in a gravelly voice.

"I came to see the old man. Is he up?"

"I'm afraid so, Mr. Michael. Much against the doctor's orders, I might add. At least he is remaining in his rooms." As Mr. Savage began to lead me into the house, the butler cleared his throat. "Ahem. Shouldn't this girl be going in through the rear, Mr. Michael? I would dislike rousing the ire of the family."

"I'll take full responsibility, Jerome."

The butler stood aside and we entered the house. The foyer was a marvel in itself. The marble floor was cool to my bare feet. The travertine-marbled walls seemed to have a life of their own, with cherubs and fawns in playful stances as they rested in concave niches in the walls. My eyes went to the plastered ceiling, where heavy wreaths waved between flowers, leaves, and fruit. It made me think of a spring garden covered by snow. Directly behind the foyer, an open doorway revealed an elaborate dining room. I was startled to see a young woman come through the open door into the foyer.

"Michael, I thought you were on your way to Falmouth," the young woman said.

"There has been a change in plans, Amanda."

Her gaze shifted to me, and her nose crinkled as though she had smelled something foul. "What's a wench like that doing in our foyer?"

"I'm taking her to see the old man."

"Really, Michael. Are you mad? She looks like a Gypsy to me."

"She is a Gypsy."

"Well, you'd better get her out of here before any of the family sees her. Really, Michael. Bringing a creature like that into this house is irrational. She probably has lice and is contagious with some dread disease." She grimaced as though a dead rat had been

121

placed before her. "And why take her to Grandfather in heaven's name? He is ill enough without you subjecting him to God knows what disease."

"I'll worry about that, Amanda. Now, if you'll excuse us."

He grabbed my elbow and steered me toward the right with a "Well, I never," echoing after us. From the corner of my eye, I could see this Amanda fleeing back from whence she came like the furies of hell were after her.

He ushered me through an open door to another wide hall, where straight flights of stairs were at right angles to each other, the second flight of stairs going in the opposite direction, leaving an open well in the center. A crystal chandelier dangled high above the well. Along the white plastered walls were various portraits in ornate, gilted frames. Mr. Savage was moving so swiftly up the stairs, I didn't have time to look at the portraits. I only had a fleeting glimpse of them.

We moved down corridor after carpeted corridor. I hoped he didn't vanish on me, for I would surely get lost in that labyrinth of corridors. Finally, he halted before a panelled mahogany door and knocked.

"Come in," a voice inside boomed.

"I'm sorry if I'm disturbing you, sir," Mr. Savage said, as he opened the door and gave me a little push into the room.

"Oh, do stop apologizing, Michael. You sound as bad as those idiots downstairs." He looked me up and down with intense scrutiny. "What have we here, Michael? You think this Gypsy might have some miracle powders to cure me?" He chuckled.

I could see he was a sick, old man. His body was thin and frail. His skin was sallow, and his hair was nothing more than white wisps clinging to an almost bald head. Still, he held himself with an aristocratic bearing. His withering features spoke of a once good-looking man, and there was merriment in his green eyes that belied his sickly appearance.

"No, sir. This girl has the mark."

The old man's expression sobered immediately, and he stared hard at me. Soon his eyes became watery, as though tears would spill forth any minute.

"Show him your ankle, girl," Mr. Savage ordered.

I lifted my skirt to the middle of my shin and thrust my foot out, turning it slightly so the star-shaped mole showed.

The old man glanced at it briefly before his gaze returned to my face. "Where did you find her, Michael?"

"She was being run out of Helston by the townfolk."

"I am James Hardwicke. What is your name, child?"

"I used to be called Jane at one time. When I went with the Gypsies, they called me Esmeralda," I answered him, bewildered by the compassion in his eyes.

"Leave us, Michael." When Michael left, he said, "Come here, child. Sit over here." He nodded to one of two chairs on either side of the fireplace.

"I am not a child," I stated firmly, as I sat down in the padded chair.

"At my age anyone under thirty is a child. I didn't mean to offend you. Would you care for tea?"

"Very much. I haven't had any breakfast."

He pulled a bell cord before seating himself next to me. In minutes a maid appeared. "Bring tea and make sure there are plenty of scones with butter and jams. Also tell Edith to prepare one of the suites in this wing. The rose one, I think. She will be having a new charge."

"Yes, sir." The maid bobbed a curtsey and, after giving me a peculiar look, departed.

Mr. Hardwicke leaned his bony frame forward,

123

elbows on knees, steepled forefingers resting on his chin. "I would appreciate your telling me all about yourself from the very beginning, in as much detail as you can remember."

The thought of a breakfast made me oblige the old man. I was still talking about the Boothes when the tea tray was wheeled in. I dispensed with my discourse. I was ravenous, and didn't try to hide my need for food. Mr. Hardwicke seemed pleased at my healthy appetite. Once sated, I resumed my tale of how I went to live with the Gypsies. By now his arms were stretched out on the chair, his head leaning back on the chair, his eyes closed. I thought he had fallen asleep, so I halted my narrative.

"Don't stop, child. I want to hear all of it." He kept his eyes closed and maintained his position.

"I thought you were asleep."

"I'm listening to every word, child."

I continued at a slower pace, thinking I might be able to stretch my story until lunchtime and get a free lunch. I was reluctantly concluding my tale when a soft knock sounded at the door.

"Who is it?" James Hardwicke called.

"'Tis me, Edith."

"Come in."

A young maid entered and respectfully curtsied. "The young lady's room is ready, sir. I also took the liberty of drawing a bath for her. What about clothes, sir?"

"Did you prepare the rose suit for her?"

"Aye, sir."

"Good. I think the clothes in there will fit her."

"But, sir . . ."

"Those clothes will do nicely, Edith." His tone indicated he would brook no argument.

"Aye, sir."

"Go with Edith, my child. We'll talk again over lunch. Edith, have someone tell Michael I want to see him."

"Aye, sir." Edith looked at me with a quizzical expression.

I rose, nodded to Mr. Hardwicke, then walked toward the maid, thinking about the glorious free lunch. Before my foot went over the doorsill, another thought struck me, and I turned to face Mr. Hardwicke.

"You know who I am, don't you?" I asked.

"Yes, I do, child."

"Tell me."

"There's a lot to tell. We'll talk about it at lunch. Now go with Edith before your bathwater is cold."

My heart pumped wildly. At last I was about to learn who I was. I only hoped the discovery would bring me happiness and not lifelong sorrow.

I went with Edith.

Ten

The rose suite was aptly named. The bedchamber walls were a pale pink with two large windows where light streamed in. The rose-colored satin coverlet on the bed was complemented by the crimson velvet drapes of the four-poster bed. The tester, which canopied the bed, was of the same crimson velvet. The bed was flanked by two nightstands. Green leaves intertwined with all shades of roses spread over the pink background of the Aubusson carpet. A chest, a dressing table, and a small table were of polished cherry wood. The small table was placed next to a pink satin chaise lounge, placed near the fireplace of pink marble.

A door opened on a small corridor that housed a lavatory on one side and an open closet on the other. At the other end of the corridor was a sitting parlor, which I didn't get to explore as Edith quickly ushered me into the lavatory where a full tub, scented with lemon verbana, was waiting for me.

As I stepped into the tub, Edith took my Gypsy clothes away. On a stand next to the tub was a porcelain bowl filled with an array of scented soaps. I felt like a princess. Edith came back to wash my hair.

She was far gentler than Zorina.

"What do I call you, Miss?" Edith asked.

"I don't know. I've been called Jane and Esmeralda. I suspect Mr. Hardwicke knows my real name. I'll probably have a new name after lunch. You'll have to wait until then, Edith. Who *is* Mr. Hardwicke?"

"He is the owner of Wyndcliffe Manor and vast amounts of acreage. He has many tenant farmers and owns the tin mines at Botallack and Cambourne. The Botallack mine is abandoned now, but he still owns the land and the minerals rights. I hear the mine at Cambourne is a large one and very productive. I always hear Mr. Savage talking about the South Crofty mine."

"Who is Mr. Savage?" I asked, as I stepped out of the tub and Edith began to towel me off.

"Mr. Savage manages the entire estate, especially the mines."

"Does he live here?"

"He does now that Mr. Hardwicke is ailing. He used to live in the manager's cottage, where he was born," Edith answered me.

"Does anyone else live here?"

"Mr. and Mrs. Nigel Lambert with their two grown children, and Mr. and Mrs. Cecil Melville with their grown daughter. Mrs. Lambert and Mrs. Melville are Mr. Hardwicke's daughters," Edith explained. "We'd better get you dressed. It's almost lunchtime, and Mr. Hardwicke detests tardiness."

With undergarments on, Edith led me to the open clothes closet. Day frocks, tea frocks, evening gowns, and riding habits were too numerous for me to contemplate, especially when I had worn the same skirt and blouse for over two years.

"I'm afraid I have no idea what to choose. Would you mind selecting a frock for me, Edith?"

"Not at all, miss." She rummaged through the day

127

frocks, pausing at each one before finally lifting one out. "I think this would be suitable."

The bodice was white lace with a V-neckline, and sleeves that billowed just above the elbow to end in gathers at the wrist. The full skirt was a deep green. A pale green sash was at the waist.

Before putting the frock on, Edith tossed several muslin petticoats over my head. I was instructed to sit at the dressing table, where Edith began to brush my hair. She parted it in the middle and intertwined two thick strands of my hair, then looped them atop my head. She secured the topknot with hairpins made of whalebone. The effect was that of a copper crown. I was ready for lunch. More importantly, I was ready to learn my true identity.

Reaching the door of Mr. Hardwicke's parlor, I raised my hand to knock and noticed it was shaking. Did I really want to know who I was? Had the last eight years of my life changed me into so different a person, that I could never go back to what I was originally? I dropped my arm and stood there staring at the door. Even though I desperately wanted to know the truth, I feared it.

I screwed up my courage. After all, I had survived the colliery and Frank Boothe's brutality. I adapted to Gypsy life without any disastrous effects. Truth should be the easiest of all to survive. With my gold chains and a frock like this, I could always leave. I made a fist and knocked rather sharply.

"Come in," Mr. Hardwicke called.

With a firm grip, I turned the knob and entered. Both men were seated at a square, linen-covered table set for lunch. The third chair at the table was empty. They turned to look at me. I had seen admiration on men's faces when they watched me dance. These expressions went beyond admiration. The look Mr.

Hardwicke cast my way was one of adoration. Mr. Savage's dark eyes communicated approval, and perhaps a latent passion.

"Come sit down, my child. Jerome will be here shortly with our lunch," Mr. Hardwicke said. Mr. Savage stood and held my chair. "Excuse me for not rising. These old bones don't take to unnecessary activity."

"You promised to tell me who I am, Mr. Hardwick," I said, trying to avoid gazing at Mr. Savage for any length of time.

"So I did, child. Your name is Jennifer Mary Hardwicke. I am your grandfather, Jennifer." Mr. Hardwicke asserted with a certain amount of pride.

I sat and stared at him while I rolled the name Jennifer around in my head, as though it could evoke lost memories. It didn't. The name didn't even sound familiar. I frowned, then asked, "Are you sure, Mr. Hardwicke?"

"Beyond any doubt. And do call me grandfather. Even without the distinctive mark on your ankle, I know you are my granddaughter, Jennifer. You have your father's eyes and your mother's hair. You bear a strong resemblence to your father, my son, Jeremy Hardwicke. Your description of the clothes you were wearing the day of that horrible accident also establishes your true identity. I had seen you in that outfit many times. I have no reservations about your heritage, Jennifer. By the way, that frock fits you nicely. The clothes may be a bit out of date, but I'm sure they'll do until you have the opportunity to obtain more fashionable ones."

"Whose are they . . . Grandfather?" If he accepted my heritage, I saw no reason why I shouldn't, even though I had no memory of Wyndcliffe Manor.

"Your mother's."

"What was her name?"

"Frances. Frances Cook Hardwicke."

"Am I in her rooms?"

"Yes."

"Did you know who I was, Mr. Savage?"

"I had a strong suspicion. I have only seen hair that color once before. And that was on your mother. And, as Mr. Hardwicke says, you bear a strong resemblence to your father."

A knock sounded at the door. Without waiting for a reply, Jerome opened the door and wheeled a tea cart to the table. Jerome lifted domed, silver lids from the trays and put them on the bottom shelf of the cart. One tray held thin slices of cold lamb, duck, and ham. Another tray held slices of tomatoes, cucumber, and pickled beets, all resting on a bed of lettuce. He placed the bread, butter, mustard, and mayonnaise on the table.

Smiles of tolerance crossed their faces, as I loaded my plate and ate like one who had been deprived of food for eons. For me, breakfast had been meager, and I was making up for it. I slowed down when I realized I was no longer a Gypsy, and would have to learn the ways and manners of the gentry if what Mr. Hardwicke said was true. I returned their indulgent smiles with a sheepish one of my own.

When the meal was over, Jerome deftly removed the dishes and served tea.

"I want to thank you again, Mr. Savage, for rescuing me from those villagers," I said.

"Please call me Michael. I suspect we'll be seeing a great deal of one another. As far as my rescuing you, I only did the gentlemanly thing."

"I daresay you *will* be seeing a lot of Michael, Jennifer. I want him to familiarize you with the house, the lands, and the mines. Do you ride, Jennifer?"

130

Grandfather asked.

"Yes. But only astride and bareback."

"Well, Michael will have to train you in the proper manner of riding." Grandfather drained his tea. "You'll have to excuse me now. Old men become dependent on their naps."

"Aren't you going to introduce her to the family, sir?" Michael asked.

"I leave that to you, Michael. I can't abide them, even though they are my daughters. Their husbands are useless wastrels. Their children worse. Spoiled, indolent brats whose every whim was indulged by their parents. Now that they are adults, they still expect to be mollycoddled like children. I avoid them at every opportunity. Now excuse me." He rose slowly and with effort, as he braced his hands on the arms of the chair to push himself out of it.

Michael came to stand behind my chair and pulled it away when I stood.

"What's wrong with Grandfather? Is he seriously ill?" I asked, as Michael and I walked along the corridor toward the main staircase.

"Rheumatism. A touch of the gout. Minor stomach disturbances. If he would follow a more stringent diet, most of the problems could be eliminated. However, Dr. Marsh assures me that he could go on for a number of years. It's the stairs that bother him most when the rheumatism is on him.

"Are you related to him?"

Michael softly laughed. "No. Not at all. I run the estate for him, as he can't physically oversee his demesne anymore. I'm what you might call his leg man."

"He seems to treat you like a son," I commented.

"The years have brought many changes."

"Who are the people I am to meet?"

"Your aunts, uncles, and cousins by marriage."

"Are they as bad as Grandfather claims?"

"They aren't the most helpful people in the world. But don't let your grandfather prejudice you against them. You must make up your own mind."

I tilted my head and smiled up at him. "I always do make up my own mind."

He returned the smile and I almost melted on the spot. "I'll wager you do, Jennifer."

"When do I meet them?"

"They all gather in the front parlor shortly before dinner. I'll call for you at the proper time."

"When's that?"

"Sevenish. I suggest you change. The ladies will be wearing gowns for the evening." He studied my face. "Though most becoming, I suggest you remove those hooped earrings. The ladies have a tendency to ridicule anything that isn't familiar."

My hands went to my earlobes. "I can't walk around with empty holes in my ears."

"Who is your maid?"

"Her name is Edith."

"Tell Edith to have Jerome get you your mother's jewelry box. I'm sure you'll find something there. A tour of the house is in order now. Are you up to it?"

"Of course."

"You and your grandfather are in the West Wing of the house so we'll tour the west ground floor first."

"Where are your rooms?"

"In the West Wing, also. The wing contains guest rooms and the suite of your late mother and father."

"Oh, dear." I stopped short.

"What is it?" Michael asked with a frown.

"I forgot to ask Grandfather what happened to my parents, and if there are any pictures of them."

"I'll tell you all about it as we move along. And I'm

132

sure you'll see many pictures of them."

Reaching the ground floor we turned left and entered the beginning of a long gallery. Instead of traversing the gallery, we turned right and walked into a room that delighted me.

Book-lined walls were interrupted only by two long windows and a fireplace. I never knew so many books existed. I no longer regretted leaving my books behind in Zorina's wagon. I could now read to my heart's content. Michael's voice cut in on my musings.

"I spend a lot of time at that desk." He pointed to the large mahogany desk in front of the windows. "I'd be happy to show you the ledgers anytime you wish."

"Thank you. Can I take a book anytime I wish?"

"Of course. Shall we move along?"

I nodded.

We began the trek down the long gallery where portraits graced the walls. I glanced at them briefly, as I had to keep up with Michael's long stride. Suddenly he put his hand on my shoulder, stopped, and nodded to two portraits.

"Your mother and father, Jennifer."

He didn't have to tell me. A deep-rooted instinct told me who the portraits represented. I gazed long and hard. My father's eyes staring down at me were my own. My mother was indeed beautiful, and her hair was exactly the color of mine. The realization that I was truly Jennifer Mary Hardwicke came to me with a sudden impact. I had a real family now. I didn't know whether to laugh with joy or cry for their loss.

"You said you'd tell me what happened, Michael."

"The three of you had taken the train to Newcastle to visit a university chum of your father's. There was a terrible train accident. All the passengers in a couple of the cars were killed, including your mother and father. There was no trace of you. When the police gave up trying to find you, your grandfather went to Newcastle and hired detectives. After a year, the search was discontinued. Your grandfather firmly believed you would find your own way home. In a way, I guess you did."

I continued to stare at the paintings until Michael cupped my elbow. His touch had a disconcerting affect on me.

"You can come and look at the portraits anytime you wish, Jennifer. For now, let's move on." He steered me down the long corridor, past the servants' staircase and into Wyndcliffe's private chapel. "Services are held every Sunday at ten in the morning," Michael informed me.

"I saw you at Newcastle a long time ago. I thought you might be the new foreman." I didn't want to mention I had actually run into him. I didn't want him remembering that dirty urchin.

"At Newcastle?" He paused reflectively. "Oh, yes. That was many years ago. Your grandfather had heard of some new type of machinery, and sent me up there to have a look. I'm surprised you remembered me."

I said nothing as we left the chapel and continued the tour on the south side of the main structure. We turned right and entered the game room, then passed into the elaborate and vast dining room where French doors led to a semicircular, outside terrace. We passed through the morning room into another gallery. Turning right, I stepped into the rear parlor and quickly surveyed it.

An elegantly appointed room with a marble fireplace. The mahogany furniture was covered with rich brocades, elegant tapestries, and velvets. The ornaments looked costly, if not priceless. I nodded that I had seen enough, and we began the trek down the East Wing gallery.

"The doors on your right lead to the butler's pantry

and the servants' staircase," Michael said, as we moved down the gallery, also lined with portraits.

"Are those my ancestors, too?" I asked, nodding to the paintings.

"No."

"Who are they?"

"Former owners."

We entered the front parlor of the East Wing, which was similar to the rear parlor. We left that room, and turning right, went into the next one.

"This room speaks for itself, as you can see. The piano, the harp, and there's a cello in that black wooden case."

Something clicked in my head. A veiled sensation of being in this room before. When I tried to pursue it, the memory faded. I was still trying to pull the memory back as we walked through the marble foyer back to the main staircase. We had made a complete circle of Wyndcliffe.

"I'll leave you here, Jennifer. I have to catch up on some work. Can you manage to find your way back to your rooms?" Michael asked with an engaging smile.

"Travelling with the gypsies has given me a good sense of direction."

"I'll see you at seven."

"Thank you for the tour, Michael."

"My pleasure." He departed as though other things had rushed into his mind. As I watched his tall frame leave, I knew he was headed for the library. I climbed the stairs.

As I was about to enter my bedchamber, I saw Jerome and a heavy woman leave Grandfather's rooms. I wondered who the woman was, but wasn't introduced as they passed me in the corridor. I shrugged and entered my bedchamber.

I looked around and noticed a cord similar to the one

135

in Grandfather's room. It hung alongside the head of the four-poster. I went over, pulled it, then sat down on the bed to see what would happen. I didn't have long to wait. Edith came in.

"Can I help you, Miss Jennifer?" she asked.

"I take it you know who I am, Edith."

"Aye, Miss. Mr. Jerome informed the entire staff this morning. I've been assigned as your personal maid. If you prefer someone else, inform Mr. Jerome and he will assign another maid."

"As far as I'm concerned, you'll do just fine, Edith. But I must warn you, I'm used to doing for myself. I'm afraid I won't keep you very busy."

"You'd be surprised how a young lady can keep a personal maid busy. Why, Miss Amanda and Miss Annabel keep their maids on a constant run, they do."

"All you can expect from me is a slow walk. But there is something you can do for me now, if you will. Mr. Savage told me I should have you ask Jerome for my mother's jewelry box. Do you mind?"

"That's what I'm here for, Miss Jennifer." She curtseyed and left.

I sat on the bed for a few minutes, then suddenly realized I hadn't explored my sitting parlor. I decided to have a good look, then go down to the library, and get a book to read.

I padded through the short hall connecting the two rooms. I was stunned when I saw the sitting parlor.

Aside from stuffed arm chairs, an escritoire, and a basket with crewel work, a table with paper, water-colors, and brushes graced the room. I was elated to see the fireplace flanked with bookcases. I wouldn't have to use the library after all, at least not for a long while. I wanted to read the books on these shelves first, in hopes of discovering what my mother might have been like. Her tastes in reading would become mine. I was perusing the titles when my bedchamber door opened. I rushed to see Edith with a large wooden case in her hands.

"Your mother's jewelry box, Miss Jennifer," she announced, and placed it on the dressing table.

"I'm not very wise in the ways of the gentry, Edith. You'll have to help me out. What should I wear at dinner tonight?"

"I know the perfect gown, Miss Jennifer." Her eyes lighted up with a new sense of importance. She went to the closet and soon emerged carrying a pale green taffeta, off the shoulder gown. The fitted sleeves stopped short of my elbows. Silk flowers of the same pale green danced around the bottom of the full skirt. A dark green velvet sash completed the simple gown. "I think this gown will set off your coloring, Miss Jennifer. I noticed most of the frocks and gowns seem a little large for you at the waist. That's why you should wear one with a sash, until you can have them altered or have new ones made."

"The gown is beautiful, Edith. My mother had lovely clothes. Perhaps you could measure my waist, then, when you have the time, take the clothes to a seamstress for me? Is there a seamstress close by?"

"In town, Miss."

"Perhaps I'd better take them myself. She might find other things that need altering."

"As you wish, Miss Jennifer."

Once dressed, I seated myself at the dressing table. While Edith tended to my hair, I poked around in the jewelry box. My mother had some lovely pieces. An emerald pendant on a silver chain and emerald earrings were the perfect complement to the pale green gown. I removed the golden hoops and my gold locket, and put them in the jewelry box. Edith fastened the clasp of the pendant behind my neck when she had finished with

137

my hair. I put the earrings on myself.

I stood and twirled around for her. "How do I look, Edith?"

"Quite regal, Miss Jennifer, quite regal." She smiled warmly at me.

Edith was neither pretty nor ugly. She had a plain oval face, nondescript features, and soft hazel eyes. A tall, angular girl whose smile was rather winsome. I learned she was two years younger than me.

"I hope the family approves of my appearance." I really didn't care about a family I didn't know. The approval I sought was Michael's.

Promptly at seven, Michael called for me. He said nothing about my appearance, but I could see pleasure in his eyes.

"Will Grandfather be at dinner?" I asked.

"No. He takes his meals in his sitting parlor."

"Are the stairs that difficult for him?"

"Not really."

"Then why doesn't he eat with everyone else?"

"You'll soon find out." He drew my hand through his crooked arm.

I was overwhelmed with joy. Being with Michael like this was as though all my dreams had come true. As he led me through the various rooms on our way to the front parlor, heady sensations trickled through me as the warmth of Michael's body seemed to flow into mine. He stopped at the entrance.

"For some reason I feel like I'm leading Daniel into the lion's den. Chin up, Jennifer."

We entered the front parlor.

Eleven

I faced a grim diorama. Seven faces stared at me, not a smile of greeting on any one of them. Expressions of instant dislike registered on every face save one. A young man of about twenty-one stared at me with neither like nor dislike, only curiosity.

"Ladies and gentlemen," Michael began, "I have the honor to introduce Miss Jennifer Hardwicke, your niece, or, as the case may be, your cousin." He turned to me. "Jennifer, may I present Nigel and Lydia Lambert, your aunt and uncle. Their two children, Amanda and Rudolph, are your first cousins. Standing by the fireplace is Cecil Melville, your uncle by marriage to your father's sister, Joyce Melville. She is seated on the settee with her daughter, Annabel."

Mumbles of restrained greetings rumbled through the room. Only the young man called Rudolph was gracious enough to rise and come toward me.

Of average build and height, Rudolph's wiry and unruly ginger hair and full mustache made him notable. Behind his gold-rimmed glasses, sparkled transparent blue eyes. As he came to stand before me, a wide, toothy smile spread across his face to reveal slightly yellowed teeth, which I presumed was from smoking cheroots or cigars. I had seen that same result many times in the Gypsy camp. He took my hand and kissed the air above it.

"Cousin Jennifer, how jolly good to have you back at last. I remember you as a fiesty tot who always tried to avoid me. Now that you have grown into a beautiful woman, I hope you have shed any need to avoid me," Rudolph Lambert said.

"I see no reason to avoid anyone. Are you aware that I remember nothing of my life at Wyndcliffe before the accident, Cousin Rudolph?"

"Oh, do call me Binky. Everyone calls me that. I detest the name Rudolph. But to answer your question, Cousin Jennifer, I believe your memory loss was mentioned." He led me to a chair.

"Why did I avoid you, Binky?" I asked, smoothing down my voluminous skirts.

"You thought I was the devil. Grandfather always called me that impish devil," he answered me.

"If your memory is gone, Cousin Jennifer, how did you find your way back to Wyndcliffe?" came a squeaky voice from the settee.

I looked at the young woman called Annabel. She was a pudgy blonde who dressed like a tart. Her face resembled that of a nasty cherub with beady blue eyes. She had a tiny bow mouth which appeared to be in a perpetual pout. She didn't exude friendliness. I forced a smile when I answered her question.

"Michael rescued me from irate villagers and brought me here."

Annabel Melville's tiny mouth fell agape, and she stared at Michael Savage as though he had no right to rescue me from anything. I turned my attention to her mother, Joyce Melville. Though she was my father's sister, I couldn't begin to fathom a resemblance. From

140

vague impressions and fleeting visions, I had believed my father to be quite tall and lean. Aunt Joyce Melville was short and stout. Her light brown hair was already graying, while her rotund face was an older version of her daughter's. Her skin was remarkably clear and smooth for a woman of her age. Her hair was coiffed in the same manner as her daughter's; hair parted in the middle with vertical curls dangling over her ears. Her gown was only a shade less flamboyant than Annabel's.

Her husband, Cecil Melville, stood near the fireplace, coat open, hands in his pants pockets. He had a paunch that would defy the constraints of a woman's corset and would precede him wherever he went. His florid face hosted a bulbous nose. I could see where Annabel inherited her beady eyes. His stance and countenance revealed a man totally without humor.

"Your mother was a very beautiful woman, Jennifer," came a woman's voice from the opposite settee.

"Thank you, Aunt Lydia. I wish I could remember her."

Lydia Lambert was a tall, lean woman with a deep mannish voice. If anyone resembled my father, she came the closest, but the resemblance was extremely slight. Her graying brown hair was parted in the middle, and severely pulled back to form a tight bun at the nape of her neck. Stretched over aristocratic bones was coarse, pale skin, which wasn't helped by the dark brown gown of bombazine. If I had met the two women under different circumstances, I never would have believed they were related to each other. I could say the same for my two female cousins.

Amanda Lambert might have been pretty if it wasn't for the scowl on her face, a plain dark gown, and the same severe hairdo of her mother. Her expression, besides the scowl, was one of haughty disdain.

141

Her father, Nigel Lambert, reminded me of an undertaker I had seen at one of the horse fairs. With his hands behind his back, he looked like a huge, black walking stick. He made little clicking sounds in his throat, as if he was about to clear it, then decided against it. His birdlike face was sallow, as though daylight was anathema to him. I felt no kinship with any of these people.

"Care for a sherry before dinner, Cousin Jennifer?" Binky Lambert asked.

"What's a sherry?" My question brought a high-pitched giggle from Amanda. I gave her one of my contemptuous Gypsy looks. I was glad to see her cringe a little.

"Sherry is a light wine with a nutty flavor," Michael explained.

"No, thank you. I have seen what wine does to Gypsy men and women."

"Did the Gypsies steal you, Jennifer?" Aunt Lydia asked, her dark eyebrows arched.

"No. I went with them willingly."

"Why would you do that, Cousin?" Amanda's voice was as deep as her mother's.

"It was a far better life than working at the colliery and living with the Boothes."

"The Boothes?" Binky queried.

I patiently explained the conditions at the colliery and at the home of the Boothes. Annabel and her mother looked shocked, but fascinated. Aunt Lydia and Amanda looked at me as though I was a creature from an alien world. When I launched into tales about Gypsy life, everyone's expression changed to one of absorption. I was aware of Michael's constant scrutiny of me. I could sense he didn't quite know what to make of me. I liked that. I wanted him to think of me as a

142

mysterious woman. Perhaps he would be intrigued enough to want to know me better. I certainly wanted to know him better. Much better.

Jerome announced dinner. Michael led me into the dining room as if I was his sole responsibility for the time being.

My feigned Gypsy bravado vanished when I saw the dining room table set with a myriad of dishes, glasses, and silverware. I couldn't help but wonder what to do with all those items. My brisk gait slowed perceptively.

"Something wrong?" Michael asked me in a whisper.

"I hope not." My eyes were fixed on the table.

Michael followed my gaze. As if assuring me of his understanding, he patted my hand resting in the crook of his arm. "Don't worry, Jennifer. Just follow my lead."

Once everyone was in the dining room, Nigel Lambert lumbered toward the head of the table. Michael put a hand on his shoulder and stopped him.

"Mr. Hardwicke insists on having a Hardwicke sit at the head of the table, Nigel," Michael declared.

"But I've always sat at the head of the table," Nigel Lambert blustered. "After all, I am the oldest male of the family."

"I'm only following Mr. Hardwicke's instructions. He made me promise to make sure his wishes were carried out."

"The old man is dotty. We all know that," Nigel grumbled.

"Nevertheless . . ." Michael stood between Nigel and the chair at the head of the table as if willing to do battle.

"Well, *I'm* the oldest living Hardwicke. If Father wants a Hardwicke at the head of the table, it should be me," Lydia Lambert argued.

143

"Let them sit wherever they want, Michael," I said. I didn't want a family argument about who should sit where.

"Sorry, Jennifer. I have my orders, and I always carry them out to the letter." Michael held the chair for me.

With an exasperated shake of my head, I took the seat at the head of the table, which threw everyone into a state of confused panic regarding where they should seat themselves. A sense of the mischievous overcame me. My next words brought pandemonium.

"If I must sit here, I want you on my right, Michael." I wasn't about to have him at the other end of the table, where I couldn't see what he was doing with the silverware, goblets, and dishes.

"But Michael always sits down here next to me," Annabel wailed in her squeaky voice, then twisted one of her blond curls around her finger.

"This is ridiculous!" Lydia Lambert declared and promptly sat down in the chair nearest her.

"I think it is a delightful change," Binky commented and sat down in the chair to my left.

Irritated mumbles ran around the room as the others sought a seat at the table. I was certain Grandfather's edict intensified the family's dislike of me. I was an intruder who was quickly disrupting their lives and the order of things.

Jerome and the serving maid stood patiently to one side. I wondered what they thought of the little family comedy. They served the meal expressionless.

Surreptitiously, I watched Michael as water and wine were poured into certain goblets. When the duck soup was served, I waited until Michael picked up the correct spoon, then followed suit.

"This soup is much too salty. You'll have to talk to

144

Cook about it, Lydia," Nigel complained.

"The meals will be much better around here when *I* run the household next month," Joyce Melville asserted.

"I doubt it. Your talent for doing anything was always nonexistent, Joyce," Lydia remarked.

"At least I know how to keep myself attractive. You forever look like some old crone from a Shakespearean tragedy," Joyce countered.

"Don't you talk to my mother like that, Aunt Joyce," Amanda warned.

"She's my sister, and I'll talk to her anyway I want," Joyce declared.

"You could use some help yourself when it comes to fashion, Amanda," Annabel said.

"I wouldn't dream of dressing like a harlot, the way some people in this house do." Amanda lifted her chin haughtily.

"Mother!" Annabel whined.

Binky smiled throughout the squabbling as he slurped his soup rather noisily. As the soup dishes were being removed, he deftly changed the subject.

"Do you think Lord Russell will be able to handle the Irish Nationalists under O'Brien, Father?"

"Militant rascals. The leadership of that faction should have stayed with someone like O'Connell, and pursued peaceful methods to solve the Irish question," Nigel said.

"I heard there is famine in the land over there," Cecil said.

"Poppycock! The Irish have an overactive imagination. They're spoiling for a fight. It's in their blood. Aren't the Americans sending corn to feed them?" Nigel asked.

"They don't know how to cook it," Michael said

145

quietly. "Besides, the mills are so busy grinding our wheat in Ireland, they don't have time to grind the maize the Americans are sending."

"Ireland is *not* the cause of our troubles here. Crop failures and the general depression on the Continent are the roots of England's difficulty. Overspeculation, especially in railroads, is tottering the Bank of France. Might even bring down the Bank of England itself," Cecil stated.

"Poppycock! It is this nonsense in Ireland. They're draining our resources, Cecil," Nigel declared.

"You never did understand the world at large, Nigel. The Continent is thrusting its woes on us," Cecil said, banging his knife and fork on the table as though to emphasize his words.

Throughout the fish and meat courses, their argument continued as, farther down the table, Amanda and Annabel resumed their squabbling. Lydia and Joyce's voices were becoming louder as they set a course for another disagreement. I felt lost in the Tower of Babel. Michael seemed to project himself into another world. Binky ate with a smug smile. He appeared pleased with himself for starting the torrent of dissensions between the older men. I needn't have worried about the proper use of the table utensils. No one paid any attention to me.

The quarrels were still flourishing when all meandered into the foyer. As the family proceeded to the front parlor for tea or more potent liquid, Michael held me back.

"Your grandfather wishes to see you, Jennifer."

I nodded as Michael escorted me up the staircase. "Is dinner always like that, Michael?"

"Always."

"No wonder Grandfather has dinner in his rooms."

"Breakfast is more peaceful, especially if you come down early. The women have trays in their bed-chambers, and the men come down late," he told me.

"Then I shall make it a point to be early. What about lunch? Quiet or noisy?"

He waved his hand from side to side. "Depends."

"On what?"

"The weather. Their moods. The women sometimes go shopping in St. Ives or Penzance. The men to the races, lawn bowling, or darts in the village."

"Don't any of them take an interest in the estate or the mines?"

Michael laughed. "They are only interested in their own needs, wants, and pleasures."

"Where do they get the money?"

"Your aunts were left annuities from their grand-mother. Your grandfather supplies free room and board, so they are free to spend the annuities as they wish," Michael explained.

"Why does Grandfather give them free room and board?"

"You'll have to ask him that. Here we are." Michael knocked softly.

"Come in. Come in," Grandfather boomed from his parlor. He was seated at the table, a tea service at hand. He waved to the two empty chairs. "Sit down."

We sat in the same chairs we had at lunch. Grandfather nodded for me to pour the tea. He didn't speak until he had a few swallows of the hot beverage.

"Michael, I want you to make sure my grand-daughter meets all the tenants and has a full tour of the mines. Make the ledgers available to her. Answer all and any questions she might have regarding the estate. I want my granddaughter to know not only the good, but the bad. Understand, Michael?"

"Yes, sir."

"Well, Jennifer, how did you find dinner?"

"A little bland, especially after eating spicy Gypsy food," I replied.

Grandfather chuckled. "That isn't what I meant, Jennifer. Was the table conversation lively enough for you?"

"Deafening. I see why you eat here."

"You and I will have lunch here. Michael is seldom around. I'll enjoy having company for lunch."

"It'll be my pleasure, I assure you, Grandfather."

"You look quite beautiful in that gown, doesn't she, Michael?"

"Yes, sir."

"When you become adjusted to life at Wyndcliffe, you must have a seamstress make more fashionable gowns and frocks for you, Jennifer."

"I intend to have my mother's clothes altered to fit me."

"But they're old."

"They're new to me."

"Do as you wish, Jennifer. This is your home. Now, Michael, I would appreciate it if you would leave me alone with my granddaughter. We have family matters to discuss."

"I understand, sir." Michael drained his tea, said good night, then left.

"I thought Michael Savage was privy to everything, Grandfather."

"Only regarding the estate, mines, and ledgers. Family matters are none of his business."

"Does he have a wife?" I tried to make my tone one of mere curiosity. But my heart was pumping furiously as I prepared to hear the worst.

"Michael is a shrewd man. He will not marry until he

148

finds a bride to suit his purpose."

My whole body relaxed and a vague smile slipped to my lips. "How are you feeling this evening, Grandfather?"

"Better than usual, especially now that you're back home. When your father was born, I adored him. I have to admit I was sorely disappointed when you were born, Jennifer. I wanted a grandson to carry on the Hardwicke name. But you were so precocious, impish, and utterly lovable, I soon fell under your spell and doted on you. I wanted your parents to leave you here when they went north. But they insisted on bringing you with them. I daresay they wanted to show you off. Who would have thought such a tragedy would ensue?" His expression saddened for a fleeting minute, then a pleasant smile curved his lips, as though a new force had pushed old and painful memories aside.

"Tell me about my parents."

"We'll have a lot of time to talk about them. Suffice it to say that they were good people and loved you and each other dearly."

"Where is my grandmother?"

"She died shortly after my son—your father—was born."

"But Aunt Lydia and Aunt Joyce? How can they be his sisters, if grandmother died so soon? Or were they born before my father?"

"That's what I want to talk to you about, Jennifer. Several years after the death of your grandmother, I remarried, much to my later regret. She was a vivacious woman, more attractive than beautiful. She had certain charms no man could resist. After the marriage ceremony, I learned she was a widow with two young daughters, Joyce and Lydia. I did my best by all of them. But I was an active man with much to do. I was

149

home very little. I sent my son away to a private school. I dread to think how he might have turned out if left to the sole auspices of my second wife, Marilyn."

"What did she do?" His tale was beginning to sound better than the *Arabian Nights*.

"She resented being left alone so often. She liked parties and lots of company. Soon she began dressing flamboyantly and going to St. Ives or Penzance. At both places she amassed friends, leaving her two daughters in the care of the staff. The staff had their own work to do, and shuffled the two girls from one staff member to another."

"Why didn't you hire a tutor or a governess for them, Grandfather?"

"I gave Marilyn the money for both, but, unknown to me, she kept the money to spend on herself."

"Didn't the staff or the girls complain?"

"Marilyn was a clever and domineering woman. She taught the girls to lie, and threatened the staff with instant dismissal if they spoke to me about it. I mistakenly presumed a tutor and a governess reigned over the girls during the day. Marilyn was against having more servants live in."

"She wouldn't have dared dismiss Jerome, would she?"

"No."

"Then why didn't *he* tell you what was going on?"

"You would have to know Jerome to understand his reticence. He is a true butler. He wouldn't have dreamed of tattling on either his master or his mistress, anymore than he would think of idle gossiping. Besides, he knew sooner or later I would learn the details myself."

"When you found out, what did you do, Grandfather?"

"I personally hired a nanny and a tutor for the girls. I stopped paying Marilyn the extra money, and she promptly stopped performing her wifely duties. By then I really didn't care. During one of our many verbal altercations, I told her she could go and live in St. Ives or Penzance for all I cared. She did, saying she would send for the girls. She never did."

"Is she still alive?"

"No. I heard she died of some terrible disease in Penzance. When I received the news, I had her body brought here to be buried in Wyndcliffe's cemetery. After all, she had been my wife, and still bore the Hardwicke name."

"Then Aunt Lydia and Aunt Joyce aren't my real aunts?"

"They are your aunts by marriage, not by blood."

"They believe themselves to be Hardwickes. There was quite a fuss when Michael said I was to sit at the head of the table."

"Sorry about that, Jennifer. They do believe they are of my seed. I would like to keep it that way for now. I not only feel sorry for them, but also a little guilty about their upbringing. They really had no dominant male figure in their lives. I suspect that is why they made such poor choices for husbands. I would appreciate your keeping this our little secret, Jennifer."

"Oh, I will, Grandfather. I am disrupting their lives enough without destroying them all together."

He smiled and reached over to pat my hand. "You are so like your father. He hated to hurt people when it wasn't necessary."

"Why are all of them living here, especially when you can't abide them?"

"Lydia's husband, Nigel Lambert, was well-to-do when she married him. They lived extravagantly in an expensive London town house. Several years ago he lost everything through overspeculation in stocks. They were penniless. Lydia wrote to me and asked if they could stay with me, until they got back on their feet. Thinking it would be only a matter of months, I consented. They've been here ever since."

"And the Melvilles?"

"I assume you've noticed how Joyce and her daughter, Amanda, dress. It put poor Cecil in dire straights. He began embezzling from the bank where he was vice president. Banks were in shaky circumstances, as they are now. They didn't want the embezzlement leaking to the public. If he maintained his silence about the embezzlement and moved faraway, they wouldn't press him to return the money. They've been here about a year now. The sisters do not get along, neither do their husbands, nor their children. But I guess you've noticed that." He sighed deeply. "I suppose it's fitting punishment for their greed."

"What about the trusts that were left to Aunt Lydia and Aunt Joyce? Couldn't they live on that?"

"Jennifer. Marilyn's mother was a fairly wealthy widow. Thinking Marilyn was well-off when she married me, she set up trust funds for the two girls. She died before Marilyn and I separated." James Hardwicke took a deep breath and let it out slowly. "Well, now you see how everything stands. Be cautious, Jennifer. Lydia and Joyce were well trained in lying. In fact, I think they've honed that attribute to a fine edge. Well, you've had a strenuous and perhaps difficult day. I think it's best you get a good night's sleep. You have a busy day tomorrow. We'll have lots of time to talk."

"I am tired, now that you mention it." I stood, bent over, and kissed his cheek. "Good night, Grandfather."

"It's so good to have you home. Good night, Jennifer."

I walked to the door, turned the knob, and opened it. Just then, Grandfather spoke again.

"Jennifer, do be wary of Michael Savage. He is not what he seems."

Twelve

I was about to ask him what he meant about Michael, when Jerome came through the open door. I quickly departed and went to my bedchamber where Edith was waiting.

I prided myself on my self-sufficiency. But I found it impossible to deal with the tiny fastenings running down the back of my gown. My mother's corsets were a complete mystery, with their hooks, eyes, and lacings in the back. I was thankful I didn't have to wear one of them. I now understood why a lady's maid was imperative.

In my nightdress I went to the sitting parlor and selected a book to read. As I walked back to my bedchamber, Edith had my clothes put away and the bed turned down.

"Can I be fetching you a glass of warm milk, Miss Jennifer?" she asked.

"No, thank you, Edith. I'll see you in the morning."

"Is there anything else, Miss?"

"Not that I can think of, Edith."

"What time shall I wake you in the morning, miss?"

"Oh, I'll be up, Edith. I'm usually up before six."

"Good night, Miss Jennifer."

"Good night, Edith."

I fluffed the pillows up against the headboard and leaned against them, my legs propped up with the book resting on my knees. I started to read, but Grandfather's parting words soon disrupted my concentration. Why did he warn me about Michael, when Michael seemed to be my mentor at Wyndcliffe? I would have to ask Grandfather at the first opportunity. I was not used to such a soft, cozy bed and was soon asleep.

Edith took up the waistband of the voluminous dark green velvet riding skirt with several stitches of stout sewing thread.

Knowing I would be spending the day with Michael, I bounced down the stairs, eager to have an early breakfast so we could be on our way.

To my dismay, the dining room was empty. Had Michael forgotten about our early morning appointment to see the tenant farms? The thought was disheartening.

"Good morning, Miss Jennifer," Jerome greeted me, and held my chair as I sat down. "Tea, miss?"

"No. I'd prefer coffee if it isn't too much trouble. Hot and strong. What is for breakfast?" I asked innocently.

"Breakfast is on the sideboard, Miss. It is the custom for everyone to help themselves. I'll serve you if you like."

"That won't be necessary, Jerome."

He pulled my chair back. I stood and went to the sideboard. Covered trays of silver were lined up and warmed by small candles underneath. The first tray held a thick porridge. I filled a small bowl with it. I was about to return to my seat when curiosity got the better of me. I began to lift the covers of the other trays. Eggs scrambled, poached, or coddled stared back at me. I remembered having a fried egg at the Boothes once. The Gypsies never ate eggs, or milk for that matter. They believed weak or slippery food had a debilitating effect on one's system. Rashers of lean bacon filled another tray. I had no idea what lay in the other tray. Holding the lid up, I turned to Jerome.

"What are these?"

"Kippers, Miss."

"What are kippers, Jerome?"

"Smoked and salted herring, Miss Jennifer."

I quickly put the lid back on. I had no stomach for fish so early in the morning. A bowl of orange slices was at the end of the table. I took the bowl of porridge back to the table.

"Is that all you're going to eat, Miss Jennifer?" Jerome asked.

"No. After the porridge, I'm going back for eggs and bacon. I can, can't I?"

A wisp of a smile flickered for an instant on his lips. "Of course, Miss. I'll get your coffee and some toast. Marmalade, sugar, cream, salt, and pepper are on the table."

"Thank you, Jerome." I had finished my porridge and had filled a plate with scrambled eggs and three rashers of bacon when Jerome returned. As he bent to pour my coffee, I asked, "Do we eat like this every morning?"

"Yes, miss."

"I shall have to be careful or I shall be as fat as a toad," I said, voicing my thoughts aloud.

Jerome left the ornate silver coffeepot on the table so I could help myself. I had finished the satisfying breakfast and was munching on a piece of marmalade-covered toast when Michael came striding in. Dressed in riding clothes, knee-high black boots shining, he was

156

particularly handsome.

"I thought you'd forgotten about our ride this morning," I said.

"Hardly. I was out in the stables seeing to the horses. Have you finished with breakfast? We have a lot of ground to cover."

"Almost. Have you eaten?"

"An hour ago. But I will join you in a cup of coffee." He sat down on my right and reached for the coffeepot. "I took the liberty of having Cook prepare a picnic basket for us. I saw no sense in riding all the way back here for lunch. I hope you don't mind?"

"Why should I? For me, lunch is a treat. The Gypsies seldom bothered with lunch."

"What were the Gypsy men like?"

"Their lives revolved around their horses, songs, drinking, and more horses."

"Do you think you'll miss the Gypsy life?" He took a swallow of his coffee.

"I don't think so. Spring, summer, and fall were nice, but the winters could be brutal, especially when the water was frozen and one couldn't bathe. Bad weather kept everyone in the wagon. During those times the air in the wagon became smelly and oppressive. One was never certain of what there would be to eat." I took a deep breath, finished my toast and coffee. "That sort of life had its good and bad points. I think I'll enjoy living here far more than Gypsy life. I know for certain I will like it better than the colliery."

"Don't speak too soon, Jennifer. Life at Wyndcliffe might not be as rosy as you think."

"What do you mean, Michael?"

He drained his cup and stood, his gaze surveying my face as though he were seeing it for the first time. "Hadn't you better have your maid do your hair, so you can wear your riding hat?"

157

I looked at him quizzically. "What's wrong with the way it is?" I had braided it in a plait hanging down my back. I wore it like that when I rode Rico's horses. I saw no reason to change.

He smiled indulgently. "It looks fine to me, but the custom for the lady of the manor is to wear her hair coiffed and crowned by a hat."

"I am not accustomed to wearing hats, especially when riding. I shall go as I am and let the people think what they will."

Still smiling, he shrugged. "As you wish, Jennifer. Shall we go?"

I nodded.

I had trouble walking across the cobblestone stableyard. I managed the slipperlike house shoes without too much difficulty, but riding boots were another thing. My feet weren't used to such rigid confinement. Even though protected by cotton stockings, my feet were being chafed by the leather. I held my head up and tried to walk straight despite the discomfort. I didn't want Michael to think I was a clumsy oaf.

The stable master led the horses out. Instinctively, I knew the black stallion was for Michael. When I gazed at the docile chestnut, I became dispirited. The saddle was grotesque. I would never be able to ride the horse properly sitting on that bizarre hunk of leather. My eyes sought out Michael's.

"That isn't a proper saddle," I declared, horror and frustration mingling in my voice.

"Henry will explain the correct use of a lady's sidesaddle to you."

Michael mounted, while Henry patiently explained how I should position myself on the saddle before he assisted me in mounting. I hooked my legs around the off-center horn of the saddle, quite sure I would fall off the beast the minute the animal fell into a trot. When we moved off, my leg was so tight around the horn it felt crampy. By the time we reached the road, I felt a little more at ease. Still, it was uncomfortable.

Stone-walled, verdant fields stretched before me. Gulls screeched stridently as they circled overhead in a clear blue sky. Crisp, salty air filled my lungs, whlie my ears were treated to the musical cadence of the sea tossing itself endlessly against the rocks and cliffs.

Michael said little until we came to the cottage of a tenant farmer. I was introduced to the family. Mundane pleasantries were spoken while we remained on horseback. At the next farm, I was surprised to see the entire family had once again turned out to greet me. And so it went until the sun was high in the sky. We urged our horses into a grassy meadow. Michael dismounted and untied the wicker lunch hamper from the back of his saddle.

I sat on the mare like a frozen statue. I couldn't get my leg unhooked. My leg had either fallen asleep or was dead from the rigid position.

"I'm sorry," Michael said, coming to the side of my horse, his arms outstretched to help me dismount.

"I can't move my leg. It seems to be locked into position." I smiled somewhat sheepishly.

"Toss me the reins, then rub the circulation back into your leg," he instructed.

I did as he suggested. After several seconds of vigorous rubbing, I managed to unhook my leg from the horn. Michael dropped the reins and once more offered me his arms. I gratefully slid into them, my hands braced on his upper biceps.

His face was inches from mine. His ebony eyes became hooded as his grip on my waist tightened. His head turned slightly as his lips parted. With the swiftness of a predator securing its prey, one arm went about my waist, while his other arm went over my shoulder so his hand could cradle my head. His lips moved over mine as he crushed me to the length of his hard body. The tentative kiss turned to an insistent demand. Without reservation, I yielded to him. My hands moved up his arms and over his wide shoulders, one hand resting on the thick cords of his neck, the other feeling the hard sinews of his back.

The world spun and twirled like a dizzy toy top in my head. I had found my prince and he loved me. I was content. But my mind hadn't completely banished reason. As Rico had taught me, men kissed women like this for reasons other than love. I quickly pulled away.

The startled expression on Michael's face quickly dissolved into a mask of contrition.

"I'm sorry, Jennifer. I overstepped my place. I have no excuses to offer you, only an apology for my boorish behavior."

"No need to apologize, Michael. I shouldn't have let you kiss me. I'm as much to blame as you."

"You're very forthright, aren't you, Jennifer?"

"I try to be. Shall we eat?"

He carried the hamper to the shade of a small, solitary oak, knelt down, and opened it. I sat down in the grass cross-legged, my skirts discreetly covering my legs. He whipped out a checkered tablecloth and began to place the food on it, along with a jar of milked tea. Cold ham sandwiches, figs, dates, and currant cakes magically appeared from the hamper. We ate in silence. The fresh air and the excitement of the morning made me hungry. I poured the tea into tin mugs and handed one to Michael.

"Thank you," he said, then stared at it thoughtfully. "I would appreciate your not mentioning this morning's incident to your grandfather."

"You mean kissing me?"

160

MORE PASSION AND ADVENTURE AWAIT... YOUR TRIP TO A BIG ADVENTUROUS WORLD BEGINS WHEN YOU ACCEPT YOUR FIRST 4 NOVELS ABSOLUTELY *FREE*
(AN $18.00 VALUE)

Accept your Free gift and start to experience more of the passion and adventure you like in a historical romance novel. Each Zebra novel is filled with proud men, spirited women and tempestuous love that you'll remember long after you turn the last page.

Zebra Historical Romances are the finest novels of their kind. They are written by authors who really know how to weave tales of romance and adventure in the historical settings you love. You'll feel like you've actually gone back in time with the thrilling stories that each Zebra novel offers.

GET YOUR FREE GIFT WITH THE START OF YOUR HOME SUBSCRIPTION

Our readers tell us that these books sell out very fast in book stores and often they miss the newest titles. So Zebra has made arrangements for you to receive the four newest novels published each month.

You'll be guaranteed that you'll never miss a title, and home delivery is so convenient. And to show you just how easy it is to get Zebra Historical Romances, we'll send you your first 4 books absolutely FREE! Our gift to you just for trying our home subscription service.

BIG SAVINGS AND FREE HOME DELIVERY

Each month, you'll receive the four newest titles as soon as they are published. You'll probably receive them even before the bookstores do. What's more, you may preview these exciting novels free for 10 days. If you like them as much as we think you will, just pay the low preferred subscriber's price of just $3.75 each. *You'll save $3.00 each month off the publisher's price.* AND, your savings are even greater because there are never any shipping, handling or other hidden charges—FREE Home Delivery. Of course you can return any shipment within 10 days for full credit, no questions asked.

"Yes."

"Why?"

"He would take a dim view of my kissing his granddaughter. It has taken me too long to get close to him to have that trust destroyed by a moment of weakness and impulse."

"I see."

"Then you will keep the incident a secret between the two of us?"

"Of course, Michael. How many more farms are we to visit?"

"Four. There's some distance between them. Are you up to it?"

"I suppose so."

"Do you find these visits to the farms a bore, Jennifer?"

"Not a bore. Perhaps intimidating is a better word. I'm not used to being a so-called lady of the manor. I've always worked for my keep one way or another. These people look up to me, and I don't feel I deserve their homage and esteem."

"You'll feel differently after a while. After all, these people owe their living to your grandfather. They are bound to respect his granddaughter."

"But I haven't done anything to merit their respect," I countered.

"Then let us hope in time you will."

"If the tenants owe respect and homage to anyone, I should think it would be you, Michael. Grandfather told me what an admirable job you do handling the estates and running the mines. And always at a profit."

"I'm glad he has such confidence in me. Shall we pack up and continue to visit your tenants?"

I nodded and helped him repack the hamper with our leftovers. I would have preferred to stay in the meadow alone with Michael. But now I had a beautiful memory I would always treasure of Michael and me kissing in the meadow. His kiss had stirred something within me. Some alien physical force had convulsed my body in a way that Rico's kisses never had. I was afraid if Michael ever kissed me again, I wouldn't want him to stop.

I was greatly relieved when the last of the farms and tenants had been seen. Once out of sight of the last farm, I stopped the mare and slipped off, causing Michael to rein in his stallion.

"What's wrong, Jennifer?"

"I can't stand this any longer." I bent down and removed my riding boots. The earth felt cool and comforting to my stocking feet. After wiggling my toes in an expression of freedom, I reached between my legs and grabbed the rear hem of my riding skirt. I pulled it through my legs and tucked it in the waistband of my skirt the Gypsy way. I remounted, straddled the horse, and instantly felt better about riding back to Wyndcliffe.

Michael shook his head and repressed a smile. "You look like a hoyden, Jennifer."

"I don't care how I look. I feel mountains better."

"You'll shock the entire countryside riding like that."

"Perhaps the countryside needs a shock."

Eyebrows were raised when we entered the stable-yard, but no one said a word. We dismounted and the grooms led the horses away.

"I'll see you at dinner, Jennifer." He strode off with Henry, the horsemaster.

I said nothing and headed straight for my rooms. I tossed the riding boots on the floor, then stretched out in the chaise. My mind quickly conjured up the image of Michael kissing me. I let the reverie consume me, as I wanted to etch the moment in my brain while the memory was still fresh.

I must have dozed, for the next thing I knew Edith was gently shaking me.

"Miss Jennifer . . . Miss Jennifer."

"What?" My sleep-glazed eyes flew open. For a second I was disoriented. My surroundings quickly reminded me where I was. "What is it, Edith?"

"Mr. Hardwicke wishes to see you, Miss Jennifer."

I pushed myself from the chaise and stood, causing a slight gasp to emanate from Edith. "What is it, Edith?"

"Your skirt, Miss. And your stockings are dirty."

"Please get me some clean stockings and my house slippers," I said as I pulled the skirt from the waistband, then called to Edith. "Should I change my clothes?"

"Mr. Hardwicke wanted to see you right away. I'm afraid you won't have time, Miss." She paused, then asked, "What gown would you like to wear this evening?"

"You pick it out, Edith. I trust your judgement." I quickly donned the clean stockings and slippers, then went to see Grandfather.

The door was open and I went in. I was surprised to see Grandfather standing tall and straight by the window. I cleared my throat to announce my presence. He turned. A smile swept across his face.

"Should you be up and around, Grandfather?"

"Why not? Your presence at Wyndcliffe has rejuvenated me. Let us sit down. I want to hear all about your tour of the farms today."

"There isn't much to tell." I sat down and he took the chair opposite me. Though I couldn't remember all the names, I recounted the day's events, including the picnic but not Michael's kiss. I wasn't one to renege on a promise.

"I haven't toured the farms in years. Are they well

163

kept? Are the animals fat and healthy?"

"From what I could see, everything looked fine. The tenants were most kind to me."

"As well they should be. You *are* my granddaughter. Tomorrow morning I will be down for breakfast early. Can you meet me there?"

"Of course."

"I do want to avoid the Lamberts and the Melvilles. Their bickering destroys my digestion. I want to go over the ledgers with you myself."

"I thought Michael was going to show me the mines tomorrow?"

"He can show you the one at Botallack in the afternoon. That one is less than an hour away. The large tin mines at Cambourne are over twenty miles away. A full day's trip, I'm afraid. He can take you there another day."

"Won't the stairs be difficult for you, Grandfather?"

"I feel fitter with each passing moment. I might even have a pipe and a whisky in my room after dinner tonight."

"Please tell me about my mother and father. What was father like when he was a little boy?"

Grandfather smiled. "He was a strong-willed tyke. He was curious about everything he saw or touched." He went on describing all my father's little idiosyncrasies in detail. He waxed fondly when he came to speak of my mother, her sense of humor and incredible beauty. His words were vivid. I felt as though I was beginning to know my parents. I longed for the day when my full memory returned.

"Well, I've kept you long enough, Jennifer. Dinner will be served soon, and you have to dress. By the way, what is this I hear about your riding skirt, no boots on your feet, and you sitting astride a horse?"

"That is how I rode the piebalds when I was with the

Gypsies. Far more comfortable than half-sitting on a horse."

"A woman sitting astride a horse!" He laughed long and deep. A healthy merriment shone in his eyes. "I suppose you're going to persist in riding like that."

"Probably. Word travels swiftly at Wyndcliffe, I see."

"Nothing escapes me, my dear." He paused reflectively. "Isn't there a way you can ride without hitching your skirt up?"

"I'll think on it, Grandfather."

"If there is a way, I'm sure you'll find it."

It was my turn to smile. "I'm sure I will." I got up, kissed Grandfather on the cheek, and started to leave.

"Jennifer . . . did Michael behave as a gentleman toward you?"

I spun around. Had someone seen Michael kiss me? Was someone spying on me? "Why do you ask that, Grandfather?"

"Michael is a man's man and quite handsome, a fact that hasn't gone unnoticed by the ladies." He hesitated, as though he couldn't find the right words. "I don't know how to put it to you, Jennifer. I guess the only way is to be perfectly blunt. Michael Savage has every reason to try and seduce you."

"Why?" I almost shouted.

165

Thirteen

I went back to the chair and sat down, my eyes lustrous with curiosity.

"Wyndcliffe Manor's demesne and the mines belonged to the Savages for centuries. The land and mines were given to Jonathan Savage by Queen Elizabeth I, for his help in destroying the Spanish Armada back in 1588."

"But how—" I interrupted.

Grandfather held up a staying hand. "Patience, Jennifer. It'll become clear to you in a moment. Old Josiah Savage, Michael's great-grandfather, had a passion for gambling. So did my father, but he was fairly lucky at it. By chance they met in a Falmouth mens' club and engaged in a game of cards. Josiah Savage lost steadily. When he ran out of cash money, his watch, and rings, he rashly put up his tin mines. My father won. Old Josiah was livid. He couldn't believe my father had won through skill and luck. He wagered everything he owned if an independent party dealt the cards. If Josiah won, my father was to return everything. My father agreed.

"A couple of men went out into the street and

grabbed a stranger, explaining the circumstances to him as they led him into the club. From the beginning the stranger proved himself to be a novice at cards. His shuffling was clumsy, and it took him longer to deal than a practiced hand would. Old Josiah trusted the man. The stranger put the deck out for each man to cut, then dealt the cards. An eerie hush shrouded the room as my father and Josiah studied their cards. At the conclusion of the game, my father had clearly won.

"Pen and paper were brought to Josiah. He promptly made good his bet and signed the mines, all his property, and Wyndcliffe Manor over to my father. A judge and several other men signed their names as witnesses to the transaction. Father wanted the mines, but didn't care about Wyndcliffe and the land. Once he thought Josiah had learned his lesson regarding gambling, he would return the manor and lands back to Josiah. But Josiah Savage did an amazing thing.

"He pulled a pistol from his frock coat, put it to his head, and pulled the trigger. He fell forward, his blood spilling on the transfer deed. I still have that deed, Jennifer. I'll show it to you someday."

"How horrible! Why is Michael working here after all that?"

"When my father came to Wyndcliffe, he found the entire estate in sad repair, the mines mismanaged. Josiah's gambling fever had drained all the resources of the farms and mines. Rents were exorbitant, leaving the tenants with less and less money for seed and improvements. Also at Wyndcliffe was Josiah's ailing wife and twenty-five-year-old son. They were shocked by the news of Josiah's death, and how he had gambled away their home and income. Josiah's son loved the land, so my father offered him the job of overseer and the use of the overseer's cottage.

"The man proved to be a capable manager, especially when my father lowered the rents. The farms began to prosper while my father ran the mines; they started to show a profit under his supervision. The son eventually married and had a boy and a girl. The girl went off to Canada when she married, but the son took over his father's job. When the son married, Michael was born. He chose to follow in his father's footsteps, only he expanded his horizons and knowledge to the mines. He's been a boon to me."

"What does any of this have to do with Michael trying to seduce me?" I asked candidly.

"Michael knows the history of Wyndcliffe. I believe he harbors the notion of getting it back into the hands of the Savages. You are a prime candidate for him to achieve his aspirations. That is why I caution you about him."

"How could *I* restore the property to the Savages?"

"By persuasion, for one thing. Michael is quite the charmer when he wants to be. Another way is by marriage."

"Neither way assures him of total ownership. What about the Melvilles and the Lamberts? Surely they wouldn't step aside because Michael wants them out of the way?"

"Michael is a determined, strong-willed, and shrewd man. Never underestimate him, Jennifer. On the other hand, Cecil and Nigel are weak and stupid men. Michael could outwit them without half-trying. Can you see why I'm cautioning you about Michael?"

"Yes, Grandfather. I'm glad you have explained everything to me. I shall keep my guard up where Michael is concerned." A heavy sadness settled on my heart. Michael's kiss in the meadow was neither love nor desire. The kiss was nothing more than part of a long-range scheme to secure Wyndcliffe. I wished Grandfather had never told me. Though he had my welfare in mind, he had cruelly crushed my romantic illusions. I stood up. "I'd better go change now."

"Perhaps after dinner you'll come back here, and we'll have a game of chess?"

"I don't know how to play chess."

"I'll teach you."

I forced a smile and kissed him on the cheek. When I reached my bedchamber, Edith had laid out a dark blue taffeta gown trimmed with pale blue lace. I remained listless while she dressed me and did my hair. I was not looking forward to seeing Michael at dinner, anymore than I relished being with my relatives. I had tolerated them because Michael was present. Now I felt deprived of that joy.

Lifting my skirts I went downstairs, across the foyer, through the music room to the front parlor. As I approached the parlor, I expected to hear my relatives loudly bickering. Instead I heard Annabel's squeaky giggling and Amanda's deep, muted laughter. I was puzzled. I didn't think either of them capable of joy.

Entering the parlor I saw the cause of their merriment. A blond, young man was regaling them with amusing stories. His back was toward me. Seeing me, Michael rose and headed for me, causing the man to turn and stand.

"Why, you must be Jennifer Hardwicke! I was told you were lovely, but they didn't do justice to your beauty. I'm Lord Jason Fox, your neighbor and at your service." He reached me before Michael, took my hand, bowed, and kissed it. "I do hope we shall become more than neighbors."

"Lord Fox." I smiled. I could feel the tensions coursing through my body as Michael came to stand close to me.

"Do call me Jason. I want to eliminate formalities immediately. May I call you Jennifer?"

"You certainly waste no time, Lord Fox."

"Jason. Remember?"

"Jason," I parroted, wondering what he was doing at Wyndcliffe. I looked at Michael.

"Lord Fox is a frequent visitor to Wyndcliffe. He likes to glean what new farming methods I might have uncovered," Michael explained, as though reading my thoughts. I hoped he couldn't read other thoughts in my mind.

"I now have another reason," Jason said, smiling fondly at me. "And aside from Michael's farming secrets, I am enchanted in the company of the lovely Annabel and the charming Amanda."

When Jerome announced dinner, Jason made a gesture of offering me his arm, but Michael had already drawn my hand through his arm. I didn't like being manipulated. But under the circumstances, I wasn't about to cause an incident as Annabel came to Jason's side and snaked her hand through his arm.

Aunts and uncles led the way into the dining room. Michael and I followed them, Annabel and Jason behind us, with Binky and Amanda trailing. Lord Jason Fox's eyebrows raised when he saw me sit at the head of the table, but he said nothing.

"How was Paris, Jason?" Nigel asked, trying to appear indifferent to the fact that his place at the head of the table had been usurped.

"A bit unsettling. Widespread unemployment, due to agricultural and industrial depression, has caused

170

many people to suffer. A number of secret radical and socialist organizations are springing up," Jason replied.

"Oh, pooh!" Annabel exclaimed. "Who cares about silly old politics. What are the fashionable women wearing, Jason?"

"I'm sorry, Bella. I didn't pay much attention to female fashions."

"But I'll bet you paid plenty of attention to the Parisian females," Binky interjected.

Jason tossed him a sly, almost lecherous, smile, then reverted to amusing tales of his Parisian adventures. With his blond hair, smooth-shaven face, and blue eyes that sparkled merrily, his patrician good looks gave him an air of perennial boyishness. He was handsome to the point of being almost beautiful. I found myself liking him, even though our acquaintance was brief. My peripheral vision caught Michael glancing at me every now and then with an enigmatic glare. I pretended not to notice.

Dinner was going remarkably well. Both the Lamberts and the Melvilles were going out of their way to be cordial, especially the women. Annabel giggled and batted her eyelashes at Jason, as though she was a paragon of seduction. Amanda appeared to wrap herself in somber intellectualism, asking what she deemed were very erudite questions. I thought her questions were silly. But I was thankful for the conviviality at the dinner table. The only time hostility hovered in the air was when Jason directed his attentions and conversation toward me.

When dinner was over, the men decided to have port and their cigars or cheroots in the dining room, while we women made our way to the front parlor. As we were leaving the morning room, Aunt Lydia put a

171

staying hand on my arm. When the others were out of earshot, Aunt Lydia spoke.

"Don't set your sights on Lord Jason Fox, Jennifer. Nigel and I have been cultivating that young man as a suitor for Amanda. It would make an excellent marriage for her. I'm giving you fair warning not to interfere. If you do, you'll suffer the consequences." She squeezed my arm viciously, and in her eyes glinted a lethal admonition which, I must confess, set my teeth on edge. At that moment I believed her capable of anything, even murder. She dropped her hand and stalked toward the parlor.

I stood there in dumb amazement. The thought of drab, bony Amanda married to the handsome Lord Fox was ludicrous! I forced myself to contain my emotions.

I entered the parlor shortly after a maid wheeled in the tea cart. Aunt Lydia did the pouring, as though it were her special prerogative.

"Isn't he the most exciting man you ever met?" Aunt Joyce queried of no one in particular.

"Did you see the way he looked at me throughout dinner?" Annabel asked, then rolled her eyes upward as though heaven was about to bless her.

Aunt Joyce reached over and patted her daughter's hand. "Anyone can see he favors you, Bella."

Aunt Lydia stiffened in her chair. "Jason's visits here are expressly to see Amanda. He's a serious, dedicated young man, who does not prize vanity and foolishness in a young woman."

"You're so filled with puffery, Lydia, you can't see the facts before you. Lord Fox likes women with life in them, not a dried-up, dreary female who is old before her time," Joyce declared.

"I suppose in your usual snide way, you are referring

172

to my Amanda."

"I am."

"My dear Joyce, if you think Bella stands a chance with a man of the world like Lord Fox, you have deluded yourself. Jason will never have anything to do with a naive woman who believes she is still a schoolgirl. He wants and needs a mature woman."

"You never did know much about men, Lydia, or you would have done much better than Nigel."

"You're being quite petty and nasty tonight, Joyce."

And on it went. They bickered back and forth while Amanda and Annabel glared at each other. I could have been a piece of furniture in the room for all they cared. I wanted to toss Jason up in the air and let whoever caught him have him. I flashed a smile when the men came into the room. At least with Jason present, they tried to be on their best behavior. To everyone's annoyance, Lord Fox came to sit beside me on the settee. Only Binky gave me a wink and a smile. Though they were smiling, I could see the other women in the room were clearly displeased by my unintentionally capturing the attentions of Lord Fox.

The more I looked at Jason, the more I could see why my aunts were so eager to have him for a son-in-law. He was wealthy, witty, charming, and extraordinarily handsome. Still, it was Michael who captivated me, regardless of what Grandfather had said about him.

"How is the old boy doing, Michael? Haven't seen him since I left for Paris," Jason said.

"Seems to be improving. I think the reappearance of Jennifer has enhanced his spirits," Michael answered.

"*We* hardly see him," Nigel grumbled.

"One would think Father never had daughters," Lydia added somberly.

173

"I go up occasionally to play a game of chess with him," Binky said. "If I don't mention the rest of the family, he tolerates me quite well."

"Still chasing the village girls, Binky? Or is there a particular one you favor now?" Jason asked, an amused smile on his face.

"With Jennifer around, I might be spending more time within the confines of Wyndcliffe Manor."

Jason looked at me with a beguiling smile. "I wouldn't blame you in the least."

"Will you be staying at Foxhill Grange for a while, Jason?" Aunt Joyce asked.

"Oh, I do hope so." Annabel was nervously twisting one of her blond curls around a delicate finger.

Her gesture caused me to look down at my rough and weathered hands. I folded them in my lap and tried to bury them in the folds of my skirt.

"My plans are to stay at Foxhill Grange until next year's spring crops are planted. Unfortunately, my plans are always tentative. I never know when business might call me away."

"What business is that, Jason?" I asked.

"Horses. Race horses in particular. That's why I went to Paris. Actually, just outside of Paris. I had heard an excellent mare was up for auction. A fine specimen. To my dismay the bidding went far beyond my purse."

"I'm sorry," I offered.

"Oh, there'll be others. Have you ever seen a race of thoroughbreds, Jennifer?"

"No. Not thoroughbreds. I've watched the Gypsies race their piebald ponies. I have to admit I found it exciting."

"You must let me take you to real races. I think you'll find them exhilarating, especially if you have a small wager on them."

"I adore the races, Jason," Annabel piped up. Her voice reminded me of a flute played out of tune by a novice.

"I find the sport of kings intriguing." Amanda was not to be outdone by her cousin.

"Then we shall make a party of it soon. I assume you'd be willing to come, Binky?"

"Naturally. Any outing to chase away the ennui here. It's good to have you back, Jason."

"What about you, Michael? Surely a day away from your chores would be a welcome relief," Jason stated.

"We'll see."

"Six is a much better complement of people than five. When the time comes, I shall insist on your presence, Michael."

"Shall we adjoin to the music room? Amanda has been most diligent in practicing the piano. This seems like a good occasion to listen to her musical accomplishments," Aunt Lydia said, rising from her chair, causing the gentlemen to stand.

"An excellent idea," Nigel added, and took his wife's arm.

Jason quickly took my arm and we joined the parade to the music room. He patted my hand on his arm and said, "Have you a beau, Jennifer?"

"No."

"Then my visits to Wyndcliffe shall be more frequent."

I should have put a halt to any aspirations he might have toward me then and there. But how could I tell him I adored Michael Savage, the prince I had dreamed of all my life?

After everyone was seated, Amanda commenced playing. To my surprise she was an excellent pianist.

175

Each note, each chord was meticulous in execution; yet, something was missing. Passion. That fiery emotion that separates a piano player from the true artist. For a change, the evening passed pleasantly.

I was up early the next morning. As I went into the dining room, I half-expected Grandfather to be there already. But he wasn't. I was glad in a way. I wanted to be there waiting for him. Michael was at the sideboard filling his plate.

"Good morning, Michael," I said cheerily.

"Good morning, Jennifer." His expression was stern.

"Grandfather is coming down to breakfast this morning," I told him as I filled my plate. He had already taken his seat.

"Oh? He must be much improved."

"When I saw him yesterday, he was walking around his parlor."

"Is he coming with us to survey the mines?"

"I don't think so." I took my place at the head of the table. "He said something about going over the ledgers with me this morning."

"What about the mines?"

"He said you could take me to Botallack this afternoon. The ride is a short one, and the visit could be completed in one afternoon."

Michael nodded. "What did you think of Lord Fox?"

"A personable young man. How old is he? Is Foxhill Grange near?"

"He is twenty-seven. Three years younger than me. The Grange is about three hours by coach. On a horse and cutting through the fields, one can reach it in less

176

than an hour. You still haven't told me what you think of him."

"I don't know him well enough to have formed an opinion. Why do you care what I think of him?"

Michael shrugged. "Everyone seems to have a different opinion of him. Are you aware Annabel and Amanda are vying to be his bride?"

"Aunt Lydia made that quite clear to me last night. Aunt Joyce and Annabel made no secret of their designs on him. Is his estate as large as Grandfather's?"

"Hardly. His holdings are about one-third the size of your grandfather's."

"Does he have any tin mines in Cornwall?"

"No. As he said, horses are his passion."

"That's an expensive passion. If his holdings aren't very large, how does he manage to maintain expensive race horses?"

"He's an excellent trainer, and his horses often win, I understand. But I don't think he's ever won a really big purse. Only enough to maintain his stables. His rents barely pay for the upkeep of the Grange. On the other hand, he does seem to do rather well for himself."

"Do you think he will really marry Amanda or Annabel?"

"Now that *you've* entered the picture, I fear their hopes in that direction are all but lost."

"Me? You don't think he is going to court me, do you?"

"I think it is highly probable. Doesn't that please you?"

"Of course, I'm flattered, but not particularly pleased. Now that I've discovered who I am and have found my grandfather, I have no intention of marrying for some time." I watched his grim expression soften. I couldn't help but think that Grandfather was right.

Michael Savage had his own plans for me. Well, I was not going to be anyone's puppet.

"Jason can be a very persuasive man," Michael said.

"Did someone mention my name?" Jason asked, striding into the dining room.

"I was telling Jennifer how persuasive you can be."

"She'll soon find that out for herself." His smile was dazzling.

"I wasn't aware you stayed overnight, Jason," I said.

"I came over yesterday on horseback across the fields. I stayed later than I should have. Taking the shortcut in the dark isn't wise. Too many pitfalls. I didn't relish spending three or four hours on the road either. I've stayed overnight before. Your grandfather has always been generous and hospitable." With a full plate, Jason joined us at the table. "Do you have any plans for today, Jennifer? I'd like to show you Foxhill Grange. You do ride, don't you?"

"Yes, I ride. But my day is quite full. Besides, I feel I should get to know Wyndcliffe before I go trotting off to visit other estates. Perhaps another time, Jason."

"I shall hold you to that, Jennifer."

I turned to Michael. "Do you have any idea what could be keeping Grandfather? He told me to meet him here early."

"When he used to come down for breakfast, he arrived promptly at six. I have no idea what could be keeping him. Jerome might know." Michael picked up the small silver bell on the table and rang it. When Jerome entered, Michael asked, "Have you seen Mr. Hardwicke this morning, Jerome?"

"No, sir. Last night he informed me not to bother him in the morning. He would be taking breakfast in the dining room. I haven't seen him since, sir. Is more coffee wanted?"

"I'll have more coffee, Jerome." While he walked away, I said to no one in particular, "If Grandfather isn't down by the time I've had my coffee, I'll go up and see what is keeping him. I wonder if his gout has come back?"

"If it has, he would have rung for Jerome," Michael said.

"Hardwicke is a tough old bird. Don't worry about him, Jennifer," Jason added.

"Have you traveled the Continent extensively, Jason?" I asked.

"After Cambridge, I took the grand tour. Don't go much now."

"Then you're a Cambridge man."

Jason laughed. "After a fashion. Only lasted a year. I'm not the studious type."

Jerome brought the coffee, poured, and departed as quietly as he came.

"Of all the places you've seen on the Continent, what was your favorite, Jason?" I asked.

"Venice," he said without hesitation.

"Why?"

Jason began to recount his fascination with Venice. Michael fidgeted with his teaspoon, then stood.

"If you'll excuse me, I have things to do," Michael interrupted.

"Michael, please wait until I've talked to Grandfather. He might want you to go over the ledgers with me, if he isn't up to it."

"All right. But hurry."

"Excuse me, Jason. We'll chat another time." I gulped down the remainder of my coffee, pushed my chair back, and stood. Lifting my skirts, I dashed from

179

the dining room, through the foyer, and up the stairs.

Reaching Grandfather's room, I knocked on the door gently. The slight force of my knuckles against the wood caused the door to inch open. I padded in calling, "Grandfather . . . Grandfather."

He was nowhere in the sitting parlor, but the door to his bedchamber was ajar. I pushed it fully open, then let go a scream that shook the plastered ceiling.

Fourteen

The screaming continued. My eyes had never seen so much blood. The white linens of his bed made the profusion of red gore even more stark in its horror. Grandfather lay in bed, his eyes open in terror, his throat deeply cut from ear to ear.

Suddenly I was filled with revulsion. Bile churned in my stomach. I had to get out of there before I fainted. I had to remain alert and get help, even though my brain told me that Grandfather was beyond help. I turned and raced back to the sitting parlor.

As Michael entered the room, I threw myself into his arms. The screaming had reduced itself to heavy breathing.

"Whatever is wrong, Jennifer?" His dark eyebrows clashed together in a frown.

Without looking, I flung my arm in the direction of Grandfather's bedchamber. Michael led me to a chair, and made sure I sat down before he went to investigate the cause of my distress. Jason Fox came in looking befuddled. Jerome stood behind him.

It seemed like ages before Michael came into the sitting parlor. When he did, he closed the bedchamber door behind him.

"What happened?" Jason asked of Michael, seeing I was in a noncommunicative stupor.

Michael shook his head as a signal he wasn't about to talk of it in my presence. "Jerome, keep everyone out of here. Jason, I would appreciate it if you would ride to town and get the constable."

"What happened?" Jason asked in a whisper.

"Mr. Hardwicke is dead."

"How?"

"Later, Jason. Please ride now." When Jason departed, Michael came over to face me. He put his hands on my shoulders and lifted me from the chair. "I'll take you to your rooms, Jennifer, and have your maid tend to you."

"I don't want to be alone, Michael. Please take me downstairs and stay with me."

"All right. I think we both could use a brandy about now anyway." He put his arm around my shoulders and led me downstairs to the rear parlor, where he poured two snifters of brandy. He handed one to me. "Drink it slowly, Jennifer."

He sat next to me on the settee and took my free hand in his. As flesh met flesh, his quiet strength flowed into me and helped me gain a momentary semblance of composure. I finished the brandy, and sat there quietly brooding before turning to him.

"Why, Michael, why?" Then the tears came.

Michael put his empty glass on the low table in front of me. He took my glass and placed it next to his. His arm went about my shoulders, and he pulled me to him. I muffled my sobs into his shoulder. He remained silent until I had cried myself out.

"Who would do such a thing? And why?" My eyes were wet, but the sobs had ebbed to an occasional croaking of my voice.

"I have no idea, Jennifer. Whoever it was has a

penchant for the brutal."

"Why? He never hurt anyone."

"I don't know."

"Did he have any enemies, Michael? The tenants or miners?"

"No. James Hardwicke was a fair man and paid decent wages. I've never heard a word against him from either source. Besides, the house is locked tight at night. I doubt if anyone could have gotten in."

The implication struck me hard and fast. I pulled myself from the comfort of his arm and sat upright. "If that is the case, then someone in this house must have done it! I can't believe that, Michael."

"It's the only logical conclusion, Jennifer. Jerome saw him late last night. He was alone until you found him this morning. Whoever it was, your grandfather must have known the person and let him—or her—in. I know he locks his doors before he retires."

"The thought that it might be someone in this house is dreadful." I paused reflectively. "Oh, Michael, everything was all right before I came to Wyndcliffe."

"Don't talk like that, Jennifer. In the short time you've been here, you gave the old boy more hope and happiness than he's known since the death of his son. Think of it this way, he died knowing a part of his son came back to Wyndcliffe."

"I'll try, Michael."

"I just heard what happened," Binky said, as he came dashing into the room. His eyes went to the snifter glasses on the table. As if an alarm went off in his head, he went to the sideboard and poured himself a brandy. "What did the old boy die of?"

I was appalled by Binky's seeming callousness. I was relieved when Michael answered him before I said something I might regret.

"The constable and the doctor are on their way. I'm

183

sure they will be able to give you a better account of Mr. Hardwicke's death."

Binky shrugged. "I thought the old boy was getting better."

"He was," Michael said.

"I guess he had a sudden setback then. Did Jason leave?"

"Yes." Michael's answer was terse. He stood as the rest of the family meandered in looking bewildered.

"Oh dear, oh dear," Aunt Joyce wailed. "Poor Father. We should have been told he was dying. We should have been with him to comfort him in his last hours."

"For a change I agree with my sister," Aunt Lydia claimed. "You were with him more than any of us, Michael. Why didn't you tell us he was so poorly?"

"His death was sudden and unexpected." Michael was clearly annoyed by the insinuation that he was somehow to blame.

"Yes. We should have been notified." Nigel nodded in agreement with his wife.

"Where is Jason? Did he leave for Foxhill?" Annabel asked, her blue eyes wide with disappointment.

"He left, Bella dear. Best he did. We don't need a stranger hanging around at a time like this," Binky said, as he went to the sideboard for a refill of brandy.

"Jason's no stranger." Annabel gave a stamp of her foot. "He's almost one of the family. He'd be such a comfort at a time like this."

"Why did he leave, Michael? Did you send him away?" Amanda asked, then primly sat down, her hands folded in her lap.

"He went on an errand."

"What errand?" Cecil asked of Michael.

"For the constable and the doctor. They should be here shortly."

184

Aunt Joyce's solemn expression turned to one of concern. "Why the constable, Michael?"

"You'll soon find out. I'd rather not go into it now. For those who haven't taken breakfast yet, I suggest they do so now. There might not be time later."

The two older men grumbled as they left the parlor, Binky trailing behind. I didn't want to be left alone with my aunts and cousins. Annabel and Amanda seemed more concerned with Jason Fox's absence than with Grandfather's death. I was in no mood to deal with their apparent apathy regarding Grandfather.

"I think I will go up to my room now," I announced.

"The constable will be here soon, Jennifer. I'm sure he'll want to talk to you," Michael said.

I looked deep into Michael's ebony eyes, hoping he could read the distress I felt at being with my aunts and cousins. He returned the stare, which soon altered to one of understanding.

"Perhaps the fresh air would do you more good than being shut up in your room alone, Jennifer."

"Yes. I'd like that."

The rear parlor, like the dining room, had French doors which opened directly onto the rear balustraded terrace. Michael led me to the terrace. I went to the balustrade and placed my hands on it. Michael followed suit. The back lawn was expansive with autumn flowers bursting with rich hues of yellow, rust, red, and orange. The topiary was neatly trimmed. The whiteness of the marble statues and benches was sharply contrasted against the deep, dark color of the evergreens. Before speaking, I filled my lungs several times with the crisp, cool air.

"No one really seems to care that Grandfather is dead."

"I don't think they've fully absorbed it. Besides, none of them was really close to your grandfather. When

185

your father died so tragically, instead of becoming closer to his family, your grandfather pushed them away. Don't blame them for their seeming indifference, Jennifer. Mr. Hardwicke was indifferent to them for many years."

I sighed audibly. "I suppose you know more about it than I do."

Michael put his hands on my shoulders and turned me around to face him. A look came into his eyes that I couldn't fathom. He was about to speak, but I never found out what he was going to say, for Aunt Lydia opened the French doors and poked her head out.

"The constable and Doctor Marsh are here," she said, then quickly popped back into the rear parlor.

"We'd best go in, Jennifer," Michael said softly, as he cupped my elbow and steered me back into the parlor.

"Well, my dear, you certainly don't look like a gypsy now," Dr. Marsh said, as he came over to greet me. He took my hands and gave me a sound kiss on the cheek.

"I hope not. Have you seen Grandfather?"

His smiling face became solemn. "Yes." He shook his head slowly. "Nasty business this. There is no way your grandfather could have done that to himself. I find it very troubling."

Under the direction of Constable John Morgan, everyone began taking a seat. Annabel quickly took a seat beside Jason Fox on the settee.

Constable John Morgan was a short, wiry man, whose thinning dark hair resembled a monk's tonsure. Sharp gray eyes lay behind wire-rimmed glasses. An unlighted pipe rested in his hand, and he occasionally used it like a baton. His sergeant, Arthur Tompson, was the opposite of his superior. A tall, stout man he had wide hazel eyes and a full head of a chestnut-colored hair. He stood in the background, assiduously taking notes.

When Constable Morgan gave a detailed account of Grandfather's death, Aunt Joyce turned pale and looked as if she might faint. But it was Annabel who actually swooned—right into Jason Fox's arms, much to his surprise and bewilderment. Once in Jason's arms, Annabel quickly regained her senses. Nigel, Cecil, and Binky made their way to the sideboard, where they helped themselves to whiskeys with trembling hands.

"If you gentlemen would care to take seats, I would like to begin my interrogation."

Once the gentlemen had secured their whiskeys, they complied with the constable's directive.

"According to Mr. Jerome Hunt, the butler, he last saw Mr. Hardwicke at eleven o'clock in the evening at which time Mr. Hardwicke indicated he was going to bed. Mr. Hardwicke also indicated that he would be coming down to breakfast, and wouldn't need Mr. Hunt's services in the morning. Mr. Hunt mentioned that Mr. Hardwicke had the habit of locking the doors upon retiring. Now, Miss Hardwicke, I would like to know at what time and under what circumstances you discovered the body," Constable Morgan said, pointing the stem of his pipe at me.

"I was suppose to meet Grandfather for breakfast first thing in the morning. I assumed he meant at six o'clock, as that is the time Jerome starts putting the breakfast fare on the sideboard. I was down at six sharp to find Mr. Savage filling his plate. We were eating breakfast when we were joined by Lord Fox.

"At seven-thirty I began to be concerned about Grandfather, and wondered if he had taken a turn for the worse. I decided to check on him. I went to his sitting parlor to find the door unlocked. After entering, I noticed the door to his bedchamber was ajar. I called his name several times before I pushed the door open.

187

Grandfather . . ." My voice cracked and I had to swallow an incipient sob. "Grandfather was as you found him. My screams brought Mr. Savage, Lord Fox, and Jerome." I could think of nothing more to say. I didn't want to remember the sight that greeted my eyes when I pushed that bedchamber door open.

"I see. From what you've told me, I assume the sitting parlor door was open."

I looked up at him. "Yes." I hadn't thought about it before. Had Grandfather opened it to come down to breakfast? No, I thought. He was still in his night-clothes.

"Will you take it from there, Mr. Savage?" the constable requested.

"As Miss Hardwicke said, I rushed upstairs when I heard her screams. Lord Fox followed me, as did Jerome. Miss Hardwicke was in a state of shock, as you can well imagine. After surveying the scene, I took her into the parlor and made her sit down. I then sent Lord Fox for you and the doctor. As I led Miss Hardwicke out of the sitting parlor, I told Jerome to guard the door and let no one in until you and the doctor arrived." Michael's deep voice delivered the information in a monotone.

"Nothing was touched, you say, Mr. Savage?"

"Nothing."

"I see." The constable tapped the stem of his pipe against his cheek. "On the face of it, Mr. Hardwicke was killed sometime between eleven o'clock last night and seven-thirty this morning. He must have known his assailant well, for he let the culprit into his rooms, then went to lay on his bed, as he was atop his bedcovers, not under them. At this point I shall need to know everyone's whereabouts from eleven at night to seven-thirty this morning."

As Constable Morgan questioned each member of

the family and Lord Fox, he received the same reply from each of them. All were asleep. Someone wasn't telling the truth, but I could see no way to prove it. I was surprised to learn my Aunt Lydia had a private bedchamber, while her husband Nigel slept in an adjoining bedchamber, as did Aunt Joyce and Uncle Cecil.

The constable's shoulders heaved in a great sigh, as though he knew there was a liar in the room. "I must insist everyone remain at Wyndcliffe Manor, until this matter is cleared up."

"Does that include me, Constable?" Jason asked.

"No, milord. But I would appreciate your keeping yourself available at Foxhill Grange." The constable received a nod of assent from Jason. "For the time being, all of you may go about your business. I'm going downstairs to question the staff. Come along, Arthur."

Dr. Marsh came over to me. "I'm sorry for your trouble, my dear. To lose your grandfather after just finding him is tragic indeed. If there is anything I can do, all you have to do is ask. Would you like me to leave some sleeping powders for you?"

"I don't think so." From the corner of my eye, I could see Aunt Lydia was fuming. It didn't take long for her to express her anger aloud.

"How dare that Constable Morgan imply someone in the family killed Father. It's utterly ridiculous!"

"Now, now, Lydia. I'm sure he didn't mean our family," Nigel offered.

"Are you saying one of us Melvilles is involved in this dastardly deed, Nigel?" Cecil sputtered, his already florid face taking on a deeper shade of red, his hands balling into fists.

"Think what you will, Cecil," Nigel countered.

"Really, Doctor. I am his daughter. I think condolences and sleeping powders should be offered to

189

me *first,*" Aunt Joyce complained.

"I am the oldest," Aunt Lydia claimed. "I should receive the commiseration first."

As arguments flew back and forth between the Lamberts and the Melvilles, Dr. Marsh shook his head and left. I went up to my rooms to grieve in private.

The wake lasted a week. The coffin was closed and rested in the chapel. Tenants and some of the mining people arrived to show their respect. Though they were sincere in their sympathy and sadness, I could see worry in their eyes. If the estate and mines were to be governed by either Cecil or Nigel, everything could take a turn for the worse. Neither of them were capable, or inclined, to supervise the estate. Jobs and tenancies could be lost.

The day of the burial was as solemn and gloomy as the occasion. Dark clouds scudded across the sky, prodded by gusty winds. A misty veil shrouded the land like a portend of the winter to come. I stared at the grim barren landscape in silence, as the carriage rolled over a rutted lane toward Wyndcliffe's private cemetery.

I rode with the Lamberts behind the casket. The rest of the family followed in carriages behind us. Michael, Jason, and Dr. Marsh brought up the rear of the cortege.

The damp, salty air assailed my nostrils the minute we emerged from the carriage. When everyone had gathered at the gravesite, the vicar began a lengthy eulogy. The wind picked up and danced in raw, chilling bursts; yet, staring at the casket, I felt nothing except emptiness. I was oblivious of the tears streaming over my cheeks. If only I had had time to know Grandfather better. Or at least remembered my childhood experiences of him and my parents. Then I would have been able to cling to memories. Now I had nothing.

My self-pitying thoughts were diverted by the strident cries of gulls circling overhead. I raised my head to look at them, and a shudder went through me as one particular gull hovered above me, its eyes seemingly boring into mine. I had the eerie sensation that the bird was trying to tell me something. Thinking my sanity was at risk, I quickly looked away. As I did, my vision caught an ominous figure standing in the background.

The small, lean man was dressed entirely in black, and reminded me of a raven ready to pounce on carrion. His long, beaked nose and black pelletlike eyes enhanced that impression. I wondered who he was and what he was doing at Grandfather's funeral. I concluded he must be one of the many overseers at the mines.

I was curious and surprised when he followed us back to Wyndcliffe Manor.

Fifteen

"Luncheon will be deferred until later, Miss Jennifer," Jerome informed me as he took my cloak, bonnet, and gloves.

"Why?"

"Mrs. Lambert's orders, Miss. She wishes to have the reading of the will first."

I looked at Aunt Lydia. She walked past me as though she refused to acknowledge my presence. Amanda and Annabel walked by me with smug smiles, as if they knew something I didn't. At that moment a knife of fear stabbed at me. Once the Lamberts and the Melvilles had established their ownership of Wyndcliffe Manor, would they throw me out? Reason soon overshadowed doubts. I had as much right to live at Wyndcliffe as they did. But they could relegate me to the status of a poor relation, and make life miserable for me. I turned back to Jerome.

"Where is the reading of the will to be held, Jerome?"

"In the library, Miss. If you'll excuse me, I have to fetch Cook."

Chairs had been arranged in the library, as though preparing for a musicale. The chair behind the desk was empty as the family took seats. Michael rushed in without Jason or the doctor.

The ravenlike man strutted in and went behind the desk. He placed a small portfolio on the desk, and made a ceremony of opening it before he sat down. He pulled a pair of glasses from his vest and put them on. He peered at our faces, as though relishing the anxiety he saw on some of them. He cleared his throat and was about to read the papers before him, when Jerome and the cook came into the library. Jerome handed him some papers and whispered something in the man's ear. The man scanned the papers. I suddenly recognized the woman with Jerome. She was the one who had come out of Grandfather's room with Jerome. After examining the papers, the man spoke.

"It seems that Mr. Hardwicke has made a new will, which nulls and voids his previous will."

"Is that legal?" Nigel interrupted.

"Perfectly legal. The will is in Mr. Hardwicke's handwriting, and attested to by two witnesses."

"Read it," Aunt Lydia demanded.

Another clearing of the throat. The man introduced himself as a solicitor, and had a raspy voice which could try one's nerves.

"'I, James Hardwicke, being of sound mind and body, do hereby revoke all and any previous wills. Having at last found my only son's child, who was believed lost or dead, I wish to revise and update my will.

"'I leave all my worldly possessions—'" The solicitor looked up and said, "At this point, Mr. Hardwicke enumerates what he means by worldly possessions. I shall have copies made for each of you. In brief, it includes the estate, lands, and mines. I shall continue, 'to my granddaughter, Jennifer Mary Hardwicke.'"

Gasps and grunts echoed around the room. I noticed that Michael rose and left the library.

Aunt Lydia jumped to her feet. "What about *us?*"

The solicitor waved her down. Aunt Lydia grudgingly resumed her seat. "I'm coming to that, Mrs. Lambert. Please let me continue without further outbursts. 'To my stepdaughters, Lydia Lambert and Joyce Melville, I leave the sum of one thousand pounds each, and a directive for them and their families within six months from the date of my demise, which I sincerely hope won't be for some time, to leave Wyndcliffe Manor. A thousand pounds should enable their husbands to find suitable employment and lodgings within the time allotted.'"

While the solicitor read minor bequests, Aunt Lydia sat straight in her chair. She was breathing hard. Despite rouged cheeks, Aunt Joyce was pale. Anger and worry mingled on the faces of Nigel and Cecil. My cousins looked bewildered. Cecil spoke when the solicitor finished.

"What if . . . er . . . something . . . er . . . happens to Jennifer?"

"In the event of Miss Hardwicke's demise, we shall have to defer to the original will, unless Miss Hardwicke makes a will."

"And how does the original will dispose of the properties?" Nigel asked.

"Everything is equally divided between Mrs. Lydia Lambert and Mrs. Joyce Melville," the solicitor replied.

"What about this stepdaughter business?" Aunt Lydia asked.

As the solicitor began the long explanation of their not being blood kin to Grandfather, I left the room in search of Michael. I would need his help now more than ever. Both Michael and Lord Fox were in the rear parlor.

"Congratulations, Jennifer." Jason left his seat and

came to kiss my hand.

"I'd rather not be congratulated on the day of my grandfather's funeral."

"Sorry. Please accept my apologies." Jason led me to a settee and sat down beside me.

I looked at Michael, who had a dark scowl on his face as he stood by the fireplace. He seemed to be angry about something. But I wasn't concerned with his anger at the moment. I was anxious to secure his continued assistance in the running of all the operations.

"You will continue in your present capacity, won't you, Michael?"

"If you wish. But I won't be living at the Manor. I shall return to my cottage."

My first reaction was disappointment. But I could sympathize with his desire to leave Wyndcliffe. I didn't look forward to eating my meals with my relatives. At least I would only have to suffer their bickering for six months.

"Will you help me familiarize myself with the tenant farms, mines, and ledgers, Michael?"

"I am at your disposal, Miss Jennifer." With that he gave a little bow, turned on his heel, and left the room.

My heart constricted a little at his sudden unfriendly attitude. Michael had always been friendly toward me, perhaps more than friendly at times. What happened? Grandfather's death? The will? Had he expected to receive a substantial sum? Perhaps he had hopes of getting the mines. My musings were disrupted as I felt someone take my hand. I had momentarily forgotten all about Jason sitting next to me.

"Jennifer, I never really got to offer you my sincere condolences. I do so now. What a shock it must have been for you to find your grandfather like that. If I can be of any help, don't hesitate to call on me," Jason said.

"Thank you, Jason. I appreciate your thoughtfulness."

"Perhaps you should get away from here for a while. Why don't I call for you early tomorrow morning, and bring you to Foxhill Grange for the day? The change of scenery would do you good. I have an excellent cook."

"That's very nice of you, Jason. But it's too soon for me to go gallivanting about the countryside. Besides, I have much to learn and learn quickly about the estate."

"One day won't matter. Michael has been virtually running everything by himself for months now. Another day or so won't mean anything to him. Please. I would like to show off Foxhill very much."

I thought about it. It would be a refreshing change. The few weeks I'd been at Wyndcliffe seemed like an eternity. Then I thought of the legacy Grandfather had entrusted to me. He had placed great confidence in my abilities. My first duty belonged to him. I couldn't and wouldn't let fanciful whims divert my attention from my duty.

"I'm sorry, Jason. For the time being, I belong right here. Perhaps another time."

"When?"

"In a couple of months."

"I'll hold you to that, Jennifer. In the meantime, I do hope you'll allow me to call on you."

"Of course. You're always welcome at Wyndcliffe."

We were interrupted by Jerome. "Luncheon is being served, Miss Jennifer."

I turned back to Jason. "You will stay to lunch, won't you, Jason?"

"I'd be delighted." He stood and offered me his arm, then led me into the dining room.

The older Lamberts and Melvilles kept a gloomy silence throughout the meal. Their children were the opposite and quite animated, especially Binky. He

196

seemed to have shrugged off the fact we had attended a funeral that morning.

"Michael tells me he is leaving Wyndcliffe Manor. Going back to live at that dreary little cottage of his," Binky said in general, then faced Michael. "Why don't you stay here, Michael? I'm sure Jennifer wouldn't mind, and it would be handy for her to have you close by where she can pick your brain anytime she wishes."

"Binky's right, Michael. You're more than welcome to stay," I added.

"Sorry. But I prefer to be at the cottage. I'll only be fifteen minutes away."

"When will you leave?" I asked.

"Tomorrow morning. I have some packing to do. I'd like to borrow one of the maids to tidy the place up and bring some food to the cottage, if that's all right with you, Miss Jennifer?"

That damn *Miss* Jennifer again. I stared into those dark eyes, trying to transmit my dislike of his using Miss before my name. I wanted him to call me Jennifer again in that soft manner of his. But he wouldn't be stared down.

"Do as you wish, Michael. Do you think you have time to show me the ledgers this afternoon?"

"I'll make a point of it. Is directly after lunch all right with you?"

"Fine." I was the first to look away. The arrogance that glittered in his eyes infuriated me.

"Why don't we play a game of whist this afternoon, Jason? I'm sure Amanda and Binky would love a game." Annabel fluttered her eyelashes at Jason, as though the gesture would melt any resistance he might have.

"I think you should first ask Binky and me if we want to play, Bella. I might have other plans," Amanda said, her expression haughty as she looked down her long, thin nose at Annabel.

"I must get back to Foxhill this afternoon, ladies," Jason told them, his smile captivating.

"Would you mind if I rode over with you, Jason?" Binky asked.

"Not at all, dear fellow."

"Why don't I come with you?" Annabel asked, determined to spend her time with Jason.

"My dear Bella," Binky began, "we're riding across the fields. Not fit for a young lady of your sensibilities."

"We could take a carriage," Annabel offered weakly, as she saw her hopes of being with Jason drain away.

"You know very well that going by the road takes too long. I'm sure Jason is anxious to get home. He's been away for a week or better," Binky said.

"Another time, Bella." Jason used his most soothing tone, as Annabel's mouth settled in a pout.

The covert glances of malice constantly cast my way by my aunts and uncles made me uneasy. I was glad when lunch was over. With Michael by my side, I quickly strode through the foyer, past the staircase, and on to the end of the gallery, where the library door stood open.

Without a word Michael went to the desk and opened one of the large lower drawers. He gathered up the books that lay at the bottom of that drawer and placed them on the desk. He motioned for me to take the large leather chair behind the desk. When I did so, he went to a sideboard, opened the doors, and removed a couple of scrolls from a lower shelf. He brought them to the desk and unceremoniously dropped them, as if he found the chore boring and tedious.

Anger churned within me, an anger I couldn't stem. "What's wrong, Michael? Why are you acting as if I were your most fearsome enemy? And why all of a sudden this *Miss* Jennifer business?"

He ran a splayed hand through his thick chestnut hair. "You are now a wealthy owner of property, and mistress of a sizable estate. I'm only showing deference to your exhalted position."

"I don't like it and wish you would stop. Whatever position Grandfather has bestowed on me, I'm still Jennifer to you. You are not a servant, Michael."

"As you wish." The expression on his sharp-boned face remained stern and enigmatic.

Anger was beginning to give way to frustration. I didn't know how to reach this new Michael, this aloof Michael. "Do you feel I'm your adversary now, Michael?"

"You are my employer. There's always a certain amount of distance between employer and employee."

"It doesn't have to be that way. Despite your sense of our business relationship, I would like to be friends with you, Michael."

"Friends?" An engaging and crooked smile flickered over his lips, then settled in a grim line. "Shall we proceed with the business at hand?" He unfurled the scrolls to reveal maps of land tenancy and the mines. With a great deal of patience, he explained the maps. When he saw I had a grasp of the territories, he rerolled them and returned them to the cabinet.

"If you have need to refer to them, you now know where the maps are kept." He came to stand by my chair as we started on the ledgers.

His head bent close to mine, as he unraveled the numerical complexities of accounts payable and receivable for the mines and the tenant farms. He was so close, the male scent of him had an unsteadying effect on me. Occasionally his warm breath would fan my cheeks. My mind kept wandering to the deep and probing kiss he gave me in the meadow, muddling my concentration. All I could think of was his strong arms around me, and the hard sinews of his body as they pressed against me.

"Are you with me, Jennifer?" he asked, his lips inches from mine when I turned my head.

"Yes." My mouth was dry. I ran my tongue over my lips to moisten them. Michael quickly pulled back and stood up straight.

"Perhaps we should have tea, and continue this after a short respite," he suggested.

He pulled the bell cord, causing Jerome to come into the library. Michael let me request the tea. When the tea and scones with clotted cream were brought, we sat in the two maroon leather chairs flanking the fireplace. Though Michael seemed content to remain silent, I was not.

"When will I see the mines, Michael?"

"Whenever you wish."

"Tomorrow?"

"I'll only be free in the afternoon, which would exclude going to Cambourne. But I could take you to Botallack. Would that be satisfactory?"

"That would be fine."

"I'll come for you at one o'clock."

I nodded. Silence cloaked the room once more. I couldn't stand it. "Is your cottage comfortable?"

"Quite."

"I'd like to see it sometime, if it's all right with you."

"You are free to visit at any time. After all, it is your property."

"My property or not, I wouldn't wish to intrude or inconvenience you. I shall wait for a proper invitation."

Michael made no reply, leaving me to assume any invitation would be a long while in coming. The next conversation I initiated was desultory, revolving mostly around the weather. When our tea was over, we went back to the study of ledgers. This time Michael kept his distance.

I continued to pore over the ledgers when Michael departed. Slowly, I was beginning to grasp the essentials. With my head crammed full of new information, I closed the ledgers and put them back in the drawer. I started to rummage through the other drawers. Sundry stationery items. Folders containing paid and unpaid bills. In the large middle drawer rested one of those new checkbooks issued by a bank. I noticed the bank was in Falmouth. I made a mental note to go there and have my signature registered with them soon. The balance of money in the checkbook was sizable. I was pleased to note Grandfather kept neat and meticulous records.

Far back in one of the drawers, my fingers touched a metal box. I pulled the drawer farther out and removed the metal box, placing it on top of the desk. To my dismay it was locked. I went to the bell cord and gave it a tug.

"Did my grandfather have any other keys?" I asked when Jerome appeared.

"I took the liberty of placing all Mr. Hardwicke's personal possessions in a box, Miss Jennifer."

"Could you bring it to me, Jerome?"

"It is almost dinnertime, Miss Jennifer."

I glanced at the clock on the mantel of the fireplace. "So it is. Then after dinner. I will sort through them privately in here."

"Yes, Miss. About Mr. Hardwicke's clothes. What would you like done with them?"

"Give his clothes, boots, and the like to the church, so they may be distributed to the needy in the parish."

"Yes, Miss."

The family was rather put out when I left them after

201

dinner and sequestered myself in the library. The box Jerome deposited was a large one. I took the articles out one by one. I put the silver hairbrushes aside, thinking Grandfather might have wished Jerome to have them. He had served the family long and well.

The daguerreotype and talbotype photographs of my grandmother, mother, and father, I would place in my rooms. A number of baby pictures were in silver frames. The name Jennifer was inked on some of them. I could see the resemblance to myself. I studied them for a while, hoping they would stir my memory. They didn't.

A small velvet case contained a gold watch and various manly rings. Finally I came to a set of keys. I took the metal box out of the drawer again and began trying the keys. I went through several before finding the one that opened it.

Inside was a large amount of cash and a small notebook. I left the cash and took out the notebook. In doing so, a paper fell out. On it were numbers. I had no idea what the numbers meant. I put the paper back in the notebook, relocked the box, and put it back. I skimmed through the notebook, and realized it was some sort of diary. I decided to read it in my room later, and slipped it into the hidden side pocket of my gown along with the ring of keys.

With the exception of the silver brushes, I started to return the other items to the box. When I came to the velvet case, I opened it again and stared at the gold watch. Thinking it would make a nice gift for a husband-to-be—if I ever decided to get married—I slipped it into the same pocket as the notebook. I rang for Jerome.

"I think my grandfather would have wished for you to have these, Jerome." I picked up the brushes and handed them to him.

For the first time, I could see a deep-rooted emotion spread across his face. He looked at the brushes, then at me. Though he was quickly under control, I could have sworn the man's eyes glazed over with incipient tears. His gaze returned to the silver-backed brushes. A warmth suffused him.

"Thank you, Miss Jennifer. I shall treasure them." He paused. "Shall I take the box now?"

"Not just yet. I haven't finished putting everything back. I must decide what to do with these things. I'll take care of it in the morning. That's all for now, Jerome."

"Good night, Miss." He was staring at the brushes as he closed the door behind him.

I was in the process of returning more of the items in the box when, without a by-your-leave, the library door swung open. In marched a militant Aunt Lydia, her pale face made paler by the black mourning clothes. Her eyes rested on the box.

"What have you got there, Jennifer?"

"Grandfather's personal items."

"You've no right to them! They should have been brought to me. Jerome will hear about this." She strode up to the desk and put a possessive hand on the box.

"You will not say a word to Jerome, or you'll answer to me. I was under the impression that everything at Wyndcliffe belongs to me, Aunt Lydia."

"Well, I never. You'll be sorry you ever spoke to me in such a manner, you guttersnipe. You can be sure I will talk to the solicitor about this." With her free hand she reached for the velvet case I had laid on the desk. Her eyes widened when she opened the case. As suddenly as they widened, they narrowed.

"Where's my father's gold watch?"

"I have it and intend to keep it. You may have the rings and whatever else is in the box." Although I knew the rings were quite valuable, I didn't care if she took them. I had no use for them.

She spied the silver-framed pictures on the desk. "What are those?"

"Pictures of my mother, father, and me as a tot. I'm sure you don't want them, Aunt Lydia."

"Certainly not. I want no memories of you or your parents. I'll never forgive Father for the way he treated my family in his will! I will find a way to avenge his gross injury to our pride and way of life." She glared at me with hate spewing from her eyes. Grabbing the box and velvet case, she stalked from the room without mentioning why she burst into the room in the first place.

Sooner or later she would remember what she had wanted to say, and I was certain I'd hear all about it.

As I climbed the stairs, I wondered what was in the notebook that made Grandfather keep it under lock and key.

Once in bed, I opened the notebook and began to read.

Sixteen

"Someone is cheating me and the amount is substantial," Grandfather began. "I am writing all this down so I won't forget each episode, and perhaps in retrospect, I can piece the puzzle together. When I find the culprit, I'll warrant he'll rue the day he ever crossed me.

"Perhaps I should go back to my original cash system, instead of using these newfangled checks from the bank. My accounts never agree with the banks. A large discrepancy is always in the bank's favor. Perhaps I am getting too old to do my arithmetic properly."

A big gap appeared, and I had to turn to the next page before I could continue.

"It's happened again. One hundred pounds missing this time. The time has come for me to get a bank employer to go over this checkbook. As soon as I feel a little better, I shall take myself to Falmouth."

A gap.

"Damn rheumatism and gout. I finally had to send for a bank clerk. He was in the library for what seemed like an eternity. We had tea when he came to my rooms. He was an extraordinarily patient man. He showed me all the checks I hadn't entered. A feed company. A tool company. A wagoneer. When I claimed I had no knowledge of those checks, he suggested someone might be forging my checks. I wondered if Michael had been ordering equipment and supplies I know nothing about. Did he think it simpler to forge my name than disturb me? First I must write these companies and find out what these checks were for. I don't want to openly accuse Michael without some sort of proof. He has become too indispensable to me."

Short gap.

"My Jennifer has returned to me. I shall put this forgery investigation off for a day or two, so I can get to know my granddaughter. I don't want to stir up any nasty business until she has become acclimated to Wyndcliffe."

The rest of the pages were blank. I closed the notebook and put it on the stand beside my bed. Was Michael the forger? Had he killed Grandfather to stop an investigation of the matter?

I placed my hands over my face and shook my head. I had to push those awful thoughts from my mind. I swung my feet over the bed, scuffed them into my slippers, and got out of bed. I donned my robe, took the oil lamp, and went into my sitting parlor. Placing the lamp on the escritoire, I sat down. With a pristine piece of paper before me and pen in hand, I began a letter to the bank in Falmouth. In it, I claimed I would be the one signing the checks for Wyndcliffe now. I also apprised them I would be using my full name, Jennifer Mary Hardwicke, as a signature. Any checks signed Jennifer Hardwicke should be considered suspicious and the bank should check with me before making payment on them. I folded the paper, put it in an envelope, and sealed it. I would have one of the grooms ride to Falmouth first thing in the morning.

Eerie dreams made my sleep fitful. A head, bloodied at the throat, hovered in a thick mist. The haunted eyes stared at me. As I gazed into the depths of those eyes, I knew it was Grandfather. The lips of the ashen face began to move, but I couldn't hear the words. In my dream I tried to get closer to the head, and called for the phantom to speak louder. But the closer I moved, the more distant the head became. I stopped advancing and yelled, "Speak up!"

The head ceased moving, but the lips continued to move. Still, I heard nothing. Suddenly, the words were all around me as though in a cavern, booming forth in circling echoes.

"Avenge me. Avenge me, Jennifer. But be wary. Remember, things and people are not always what they seem to be. Avenge me, so I can rest in peace."

The words reverberated in my brain. When dawn came, I remembered each word and vowed to carry out my grandfather's wishes.

With the letter to the bank resting in the pocket of my skirt, I went directly to the stable and gave instructions to a groom. Not until I saw him gallop off, did I go into the dining room for breakfast. To my surprise Binky was already at the table, his plate full.

"Don't look so startled, Jennifer. I'm not a complete wastrel who sleeps the morning away."

I smiled at him, filled my plate, then took my seat. "Why so early, Binky? It's not like you."

"Thought I'd ride over to St. Ives. I have some artist friends there. Why don't you come with me, Jennifer?"

"I have too many things to do. Thanks anyway. Do you go to St. Ives often?"

"At least once a week. They have the best herring pasties in all of Cornwall. I'll bring you back some."

"I'm not fond of herring, Binky, but I appreciate the thought."

"Then I'll bring you some rabbit pasties. They're excellent, too."

"I take it you'll be gone for the day."

"I hope so."

"Why?" I looked at him curiously.

"Oh, Aunt Joyce is in a snit over my mother getting a box of Grandfather's personal items. If it had been me, I wouldn't have let Aunt Joyce know I had them. Mother does like to tease her whenever the opportunity arises."

"I'm afraid I'm at fault. I was going through his things when your mother walked in. She insisted she was entitled to the box. I had what I wanted, and didn't care if she took it. I assumed she'd share it with Aunt Joyce."

"You don't know Mother. She shares nothing, especially with Aunt Joyce. What did you take, Jennifer?"

"Some old photographs which only have value to me. Did your mother show you the rings?"

He held his hand up to display an elegant gold ring. "She gave one to me and one to Father. I think she intends to sell the rest."

"I'm sorry Grandfather's will was entirely in my favor. I had no idea he'd do that."

Binky shrugged. "It doesn't matter. He was bound to kick us out sooner or later. Couldn't stand the constant arguing."

"What will you do, Binky?"

"I really hadn't thought about it. Guess I'll have to find me a rich widow, spinster, or young lady of the peerage. I don't suppose you'd care to apply for the position."

I started to laugh, but quickly smothered it when I realized that Binky was serious. "I have no plans to marry for some time. I'm flattered by your offer, but I'm waiting for the prince of my dreams."

"And who might that be?"

"Oh, I'll know him when I see him." I certainly wasn't about to tell him I found my prince in Michael Savage, a man I might have to accuse of forgery.

"What keeps you busy today?"

"Business in the morning, then a tour of Botallack."

"Botallack? I thought Grandfather was going to sell that old place."

"I wouldn't know." I finished breakfast and stood. "I'll see you at dinner, Binky."

He nodded and poured himself more coffee.

I went to the library to find those forged checks. I found all the checks in a large envelope of heavy paper. I began to sift through them. The forged ones weren't difficult to find. The bank examiner had put a small red check in the upper right-hand corner. I pulled all those checks with that red mark, and made note of who they had been made out to.

I studied a map of Cornwall and discovered that two of the places were within riding distance of Wyndcliffe. I would be back before lunch. The feed company was in Falmouth. I would leave that for another day.

I changed into my riding habit. Though I wasn't fond of the sidesaddle, I let the groom put it on the mare. I supposed I would have to get used to it. I certainly couldn't ride to these places with the rear of my skirt tucked into my waistband. I didn't care what people thought of it, but I did care about being a proper representative of Grandfather.

The wagoneer's place had a small office to the side of the sheds where the wagons were constructed. I entered the office, causing a burly man to look up at me.

"What can I be doing for you, missy?"

"Are you the owner of this establishment?"

"That I am. John Wilson at your service, missy. And who might you be?"

"Jennifer Hardwicke."

"Old Hardwicke's granddaughter, eh? I'd heard you'd returned. I suppose you've come to tell me that Michael Savage is no longer estate manager."

"What makes you think that?"

"Michael is a hot-tempered and strong-willed rascal. I doubt if a lass of your tender age could deal with him for long."

"Mr. Savage will continue in the same capacity he had under my grandfather. I came here on another matter." I resented his opinion of Michael.

"And what might that be, missy?" he asked, leaning back in his chair and hooking his thumbs in his vest pockets.

"This." I put the check on his desk.

He sat upright, picked up the check, and studied it before placing it back on his desk. "What about it?"

"Do you remember what it was for?"

"Of course. James Hardwicke was a good customer. Paid his bills promptly, he did. I always do him a favor whenever I can. He said he needed cash to pay some itinerant workers. I gave him the cash for the check."

"My grandfather came himself?"

"Oh, no. He hasn't been here in a long time. He sent an emissary."

"Do you know who this person was?"

"One of the grooms from his stable."

"What was the groom's name?"

"I never asked. Hardwicke's check with his name on it was good enough for me."

"What did this groom look like?"

He laced his hands behind his head and again leaned back in his chair. "Scrawny lad with unkempt hair."

"Anything else? His clothes?" I was desperate for some definite information.

"Let me think. That was a number of weeks ago." His eyes remained fixed on his desk. Suddenly he sat up straight, his elbows coming to rest on the desk as he looked up at me. "Come to think of it, missy, I remember thinking at the time that the lad was poorly dressed for a groom at Wyndcliffe. He looked more like a stray urchin than a proper groom. I remember thinking to meself to tell Hardwicke about it the next time I saw him."

"What else do you remember?"

"That's about it, missy. What's this all about? Why the questions?"

"Oh, nothing important. Family matters. Thank you for your time, Mr. Wilson."

"I hope the Hardwickes will still be doing business with me now that the old man is gone."

"Of course, we shall. Goodbye and thank you again."

I departed quickly, before he thought of more questions to ask me. My trip to the toolmaker had the same results. A nondescript lad with a check and requesting cash for it. The toolmaker reenforced Mr. Wilson's description of the lad. Unkempt, not like a groom at all. I had the feeling I would get the same answers from the feed store in Falmouth.

I headed back to Wyndcliffe with a sense of defeat. I had seen all the grooms at Wyndcliffe, and none of them fit the description given to me. My guess was whoever was cashing those checks gave a shilling or two to a stray waif to get the check cashed. The man or

211

woman who had the checks was never seen by the tradesmen. I had such hope for solving the mystery of the forgeries. Now those hopes were dashed.

I arrived at Wyndcliffe in plenty of time to change for lunch, but, seeing I would be riding again to Botallack, I decided against changing.

I was surprised to find only Uncle Cecil at the luncheon table. I knew Binky was away for the day, but where was everyone else? I voiced my question to Uncle Cecil.

"The Lamberts have gone to St. Ives, and took Annabel with them. My wife has a severe headache and remains abed."

"Have you any plans as to where you will go when you leave Wyndcliffe, Uncle Cecil?"

"Are you rushing things, Jennifer?"

"Not at all. I am concerned."

"You needn't be. A man of my caliber is in demand. I'm sure I can find a suitable position."

"Will you go back into banking?"

He winced. The nostrils of his bulbous nose flared. "Perhaps. I'm rather good with figures. I might take a position as an accountant with some major firm. I hear new businesses are being ventured all the time near Liverpool. Of course, if Annabel was to marry here in Cornwall, it would put matters in a different light."

I knew he was thinking, and perhaps hoping, that Annabel would marry Lord Jason Fox. I wondered if Jason was of the same mind.

"I hope Aunt Joyce's headache is gone before dinner."

"If it isn't, it will be your fault, Jennifer."

"What makes you say that?"

"You shouldn't have given all Father Hardwicke's effects to Lydia."

212

"I thought she'd share with Aunt Joyce. I never dreamed she'd keep them all to herself."

"You don't know Lydia. All the Lamberts are a greedy bunch. Those rings are worth a pretty penny, you know."

"If there's such animosity, I'm surprised Annabel went with them to St. Ives."

"What Annabel does is none of your concern, Jennifer. Your interference in our lives has been most distressful to us, to say the least. You left here years and years ago, and now you have taken everything from us. We don't forget or forgive such callousness."

"I had no control over Grandfather's actions. I don't see how you can hold me accountable." I was beginning to become annoyed. Without the Lamberts and Aunt Joyce present, I thought lunch might be a pleasant interlude. I should have known better. These people were as attuned to argument as the tides to the moon.

"Well, we do, especially Lydia. If you hadn't returned, the old man never would have made a new will, and we'd be comfortable for the rest of our lives." His tone was bitter, his eyes reflecting sheer hatred.

I was about to tell him it was time that both families stopped sponging off Wyndcliffe Manor, and pulled their own weight. But I knew he was baiting me. He wanted an argument so he could tell everyone I was a devilish and nasty person. I wasn't about to fall into his trap. I remained silent through the rest of lunch. I finished as quickly as I could, then went to my rooms to wash and comb out my hair. I let it dangle down my back, then secured it at the nape of my neck with a ribbon.

With thoughts of putting the notebook back in the metal box, I took it off my nightstand. As I did, that piece of paper fell out again. I picked it up and went

213

down to the library to await Michael. After I had locked the notebook away, Michael arrived.

The sight of him caused me to smile. "Have you settled into your cottage?"

"Yes."

"Who cooks your meals?"

"Breakfast and lunch I manage on my own. Cook usually sends supper down for me. Shall we go? They're saddling the horses now."

"In a minute, Michael. I would like to know what these numbers mean." I handed him the piece of paper.

He studied the paper for a moment. "I believe they are the combination to your grandfather's safe."

"I didn't know he had a safe. Where is it?"

"I don't know. Perhaps Jerome does."

I rang for Jerome. When he appeared, I asked, "Do you know where Grandfather's safe is, Jerome?"

"Yes, Miss Jennifer." Jerome went to a picture of a landscape on the wall. He swung it open as though it were a door. "There's a small latch on the side, Miss. Press it and the picture is released. I'm afraid only Mr. Hardwicke had the combination to it, miss."

"That's all right, Jerome. Thank you." Hearing the dismissal in my voice, he left. "Michael could you open it for me? I don't know a thing about safes."

"Are you sure you want me to? I might remember the combination and use it at a later date."

"I trust you, Michael."

A peculiar glimmer came into his eyes. For a second I thought he was going to embrace me. His eyes quickly clouded over, and the moment was lost.

He went to the safe and opened it. As the safe was too high for me, Michael emptied it and placed everything on the desk. Papers and a large velvet box. I opened the box first. Fabulous jewels greeted my eyes. Pearls, diamonds, emeralds, and rubies, all in various settings. Rings, earrings, necklaces, bracelets, and brooches. I looked at Michael quizzically.

"I believe they were your mother's and grandmother's," he told me.

"But Jerome brought me my mothers jewel box."

"Those were probably your mother's own pieces. I believe these belonged to your grandmother, and your mother inherited them when your grandmother died," he offered in explanation.

"Why weren't they with my mother's jewels then?"

"I have a suspicion your grandfather wanted to keep them from the clutches of your aunts. They knew about your mother's jewels and wouldn't touch them—at least not while your grandfather was alive. I don't believe they know about these. I suggest you keep it that way, or you're liable to have a war on your hands."

"I already have one. Aunt Lydia didn't share Grandfather's personal effects with Aunt Joyce." A crooked smile flickered across his face, and my heart beat a little faster. He had a powerful effect on me. I nodded and closed the velvet box. "What are these papers, Michael?"

He shuffled through them slowly. A sardonic smile pulled at his lips as he looked at a particular sheet. He handed it to me.

"What is it?"

"The original transfer of the estate and mines from Savage to Hardwicke. Did you know Wyndcliffe originally belonged to my family?"

"Yes. Grandfather told me."

"Doesn't that make you distrustful of me? I might be contemplating any means to get it back."

"Grandfather said you might."

"And you're keeping me on?"

"Why not? You knew who I was before bringing me to Wyndcliffe. You never would have brought me here if you had some devious plot."

"Perhaps I thought I could wrest it from a chit of a girl more easily than I could from your grandfather." His chin had a hard set to it. His eyes bore into mine with a rare intensity.

"I don't think you capable of anything dishonest, Michael." I gave the sheet back to him.

"I could tear this up."

"I don't think you will. What are the other papers?"

He sighed heavily, then put the paper down. "Deeds, stocks, and quite a few loan chits."

"From who?"

"Mostly from Binky. A few from Nigel Lambert."

"I'm surprised Grandfather lent either of them any money."

"He probably did it to stop their whining. Although, Binky had a way of charming your grandfather. If he tolerated any of them, it was Binky. We'd better go."

"Would you put all this back in the safe for me?"

He did so, locked the safe, then handed the piece of paper back to me. "You'd better keep that number in a safe place."

"Any suggestions?"

"Perhaps in one of your favorite books."

"I'll keep it in mind." I tossed the paper into a desk drawer.

I was stunned by the bleak scene before me. Wind from the sea groaned through the gaps that were once windows. Green and yellow lichen marched upward and over the stones of roofless buildings. A lone, narrowly rounded chimney stood atilt, as though its weary stones wanted to return to the earth. Once precisely constructed stone walls had begun to crumble. With the sun passing its zenith, the ghostly, empty buildings cast eerie shadows of a time long past.

I didn't notice Michael had dismounted until he was alongside my horse, his arms outstretched to help me down. The minute my feet touched the ground, he released me and stepped back. Seeing he lacked interest in me, my attention returned to the decaying buildings of the Botallack mine.

"Why did Grandfather want me to see this mine? There's nothing here."

"He felt that it is part of the history of the mining in Cornwall. He said viewing it on occasion kept him sensible. 'What no longer produces, or is too costly to keep producing, must be abandoned in favor of new ventures' he used to say. He'd often come here just to meditate. I can only assume that is why he wanted you to see it. Perhaps he thought you, too, might find solace here, if you needed it. Care to walk around?"

"I'd like that."

"Be careful of the stones," Michael warned.

Gorse and briars tugged at the hems of my skirts. The wind whipped my hair into tangles of coppery strands. I lifted my skirts and quickened my pace to keep up with Michael. The terrain was rough and strewn with stray rocks and stones. He seemed to be heading toward one particular dilapidated building. I caught up with him just as he was about to enter. As we stepped in, a flock of raucous rooks flew up at us. With a startled gasp, I clutched Michael's arm. He put his hand over mine and gave me a reassuring smile.

"They're only birds," he said.

I drew my hand away. "They frightened me for a minute. Why have you come here?"

217

"See that slab? Underneath it is an old shaft that reaches out under the sea. Years ago, when men worked in that shaft, they could hear the force of the sea rolling stones over the ocean's floor."

"That must have been pleasant."

"Cornish men have mining in their blood. They've carried on tin mining since the times of the Phoenicians, centuries before the birth of Christ. Ships from the Mediterranean sailed to Cornwall for tin for centuries. I think there is a book in your library on the history of Cornish tin mining."

"I shall make a point of reading it."

We wandered about the ruins. I could understand why Grandfather found the place suitable for thinking. The solitude among the old stones had a soothing affect on one's soul.

Michael was quiet, as though his thoughts had strayed elsewhere. The expression on his face was austere, almost forbidding. Suddenly his expression changed, as though he had come to a decision.

"Would you care to walk to the promontory? One can see the vast expanse of the Atlantic Ocean from there," he suggested.

"What about the horses?"

"We can leave them. It isn't that far."

I agreed. The day was delightful and the air crisp. A good day for a bit of a walk. Even the wind felt fresh on my face. Besides, Michael was with me.

The sound of the sea assailing the rocks increased, and became a dull roar in my ears as we came closer to the edge of the cliff. Once there I marveled at the endless sea and its assault on the jagged rocks below. The roar now thundered in my ears. I was fascinated.

Suddenly the spray took on a gauzy form. I swallowed hard as I recognized the face of my

218

grandfather softly molded by the watery mist. His lips moved and I heard the hoarsely whispered words, "Beware . . . beware . . . beware." The voice seemed to be saying something else, but a sweeping dizziness came over me. The dizziness fled when I felt strong hands tighten on my shoulders.

Oh, dear God, I thought. Michael was behind me. He was going to push me off the cliff.

Seventeen

"Hey there! What's going on?" came a voice and the thudding of horse's hooves.

Michael's hands left my shoulders and both of us spun around. I dashed away from the edge of the cliff, my heart beating wildly. Lord Jason Fox dismounted and came toward us holding the reins in his hand, his horse meekly following.

"I say there, Michael, what were you up to?" Jason asked, a frown on his handsome face.

"Jennifer was swaying. I thought she was going to swoon. I tried to steady her, if you must know."

Jason arched his eyebrows at Michael, then turned to me. "Are you all right, Jennifer?"

"Yes. As Michael said, I became dizzy for a moment."

"What brings you here, Jason?" Michael asked none too pleasantly.

"I was looking for Jennifer. Jerome told me she went with you to Botallack. Being a nice day, I thought I'd ride out and join you."

"What did you want to see me about, Jason?"

"I thought I'd have a little soiree to welcome you to Cornwall," Jason said.

"I don't think a soiree is suitable so soon after Grandfather's death."

"He'd want you to enjoy yourself, Jennifer," Jason claimed.

"I'm still in mourning, Jason. I appreciate the gesture. Perhaps another time."

"How about All Hallow's Eve?"

"We'll see."

Jason walked with us back to our horses. Once mounted we leisurely started for Wyndcliffe together. It wasn't long before a scowling Michael claimed he had pressing business elsewhere. With a kick to the flank of his horse, he galloped off and soon disappeared on the horizon.

"Michael can be a surly fellow. Never did care for the chap. You really should replace him, Jennifer."

"Why? He does an admirable job running everything for me. Grandfather thought him indispensable."

"I don't trust him. Why did he bring you to that desolate mine?"

"He said it was my grandfather's favorite place for meditating."

"And you believed him?"

"Could we talk about something else, Jason?" I didn't want to hear anymore about Michael, especially anything bad. I wanted to believe Michael's explanation for the incident on the promontory. Of course, he was trying to protect me, not push me off. But what would have happened if Jason hadn't come along?

On the way back to Wyndcliffe, Jason regaled me with stories of Paris and some of his dealings with horses. I told him about the Gypsy horse fairs and how they fooled unsuspecting farmers.

"You must have learned a lot living with the Gypsies. Can you tell fortunes from cards or the palm of one's hand?"

"No. I was never interested in it. I liked the Gypsy dancing."

"Can you dance like a Gypsy?"

I nodded. "In fact, I used to be pretty good at it." We started up the driveway to Wyndcliffe. "Would you care to stay for dinner, Jason?"

"I thought you'd never ask."

While I went upstairs to wash and change, Jason said he would be in the rear parlor. He was thumbing through an issue of *Punch* when I came down. He stood and came to me when I entered the parlor.

"You look positively lovely, Jennifer." He took my hands in his and, at arm's length, scanned me up and down. "Let's go out on the terrace and watch the sun go down."

"The terrace faces south. We can't see the sun go down from there." I smiled. Jason was a true charmer.

"Let's go out anyway. We don't have many days left of this balmy weather." I relented and he led me onto the terrace. He rested his forearms on the balustrade. "Wyndcliffe is a beautiful estate, Jennifer. How does it feel to be mistress of it?"

"I really don't know. I don't feel any different than I did when I first came here."

Jason stared out over the rear gradens and remained silent for a long spell. As though reaching some conclusion, he stood erect, faced me, and put his hands on my bare shoulders.

"Jennifer, I want you to know that if your grandfather were alive, I would ask his permission to court you. Since he is no longer with us, I ask your permission."

I was stunned. I thought he was seeking the hand of either Annabel or Amanda! Besides, I didn't feel as though I really knew him. I didn't know what to say. Finally I managed to speak.

"I'm flattered, Jason. But I'm not interested in marriage now."

"I shall court you anyway, Jennifer. No matter how long it takes, I will win you over in the end."

"When did you get here, Jason?" came Amanda's voice from the open French doors.

We turned to see a disgruntled Amanda with Annabel peering over her shoulder. The two of them came out on the terrace. From the look on their faces, I knew they had heard Jason's declaration to court me. I also knew they would tell their mothers, and I'd be in for a lecture from both of them.

"Ladies." Jason bowed and gave each of them a devastating smile. "We returned over an hour ago."

"We?" Annabel squeaked, then pursed her lips.

"Jennifer and I."

"Where have you been?" Amanda's expression was as grim as her mother's.

"Botallack. Looking over the old mine there," Jason answered, giving them the impression he had spent the entire afternoon with me.

"Why ever would you go there?" Amanda asked.

"Michael and Grandfather wanted me to see the place," I said.

"What does Michael have to do with it?" Annabel looked confused.

"Michael took me there. Jason joined us later." I hoped that reply would correct any earlier impression they might have had.

Annabel gave a toss of her head, her golden curls springing up and down. She sashayed over to Jason and snaked her hand through his arm.

"When are you going to have us at Foxhill Grange, Jason?" Annabel fluttered her eyelashes at him.

"You're welcome anytime—all of you." He led her back into the rear parlor, Amanda swiftly following. I took my time, arriving in the parlor as Jerome announced dinner.

Aunt Joyce joined us for dinner, where she trembled like a volcano about to erupt as she glared at Aunt Lydia. Uncle Cecil and Uncle Nigel wore expressions of annoyed disdain, while Annabel and Amanda vied for Jason's attentions.

"Aunt Lydia," I began causing everyone to look at me expectantly, "didn't Binky come back with you?"

"No. He had ridden his horse to St. Ives. He wasn't sure when he'd be back. Why do you ask, Jennifer?"

"Just curious."

When asked, Jason agreed to spend the night. After dinner, we trooped to the music room where Amanda consented to play the piano. She was on her third piece when Binky burst into the room.

"Have you heard? There's been another murder," he exclaimed breathlessly.

Shock registered on everyone's face. Aunt Joyce snapped her fan open and flapped it vigorously.

"Who?" I asked, almost fearful of the answer. prayed it wasn't Michael.

"Nobody we know. Some lad about twelve. No one seems to know who he is. From none of the families around here. Strange thing though. He had his throat slit open, just like Grandfather."

"Where did they find him?" Uncle Nigel asked.

"In a ditch outside the village," Binky said.

"How did you find out about it?" I asked.

"Ran into Dr. Marsh. He was returning home after viewing the body."

"How horrible!" Aunt Lydia's countenance turned to her usual austere expression.

"Horrible? It's positively scandalous," Uncle Nigel said. "What is the constable going to do about it?"

Binky shrugged. "I didn't see the constable."

"Oh, dear me," Aunt Joyce gasped, her fan fluttering faster. "We'll all be murdered in our beds with this fiend mucking about."

"There, there, Joyce. I'm sure the constable will get to the bottom of it soon," Uncle Cecil soothed.

"When did this happen, Binky?" I asked.

"Shortly before noon. I don't think Constable Morgan will get any further with *this* murder than he did with Grandfather's."

Conversation continued to revolve around the two murders. When I went to bed, I had an intuitive feeling that the murdered lad was the same one who had passed the forged checks. In the morning I would ride into Penzance and ask the constable to let the wagoneer and toolmaker view the lad's body.

I was already dressed in my riding habit, when I came into the foyer from the dining room.

"Where are you off to so early, Jennifer?" Jason asked.

"To Penzance."

"Whatever for?"

"To see the constable and visit a dressmaker."

"Do you have information about the murder of the lad?"

"No." It was a small fib. But as a Gypsy, I learned to be cautious about divulging my private thoughts.

"Then why are you going?"

"To see if he has any clues regarding my grandfather's murder. Actually, the dressmaker is my primary objective. I must get some clothes altered and order some new ones."

"I'll go with you."

"You needn't bother, Jason."

"I insist. I don't like the thought of you riding alone

225

with a murderer on the loose."

"What about your breakfast?" I didn't want him coming with me, but I didn't dare protest too much, lest he think I had an ulterior motive, which I did. I didn't want anyone to know what I was about to suggest to the constable.

"I can get some when we reach Penzance." When I headed for the door, he asked, "Where are your frocks for the dressmaker?"

As I hadn't really thought about going to a dressmaker, I had no frocks with me. I smiled at him while my mind went to work. "I couldn't possibly carry them on the seat of a horse. I only intend for her to take my measurements. I'll send the frocks with a maid."

He smiled. My answer seemed to satisfy him. He extended a crooked arm. "Shall we go?"

On the ride to Penzance, I tried to think of a way to rid myself of Jason's company while I went to see the constable. I needn't have bothered. When we reached the bustling seaport, Jason left me to have his breakfast at a tea shop.

Though not as large as Falmouth, Penzance was a busy port and had a population of almost nine thousand. Wyndcliffe Manor was located south of St. Just, making Penzance the nearest sizable town. Eight miles north of Penzance was the more populated fishing town of St. Ives. But a lot of our tin was shipped from Penzance, so I thought it best I should come to know it better.

I had to pass the handsome edifice of St. Paul's before arriving at police headquarters. I waited several minutes before I was shown into the constable's cramped and tiny office. He rose and remained standing, until I was seated.

"What can I do for you, Miss Hardwicke?" Constable Morgan puffed on the pipe dangling from the side of his mouth.

"First of all, do you have any news regarding the murder of my grandfather?"

"I'm afraid not. If only we had the weapon, it might be a start. Now this similar business with a stray lad." He shook his head solemnly.

"That's what I really came to see you about." I went on to relate the tale of the forged checks, and my conversation with the wagoneer and toolmaker. "Perhaps they might be able to identify the lad."

"Are they the ones here in town?"

"No. They're located on the road between St. Just and Botallack."

"You can be sure I will contact them, Miss Hardwicke. Anything else?"

"Not that I can think of at the moment. You will let me know, won't you, Constable Morgan?" I stood, causing him to rise from his seat.

"Of course, Miss Hardwicke. Good day."

"Good day, Constable." I walked to the door and was about to turn the knob, when I turned around. "Could you tell me where I might find a good dressmaker?"

I listened to his instructions, then went on my way. His directions were precise and I was soon at the dressmaker's. I told her about the frocks and gowns that needed altering. As she took my measurements, I mentioned the possibility of some new apparel. Before I left, she handed me several magazines containing the latest in women's fashions.

Looking splendid in a dark green frock coat and brocaded silk vest, Lord Jason Fox was waiting outside the dressmaker's shop.

"What do women do in a dress shop that takes them so long?" he asked good-naturedly.

"Dawdle."

He smiled broadly. "Want to stay in town and have lunch?"

"I'd rather go home."

"Where is your horse?"

"I left the mare at the stable of the Three Tuns Hotel. And yours?"

"At the Queens. We could stop at Foxhill on the way to Wyndcliffe," Jason suggested, as we walked to our respective stables.

"When I'm properly chaperoned. I've caused enough gossip by coming to Wyndcliffe as a Gypsy. People will think I'm a through and through wanton, if I go to Foxhill without at least one of my aunts being present."

"Don't be so prudish, Jennifer. What do you care about silly gossip? Besides, if the gossip is nasty enough, you might have to consent to be my bride."

"Really, Jason." After living with the Gypsies, I didn't think I could still blush. "If you persist in talking about courting and marriage, I shan't see you again."

"Well, we can't have that, can we now? I shan't mention the subject again. But I shall become your constant companion, until you can't resist me." His smile was confident.

I wanted to laugh out loud, but only managed a soft giggle. Though Jason was pleasant and amusing company, the thought of him being my constant companion didn't appeal to me.

We parted to retrieve our horses, agreeing to meet at the edge of town.

I was approaching the Three Tuns Hotel, when my arm was grabbed from behind by a strong hand. Though apprehensive, I stopped and turned around.

"What are you doing here?" came Michael's brusque voice.

"I came to see the dressmaker."

"How did you get here?"

"By horse."

"Alone?" He frowned. "There are brigands who would like nothing better than to accost a woman alone. And now there is a killer at large. Don't you have any sense, Jennifer?"

I glared at him. I didn't like his presumptive manner. "I didn't come alone. Jason is with me." His hand tightened on my arm. "You're hurting me, Michael."

His hand dropped to his side. "That popinjay couldn't defend himself. How can you expect him to protect you?"

"Why don't you like Jason? He's a fine man," I declared.

"Jason Fox is a fraud as a man. He's never done a day's work in his life. If he didn't have money and a title, he'd be a leech or a mendicant on the streets."

"Why, Mr. Savage, I do believe you are jealous of Lord Fox," I teased.

"I have no reason to be jealous of him."

"But you are, aren't you, Michael?"

"You're talking nonsense, Jennifer. What are you doing in Penzance with him?"

"He came to keep me company."

"I should think you could find someone better."

"I see nothing wrong with Jason. He's a delightful companion. Besides, he fancies himself my suitor." I found I liked teasing Michael. He was endearing when he scowled.

Michael's dark eyes became hooded, and his dark eyebrows arched. "Does he now? And what do you say about that?"

"I haven't made up my mind." His scowling no longer enticed me. A perverse mood overcame me as Michael's manner began to prod my indignation.

"You're a foolish young woman, Jennifer. Perhaps you and Jason deserve each other."

"You have no right to talk to me like that, Michael. It's my life, and I'll do as I please with it."

"I suspect we have nothing more to say to each other, Jennifer." He spun around and stalked away.

Go. I hope I never see you again, I thought. As I watched his tall frame and straight shoulders recede, tears began to well in my eyes.

Eighteen

The inclement weather kept me inside for over a week. I put the time to good use by studying the maps, ledgers, and checkbook, until I had a thorough knowledge of them. I calculated over a thousand pounds had been pilfered from Grandfather's checking account. I strongly suspected Uncle Cecil. Aunt Joyce and Annabel never seemed to want for anything. New frocks, gowns, bonnets, boots, and trinkets appeared on their persons with increasing frequency.

Despite the weather, Lord Fox came to Wyndcliffe several times, making his desire to see me quite apparent. More often than not, I left him to the tender mercies of Amanda and Annabel, while I sequestered myself in the library, much to his annoyance.

For the most part, I avoided the Lamberts and Melvilles, which seemed to suit them. In Binky's case, I made an exception. He was an ardent gossip and kept me informed about events in the household, village, and nearby towns.

I was scanning some maps for the best road to the tin mines at Cambourne, when a knock sounded at the library door.

"Come in," I called.

Binky sauntered in saying, "This weather is bloody beastly. If this rain doesn't let up soon, I'll go dotty. What are you scrutinizing so carefully, Jennifer?" He came over to the desk and peered at the map.

"I'm trying to decide what would be the best route to Cambourne. Any suggestions, Binky?"

"Either the St. Ives road or through Penzance. It doesn't make much difference. I think one is just as long as the other." He went to the sideboard, fixed himself a whiskey, then sprawled in a leather armchair. "I'm so bored, Jennifer. When are you going to Cambourne?"

"The next nice day. The ride is too long to go in the rain."

"Then take the road to St. Ives, and I'll go with you that far."

"Why not all the way to Cambourne?"

"The mines are tedious and bore me. St. Ives offers more divertissements." He paused to sip his drink. "I suppose you know Jason is quite displeased with you."

"Oh, why?" Though I kept an innocent expression on my face, I smiled inwardly.

"Leaving him to entertain my sister and Annabel. I do believe he is trying to court you, Jennifer. You might be wise to accept his ardent attentions. He *is* quite a catch, you know."

"Unfortunately, I'm not interested."

"Why not? Jason is handsome, wealthy, and titled. Any woman would leap at the chance to marry him. I know my sister or Annabel would. Is there someone else you favor?"

"That is none of your business, Binky Lambert."

"Aha! Who is it? You can tell me, Jennifer. I won't breathe a word to anyone."

I laughed. "Telling you anything would be like announcing it to all of Cornwall."

"Really, Jennifer. You cut me to the very quick. I daresay it is one of those Gypsy men that caught your fancy. I hear they are rakishly handsome, and women find them most appealing. Am I right?"

I answered him with an enigmatic smile. Better he thought I was enamored of a distant, unknown Gypsy, than have him know it was Michael Savage. After my last encounter with Michael, I'd be more than embarrassed if Michael knew I was in love with *him*.

"Well, that solves a problem." Binky grinned impishly, and I knew he could hardly wait to tell Jason.

A few days later the weather turned into a splendid fall day, not a cloud in the sky. I rose early and was eating breakfast when Binky came into the dining room.

"I had a suspicion you would be up and off early. I'll scamper through breakfast, then we can leave for St. Ives. Aunt Joyce and Bella mentioned they'll be going to St. Ives also. I hope we can leave before they come down. I don't relish their company."

"They'll probably take the carriage and we'll be on horseback, so we won't be in their company anyway."

"Knowing them, they'd want us to keep pace with them. I can't stand Aunt Joyce's whining." He sat down at the table, a full plate before him.

"Why are they going to St. Ives?"

"New gowns or some such thing. I heard Jason is giving a small ball on All Hallow's Eve. Didn't you hear?"

"Come to think of it, he did mention it some time ago. Where does Uncle Cecil get his money from?"

Binky shrugged, then crammed a rasher of bacon into his mouth. "Aunt Joyce receives the same amount from an annuity as my mother. I know my mother and sister can't afford such extravagances. Perhaps Uncle Cecil is lucky at wagering."

Or embezzled from Grandfather's checkbook, I thought. But no forgeries had been executed since I took over the checkbook, and he still seems very comfortable. Perhaps Binky is right. Uncle Cecil is lucky at wagering.

We left and headed for St. Ives at a good canter. I had never been to St. Ives and found it a quaint fishing village, far more lively than Penzance. Binky treated me to a light tea of scones and clotted cream. Leaving the tea shop, he pointed me in the direction of Cambourne, and I was off.

At the small village of Hoyle, I inquired at the butcher's if I was on the correct road to Cambourne. He told me to bear right as the road forks when leaving Hoyle. The road was fairly busy with merchant wagons, carriages, and coaches with passengers. I felt quite safe. Besides, I believed brigands would keep to the lonelier roads.

I secured directions to the mines from a lad in the streets of Cambourne. Excitement filled me, as silhouettes of buildings and mining equipment stood gaunt against the blue sky. I went directly to the office and introduced myself to the manager, Bob Thomas. He was most hospitable, and insisted I have tea before he showed me around the mine.

"We have been anticipating your visit with pleasure, Miss Hardwicke," Bob Thomas said. "Mr. Savage said you were anxious to see this mine."

"Did he say anything else?"

"Only to show you every courtesy."

"How long have you managed this mine, Mr. Thomas?"

"Ten years." He went on to tell me about the tradition of mining in his family, and how he had started out digging in the mines like his father and grandfather before him. The conversation was pleasant and informative. Our tea finished, we went outside where he gave me a tour and explanation of the mine's works.

Behemoth machines groaned and rattled like hungry monsters, as the great wheels of hauling machinery brought up the ore and dumped it into conveyer belts, endlessly moving toward great grinding machines. The resultant brown sludge was poured into huge vats. The noise was deafening, and the ground trembled from the exertions of the gigantic machinery.

"The ore at this mine is rich in tin, Miss Hardwicke," he informed me, his voice bellowing over the din of an active mine.

"Let's hope it remains that way," I commented, as my eyes gazed at the huge wheel near one of the shafts.

To my astonishment, a half-naked Michael emerged from the shaft. His deep chest was matted with darkly burnished hair. His arms were heavily sinewed, his skin glistening with sweat in the bright sun. His black breeches and boots were spattered with a muddy substance. He spoke to one of the men, then went to a table where a basin and ewer rested. He poured water into the basin and splashed his naked torso with water. A young lad handed him a towel. After he dried himself, he pulled a black sweater over his head. I couldn't keep the admiration from sparkling in my eyes. The sight of him half-dressed stirred warm physical sensations in me. I swallowed hard when he spied us. He tugged his sweater down and, after running a splayed hand through his hair, came toward us.

His physical appearance and manly appeal sent my blood singing in my ears. The closer he came, the more knots formed in my stomach. I hoped he had forgotten our quarrel in Penzance, but when his eyes locked with mine, I could see he still retained a smoldering rage where I was concerned.

"What do you think, Mr. Savage?" Bob Thomas asked.

"A number of veins are extremely rich in tin. I expect we should do well."

"Will there be an extra packet of wages for the men?" Bob Thomas asked.

"That will be up to Miss Hardwicke."

Bob Thomas looked at me.

"If it's standard practice to give the men a bit of extra pay when a rich vein is uncovered, then I see no reason to discontinue the practice," I said. "Is it possible for me to go down?"

"I wouldn't advise it, Miss Hardwicke. The temperatures down there get to be over a hundred degrees. Boiling hot water is dripping all over those deep shafts," Bob Thomas warned me.

"I see. Is there anything more for me to see?"

"Well, there are the maps and descriptions—depth and extent—in my office."

"Shall we have a look at them?"

"By all means, Miss Hardwicke." Bob Thomas started to stroll toward his office.

I began to follow him, when Michael put a restraining hand on my arm. I managed to put a haughty, yet inquisitive, expression on my face. Bob Thomas stopped and turned around, looking for me.

"We'll catch up with you later, Bob," Michael called as I pulled my arm away, then he looked down at me sternly. "Where is your ardent admirer?"

"If you mean Jason, I have no idea where he is."

"Didn't he accompany you here?" He frowned, his dark eyebrows clashing together over the bridge of his sharply chiseled nose.

"No. Jason is not my keeper. I told you. I go when and where I please."

"Haven't I warned you about traveling alone?"

"I wasn't entirely alone."

"Oh?"

"Binky came with me as far as St. Ives."

"Why didn't you talk to me? I told you I would bring you to Cambourne."

"I'm no more accountable to you, Michael, than I am to Jason. I'm certainly not going to hunt you down everytime I want to go somewhere."

"You may not feel accountable to me, but I feel accountable to your grandfather. I promised him I'd watch after you, and I intend to keep that promise."

"My grandfather is dead, which I believe relieves you of that promise. I don't want to be an imposition on your freedom. Besides, I've never had a chaperone, and certainly don't need one at this stage of my life. You are free to go your own way, Michael."

"Are you trying to tell me you no longer require my services?" His chin lifted in a prideful manner.

"Don't be ridiculous, Michael. I'm only saying you needn't be attendant on me personally. I don't need someone hovering over me every minute," I declared.

"You don't seem to mind Lord Fox hovering over you. He is a rather constant visitor to Wyndcliffe. But then, I'm not a peer. Just a ridiculous fellow to you, Jennifer."

"Why do you twist everything I say, Michael?"

"You speak quite clearly, Jennifer. I have no need to twist your words."

"You're impossible, Michael. I'm going to the office."

"Just a minute." Once again his hand closed about my arm. "I'm riding back to Wyndcliffe with you, whether you like it or not."

237

"Suit yourself." I wrenched my arm free and stalked toward the office, Michael trailing behind me. Why did we quarrel so? Whenever we were within two feet of each other, our conversation eventually became argumentative. Since Grandfather died, Michael seemed to resent me. Why? The question whirled in my head like a tune whose name I'd forgotten.

Patience was another name for Bob Thomas. He explained the various maps while Michael stood aside with a brooding expression. Mr. Thomas answered my questions with detailed explanations.

"What happens to that brown sludge in the vats outside?" I asked.

"We cook it until it releases its sulfur and arsenic content, creating about an eighty-five percent stannic oxide, or tin. Then we put in in a blast furnace for further purification."

"I see. Well, I'll detain you no further, Mr. Thomas. I'm sure you have more important work to do. Thank you for showing me around. I appreciate it."

"Anytime, Miss Hardwicke. Good day to you."

I went outside to my horse and could feel Michael directly behind me. We rode in an uneasy silence toward St. Ives.

"I don't know about you, but I'm famished. I didn't have any lunch," I said, as we rode into St. Ives. "Can you recommend a good tea shop?"

"I'll take you to one," he said grumpily.

The shop was a pleasant one, almost cozy. I settled on a ham sandwich and tea. A plate of pickled cucumbers and beets accompanied our orders.

I decided to make a stab at friendly conversation. "Do you go down into the mines often, Michael?"

"Whenever I'm at the mines."

"Why?"

"I like to know the conditions the men have to work

under. It makes them think management cares. By the way, I'm glad you went along with the extra money in the pay packets. Not only is it a tradition that your family started, but the men appreciate it, especially when the Christmas holidays are at hand."

"Don't they get a bit extra on Boxing Day?"

"No. They get a three-day holiday. They seem to prefer that."

"With or without pay?"

"Without."

"Can the mines afford to pay for two of those days?"

"You've seen the books. You be the judge, Jennifer."

"I'll look into it."

Though Michael ignored the pastries, I couldn't resist taking a raspberry tart when the three-tiered tray came around. I knew he was watching me, but when I lifted my gaze to meet his, he quickly looked away. Suddenly, his bland expression became hard and set, his eyes exuding a seething inkiness.

"I should have known you wanted to stop in St. Ives for something other than food."

"What are you talking about, Michael?"

"Well, well. What a pleasant surprise! Fancy meeting you here, Jennifer."

I looked up slowly. I really didn't have to see him to know it was Lord Fox. He had a distinctive voice with a slight rasp to it.

"What brings you to St. Ives, Jason?" I asked.

"I accompanied Annabel and her mother. They told me you had left earlier with Binky." He neither looked at nor acknowledged Michael's presence. "What have you been doing all morning in St. Ives?"

"I wasn't in St. Ives. I went to Cambourne to visit the mines," I explained, wishing he'd go away. My conversation with Michael was becoming pleasant for a change.

"How naughty of you, Jennifer. You should have let me know. I would have come with you, and we could have had a picnic lunch," Jason said, giving me his beautific smile. "Where are you going now?"

"Home."

"Oh, do stay. The carriage holds four people," Jason urged.

"I came on horseback."

"Savage here can take your horse back. Your presence would make the trip back more enjoyable. Besides, we could spend the afternoon browsing through the shops. I know a particularly fine antique shop, which I'm sure would interest you, Jennifer."

"Not today, Jason. I'm tired and want to get home." I gulped down the remainder of my tea and stood. "If you'll excuse us, Jason. We were just about to leave."

"Alas. I promised Mrs. Melville and Bella I would meet them here for tea. Perhaps I will see you when we get back to Wyndcliffe."

"Perhaps. Goodbye, Jason."

I quickly walked from the tea shop with Michael at my heels.

"What was that all about?" Michael asked, after we mounted our horses.

"What do you mean?"

"I thought you would have jumped at the chance to spend the afternoon with his lordship."

"You haven't been listening to me, have you, Michael? I am not enamored of Jason Fox, and never will be. Are you so dull you can't understand that?"

"First I was ridiculous, now I'm dull. I'm sorry you don't have a higher opinion of me, Jennifer."

"Oh, Michael," was all I could think of to say. I had the feeling if I said anything further, the result would be another bitter argument. Silence dominated the ride

240

back to Wyndcliffe. As we reined the horses to a halt before the entrance, I found myself reluctant to part from Michael, regardless of disputes.

"Bob Thomas gave me the monthly sales and expense ledger for the Cambourne mine. Would you care to go over it with me, Michael?"

"If you'd like."

"Only if I'm not imposing," I said tartly.

"Touchy, aren't you?"

"Well, you act as though you're doing me a favor."

"Bob usually gives the ledger to me. I would bring it to your grandfather, and we'd go over them together. It's become a habit with me. I didn't know if you wanted to continue the custom."

Somewhat mollified, I apologized. "I'm sorry. Under the circumstances, I think it best we continue the custom."

A groom took our horses and we went into the house. In the library we began the study of the ledger. I was glad Michael was there, as Bob's handwriting was difficult to decipher, and I had no idea what many of the abbreviations stood for.

"Oh, dear. Look at the time," I declared after a brief glance at the clock. "I have to change for dinner. We can finish this later."

A wry grin spread across his face. "Your grandfather usually asked me to stay to dinner, and we would finish up after dinner."

I smiled. Whether it was from happiness or embarrassment, I didn't know. "I took it for granted you would be here for dinner. I'd forgotten you've moved into the cottage. I do hope you'll stay and take dinner with us, Michael?"

"I'd be delighted. I could do with a bit of cleaning up. Is my old room still available?"

"As far as I know. Perhaps you should check with Jerome."

"I will."

I was surprised to see Lord Fox at the dinner table. Evidently Aunt Joyce and Annabel had asked him to stay. I should have resented their presumption in asking guests without my permission, but, for once, everyone seemed in a festive mood, so I let it pass.

"How was your shopping trip to St. Ives, Joyce my dear," Uncle Cecil asked, his bulbous nose more red than usual. I suspected he had a few brandies before dinner.

"Delightful. Just delightful. Don't you agree, Annabel?"

"Oh, yes, Mother. We bought two new gowns each and new bonnets. Jason was a dear, helping us with the parcels. He also took us to tea. Wait until you see my new gown for the All Hallow's Eve ball at Jason's. Are you going to get a new gown for the occasion, Amanda?"

"I haven't decided." Amanda's scowl became more prominent.

"You'd better hurry and decide. There isn't much time left," Annabel warned.

"I say, Savage, have you moved back into the house?" Jason asked, his hair shiny and slick with French pomade.

"No. I've been helping Jennifer with the ledger from the Cambourne mine. We haven't finished, so she invited me to stay and dine, so we could continue later tonight."

The animosity between Jason and Michael was apparent, but they kept it on a polite level. I noticed Binky eyeing Aunt Joyce and Annabel. His gazed then

242

turned to Uncle Cecil, and he stared at him with a peculiar glint in his eyes. Uncle Nigel also stared at his brother-in-law, but hatred born of jealousy was easily discerned in *his* eyes. Aunt Lydia was as solemn as ever, a good match to her brooding daughter. I sensed something was afoot between the Lamberts and the Melvilles. I was glad when dinner was over, and Michael and I retired to the library in the West Wing. I wanted no part of a quarrel between my relatives.

Two hours passed before we finished with the ledger.

"I must leave," Michael said.

"I appreciate your help. I never would have understood it on my own. As way of compensation, let me offer you a nightcap."

"Thank you." He helped himself to a brandy, then headed for one of the chairs flanking the fireplace. I left the desk to join him. I was halfway there when I twisted my ankle and almost fell. He immediately put his drink down and came to assist me. His hands closed about my shoulders to steady me. "Are you all right, Jennifer?"

The warmth of his hands on my bare shoulders made me all limp inside, and caused an idiotic smile to curl my lips. "I'm fine."

For a minute I thought he was going to give me the kiss I so desperately yearned for, but my peripheral vision caught a movement at the window. I turned to look. An indistinguishable face and figure was looking in at us. I gasped and rushed to the window, leaving a startled Michael in the middle of the room.

"What is it, Jennifer?" he asked, rushing up behind me.

"Someone was at the window watching us! A sinister creature. I wonder if Aunt Joyce was right about us all being murdered in our beds."

243

Nineteen

"Don't talk like that, Jennifer. Don't even think it. Let me have a look."

I moved to the side and said, "Whatever it was, it's gone now."

He peered into the darkness, looking right then left. "It's too dark to see anything now." He turned to me. "Did you see who it was?"

"No. I was too faraway. By the time I got to the window, the creature was gone. Do you think it might be the murderer, Michael?"

"Of course not. You're perfectly safe at Wyndcliffe."

"Wyndcliffe didn't protect Grandfather."

He gazed deep into my troubled eyes. "Would you like me to stay the night, Jennifer?"

"Would you? Now that Grandfather is gone, I'm alone in the West Wing. Knowing you're there would be a comfort to me."

"Then I'll stay. But I would like to have that nightcap first."

"Of course." We sat in the chairs by the fireplace. Michael talked to me of my grandfather and what he remembered of my parents.

244

*   *   *

As Jerome poured my morning coffee, I asked, "Did you hear anyone prowling around last night, Jerome?"

"No, Miss Jennifer."

"Did Lord Fox stay the night?"

"Lord Fox and young Mr. Lambert left directly after dinner, Miss."

"Oh? Where did they go?"

"I believe Lord Fox went home, and Mr. Lambert said something about playing darts at the village pub."

"I see."

Jerome placed the silver coffeepot on the table and was about to leave, when Michael entered. He waited until Michael helped himself at the sideboard, then poured his coffee before leaving.

"I see you made it through the night without being murdered," Michael said with a crooked smile.

"Thank you for staying."

"What are your plans for today, Jennifer? More riding alone?"

"I had planned on going to Penzance to get my clothes from the dressmaker, but decided against it. I told my maid, Edith, to have a groom take her to Penzance in a carriage."

"You must be anxious to get your new frocks."

"I only ordered two new gowns. The other clothes were my mother's. I had them altered to fit me. The seamstress said she would bring them up to date. I saw no reason for me to go. I thought Edith might enjoy the trip. I gave her a pound to spend on herself, and told her she needn't come back until late afternoon."

"I'm sure she appreciates the time off. Seeing you're free, would you care to see the other mine at Cambourne?"

"Yes." My heart sang. Another day alone with Michael. I vowed to hold my tongue and not get into an argument with him. "Could we also see Land's End? I've heard so much about it."

"Then we'll make it a day at Land's End and the surrounding countryside."

"Can't we do both?"

"They are in two different directions. We'd have to rush around too much. I think you might like to spend some time at Land's End."

"I'll go change."

Neither my day frock nor my dark green merino riding habit required the assistance of another pair of hands. I dressed quickly and secured my long loose hair with a ribbon at the nape of my neck. Feeling elated, I bounced down the stairs to find Michael waiting for me at the bottom. He had a peculiar gaze in his eyes as he watched me descend. Wanting to start our trip off on a good note, I gave him my best and warmest smile. As I reached the bottom step, his hand reached out for mine. What could have been an intimate moment, was shattered by a piercing scream coming from the vicinity of the dining room.

Michael sprinted toward the unearthly screech, while I hurried behind him.

The dining room's French doors stood ajar. A maid, her hands to her cheeks, was screaming and staring at a figure sprawled on the stone floor of the terrace. Reaching the prone figure, Michael bent down and rolled the body over, just as Jerome dashed onto the terrace.

I stared down at the bloated face of Cecil Melville, his eyes wildly staring into space, his throat slit from ear to ear. As Jerome led the hysterical maid away, Binky came out, his eyes still sleep-glazed.

"What the devil is going on, Jennifer?" Binky asked.

Horror had paralyzed my voice. I pointed to Uncle Cecil's body.

"Good Lord!" Binky exclaimed. "Do Aunt Joyce and Bella know?"

"I don't think so," I managed to mutter.

"Better send a groom for the constable and doctor, Jennifer," Michael said.

I nodded and went back into the dining room. Jerome followed me. After I told him to send a groom abroad, I said, "And, Jerome, please bring another pot of coffee."

"Yes, Miss Jennifer."

I sat down at the dining room table, my head in my hands. I wasn't overly fond of Uncle Cecil, but I wasn't totally insensitive and felt the loss. Three people with their throats slit. I shook my head and wondered what sort of monster was loose. I hardly noticed Michael and Binky taking seats at the table. I finally came to my senses, when Jerome came in with the coffee.

"Where did you put Uncle Cecil?" I asked Michael.

"I left him where he was. I don't think the constable would want him moved."

"We covered him with a blanket," Binky added, then asked, "Who's going to tell Aunt Joyce?"

"I think she best hear it from her sister," I suggested. "You'd better go tell your mother and father, Binky."

"As soon as I've had my coffee."

"Damn it, man!" Michael boomed. "A murder has been committed! Your coffee can wait."

"If you think it's so important, you go tell them," Binky tossed back at Michael.

Michael sighed and shook his head. We drank our coffee in silence until Binky left.

"Under the circumstances, Jennifer, I think we'll have to postpone our trip to Land's End."

"Of course. But you will stay, won't you, Michael?"

"If you want me to."

"I don't want to be alone today."

"You have your family."

I was about to say I felt closer to him than anyone else. Instead I said, "They have isolated me from the very beginning. They are no more family to me than Cook's pots and pans." I paused to choke back nascent tears. "What's happening here, Michael? Why Grandfather? Why that young boy? Why Uncle Cecil?"

He reached across the table and took my hand. "I don't know, Jennifer. I wish I did. Perhaps it would be best if you went away for a while. You've never been to the Continent. Why don't you take your maid and do a tour? I can manage things here."

"Are you trying to get rid of me?" A smile started to form, but quickly died.

"I was thinking of your safety."

"Do you think I'm next on this fiend's list?"

"When dealing with a madman, it's better to be safe than sorry."

I thought of the misty visions of my grandfather, and instinctively knew he would be disappointed in me if I left without trying to avenge his murder. "I can't leave, Michael. I must see this thing through, or Wyndcliffe Manor will forever be tainted with murder."

"Isn't your life more important than Wyndcliffe Manor?"

"Not if it means my grandfather's soul would never rest. Besides, these murders don't seem to have anything to do with me."

"Your grandfather is dead, Jennifer. His soul is already at rest."

"No, it isn't, Michael."

He frowned. "What do you mean?"

I hesitated for a moment. I didn't want to sound dotty. I decided to plunge on. "I have visions of

Grandfather. In them, he pleads with me to avenge him. I can't leave here, Michael. I'd always feel guilty about deserting my grandfather."

"You're being ridiculous, Jennifer. Perhaps some of that Gypsy nonsense has seeped into your brain."

"It's not nonsense!" I said too loudly. "And it's not my imagination. I really see and hear him."

"You're creating phantoms that aren't there. You need a rest. A change of scenery."

"Don't patronize me, Michael. I know what I saw and heard. I need neither a rest nor a change of scenery."

"Since coming to Wyndcliffe, you have witnessed events horrible enough to undo anyone's nerves. You're on edge, Jennifer. You really should get away from here. Don't you trust me to handle the estate?"

"Of course, I do," I replied, but a small doubt began to tug at the back of my mind. "Let's not talk about it anymore. I don't want to argue with you today."

"We do seem to have an unusual number of disagreements," he commented, removing his hand from mine.

"Can we go into the front parlor to wait for the constable and Dr. Marsh? Everytime I look up, I see Uncle Cecil's body."

"Of course." He stood, then came to hold my chair.

Shortly before noon, the constable, his assistant, and Dr. Marsh arrived. Michael led them to the terrace. Neither the Lamberts nor the Melvilles—what was left of them—had come downstairs. Dr. Marsh was the first to come into the front parlor.

"Nasty business this. Do you mind if I help myself to a whiskey, Jennifer?"

"Not at all. Do you think the same person is responsible for all these killings, Dr. Marsh?"

"No doubt about it." He poured whiskey into a glass, looked at it, then poured another dollop in. He took a seat and sighed heavily. He removed his glasses and pinched the bridge of his nose with his thumb and forefinger. He looked tired.

"What did Constable Morgan have to say?" I asked.

"Not much. He has a tendency to keep things to himself, especially when he's baffled."

"Doesn't he have any clues?"

"Not a one to my knowledge. By the way, he wants everyone in here for questioning."

"Including Aunt Joyce and Annabel?" I asked, as I rang for Jerome.

"He said everyone."

I relayed the message to Jerome as Michael and the constable entered.

"You say you've moved back to the cottage, Mr. Savage? Can you explain why you stayed at Wyndcliffe last night?" Constable Morgan asked.

"Miss Hardwicke saw a face at the library window. She was frightened. Since the death of her grandfather, she is alone in the West Wing. She asked me to stay."

"You stayed in the West Wing?"

"Yes. When Mr. Hardwicke took ill, he requested my presence at Wyndcliffe and subsequently a room was prepared for me near his own in the West Wing. I used that room last night."

The constable nodded, then directed his attention to me. "Did you recognize the face you saw last night, Miss Hardwicke?"

"I'm sorry to say I didn't. It was dark, and the face was there for only a second."

"Why did it frighten you?"

"The thought of a prowler outside brought to mind

the recent murders, and I became fearful."

The constable took out his pipe and put it in his mouth, but neither filled nor lighted it. He began to pace about the room, but stopped when the others began to drift in and take seats.

"Where is Sergeant Thompson?" Dr. Marsh asked.

"He's seeing about having the body removed," Constable Morgan answered.

Aunt Joyce was a quivering mass of flesh. A lace cap covered her head, which led me to believe her golden curls were fake. Her eyes were swollen and red. A fan of deep wrinkles radiated from the corners of her eyes. She constantly twisted a handkerchief as she took a seat. Annabel appeared dazed, as though she had no idea what had happened or where she was.

Aunt Lydia and Amanda were expressionless, their somber faces revealing no emotion. Uncle Nigel was clearly puzzled, while Binky made no secret of his boredom. Occasionally he would look over at me and smile, while the constable interrogated everyone.

Aunt Joyce swooned slightly when questions were directed her way. With the assistance of a maid and Dr. Marsh, both Aunt Joyce and Annabel were led up to their rooms.

By the time the doctor came back down, the constable and his assistant had left. At my invitation, Dr. Marsh stayed to lunch.

As we waited for the noon meal to be served, questions were bantered about with no satisfactory answers. While we were thus engaged, Lord Fox came dashing into the front parlor without waiting to be announced, much to Jerome's consternation.

"I just heard about the trouble here. I am so sorry. Is there anything I can do?" Jason asked.

"I don't think there is anything anyone can do at this point," I said.

"Where are Mrs. Melville and Bella? I would like to express my sorrow at the tragedy."

"I have given them a sedative of laudanum. They'll sleep for a while. They were in shock, which is normal under the circumstances," Dr. Marsh explained.

"Would you care to stay for lunch, Jason?" I asked, only to see Michael's face darken with anger.

"If it's not inconvenient."

"Of course not."

Jerome announced lunch and everyone rose. Jason started to stroll toward me, as if he intended to escort me into the dining room. I quickly took Michael's arm. He smiled down at me and patted my hand. Jason gallantly smiled and offered his arm to Amanda.

The wake was exceptionally trying. Aunt Joyce wailed and moaned constantly. Aunt Lydia was of no help. She avoided her sister and declined to give her any consolation. If Jason Fox was present, which he frequently was, Annabel would cling to him as though he were a lifeboat in a storm-tossed sea.

The day of the funeral was crisp and clear. A salty breeze wafted over the land from the sea. The strident screams of gulls soaring in the air punctuated the vicar's eulogy at the gravesite. At Aunt Joyce's request, the service had been a long one. I was surprised by her sudden calmness. In fact, no one cried at the grave.

I didn't want to think about the funeral, as it reminded me of Grandfather's untimely demise. I turned my thoughts to the face at the library window. I tried to recall it as sharply as I could, but the moment had been too fleeting. I began to wonder if I had really seen a face or imagined it. Then an ugly notion pressed in on me.

Michael was living at Wyndcliffe when Grandfather

was murdered. Now, the one night Michael stayed overnight, Uncle Cecil was murdered in the same manner. But what could Michael gain by the death of either man? If indeed he wanted Wyndcliffe to be under the Savage name once more, their deaths would gain him nothing. My thoughts dribbled off into a muddle.

As the days passed, a gloom settled over Wyndcliffe. I saw little of Michael, but Jason was in constant attendance. When I showed little interest in his gallantries, he resorted to consoling Annabel, much to Aunt Joyce's delight.

Aunt Joyce made a remarkable recovery from the death of her husband. She wandered about the house with a vague smile, nodding graciously to everyone, even Aunt Lydia. I suspected she had cajoled Dr. Marsh out of more laudanum than was good for her. Youth played a role in Annabel's rapid recovery. Jason's seeming devotion also helped.

I was continually treated as an interloper in my own home. Even though I would be alone in the large house, I looked forward to the day they all left. Their glares of dislike unsettled me. I dreaded the onslaught of winter, when we'd all be confined indoors.

As I stared out the library window at the cloudy day, I decided to go to the Botallack mine regardless of the weather. If Grandfather had found it a place of solace, perhaps I would find peace there, too.

I told Jerome to have my horse saddled with a standard saddle, not a sidesaddle. I went upstairs to change into my remodeled riding habit. The seamstress had done wonders with my mother's old wardrobe, and the two new gowns were lovely beyond my expectations. She had even cut the skirts of the riding habits, and sewn them into very loose pants. When I stood, they took on an appearance of a full skirt, but I could now swing my legs over the saddle without having to hitch the skirt between my legs.

Eyebrows were raised in the stableyard, but nothing was said. I paced the mare slowly down the driveway. Once on the road, I urged her into a full gallop. The sensation was soothing. As I came closer to the sea, a salty mist kissed my face.

Once there, I dismounted and tethered the horse. I was inexorably drawn to the rim of the promontory, where I stared at the turbulent sea. The rising swells would hurl themselves on the jagged rocks in a valiant effort to demonstrate their superiority. The mist from the foamy assault rose high in the air. I watched expectantly.

My patience was rewarded as the mists swirled higher and higher, until a gossamer form took shape. I had no doubt it was another visitation from my grandfather.

"Jennifer . . . Jennifer . . ." the disembodied voice called, as though deep in an echoing cave.

"Yes, Grandfather. I'm here."

"Avenge me . . . put my soul to rest. Avenge me."

"How? Tell me how? Who murdered you?"

"Evil . . . an evil one is near you. Beware . . . beware . . . beware . . ." called the fading voice. The mist fell into the tumultuous sea.

What did he mean by evil is near me? Right now? Or at Wyndcliffe?

The cry of an animal in pain halted my musings, and I turned toward the mine. No human was in sight.

Approaching closer to the mine, I discerned the mournful cry of a cat in agony. I finally pinpointed the sound as coming from the half-ruined hovel where a shaft had been housed.

I entered the ruined, roofless building, where autumn leaves had created a thick carpet over the floor. Huddled against the far wall was a kitten, dragging her legs as though they had been broken. Heedless of anything except the miserable creature, I trotted across the floor with the intentions of taking the kitten back to Wyndcliffe and seeking help for the poor animal.

When I reached the middle of the floor, I heard the snapping of twigs, just before the floor opened up and I went tumbling down the endless shaft.

Twenty

I don't know how long I lay in the damp, black shaft. My heard hurt. I did know that. When I put my hand to my head, I felt a warm, sticky spot. Feeling around, my fingers touched a large rock by my head. I assumed my head had hit it, causing me to sink into unconsciousness.

As my senses became fully alert and attuned to the darkness, I could hear a heavy rumbling above me, like the carriage of an enormous giant. For a few minutes I was fearful and puzzled, until I remembered Michael telling me of the deep shaft under the sea, and the miners hearing the ocean rolling huge boulders over the sea floor.

With that fear assuaged, my next worry was my physical state. I had no fear of the dark. Slowly I felt my arms, torso, and legs. Nothing appeared to be broken, even though I was aware of some sore bruises. But I had been sore and bruised before, without having my physical actions hampered to any great extent. I certainly had no fear of the mine shaft. My past experiences had taught me how to climb out of one.

I began the slow, arduous climb on my hands and feet. Even though my hands were no longer calloused and soft—from living the life of a lady—at least I had boots on my feet and no chains lugging a coal cart. It was an unusually long shaft and, not being accustomed to such physical strain, I had to stop and rest frequently. I consoled myself with the knowledge that the muck on my hands consisted of water and dirt, not someone's leaky bladder turning the earth to mire.

As I slowly progressed in the dark, my thoughts were with the kitten and my mare. I should have been thinking about how I came to fall in the mine shaft. My hands were becoming painful, and I began to lose heart. My spirits began to flag, until I saw a point of gray light high above me.

With the end in sight, I didn't want to do something stupid, like carelessly rushing toward the light. At the colliery in Newcastle, I learned slow and steady was the best way to proceed. I had seen too many who tried to hurry, only to slip and fall back.

I sat down and tore strips off one of my petticoats, then bound my hands. I now had the steeper section of the shaft to climb. I took a brief respite before beginning that assault.

Reaching the opening, I placed my forearms on the ground and hoisted myself out. I dragged my sore and aching body to one of the dilapidated walls. I leaned against it, my eyes searching for the kitten. It had vanished. The pearl gray sky was turning the color of slate. I must have been down the shaft for the whole day, and decided to head for home before night descended.

I got to my feet and, cautiously stepping around the gaping hole in the ground, went to get my horse. My horse was not where I had tethered her. I called several times, then began a search for her, loudly calling her name—all to no avail. In the distance I heard the sound of horses' hooves on the road. Perhaps my calling hadn't been in vain after all.

Expecting to see the mare come bounding over the knoll any minute, I was startled to see a trap heading my way. As it approached, I was stunned to see Michael at the reins. I stood dumbfounded as he pulled alongside me and jumped down from the seat. He dashed toward me.

"Are you all right, Jennifer?" His eyes roamed over me.

"I'm fine. Well, maybe a little sore."

"You look awful. What happened to your hands?"

"I had to climb out of the mine shaft."

"What were you doing down there?"

"I fell in."

"That's impossible. No one could fall through a stone cover."

"Oh, no? Come and see."

Michael stared incredulously at the opening. He bent down to examine it. "Someone has made a lattice of light twigs, then covered it with leaves." He looked up at me. "I don't understand."

"Neither do I."

He straightened up. "What were you doing here? What made you come into this old building?"

Leaving out the misty vision of my grandfather, I related the events of the day. "My horse seems to be gone. Could you take me home, Michael? I might make it in time for dinner."

"Dinner? It's morning, Jennifer. I had men out searching the countryside for you all day yesterday, including myself. You've been gone all night."

"All night?"

"Your horse managed to break loose and came back this morning. I examined her hocks and found bits of gorse on them, the kind of gorse that is plentiful here. Thinking you were thrown and gravely injured, I brought the trap. I sent for Dr. Marsh before I left Wyndcliffe. He should be at the house by the time we get back."

He assisted me into the trap. I had to admit I felt wobbly. I hadn't used those particular muscles in some time.

"What have I told you about riding off alone?" With a frown furrowing his brow, he snapped the reins, and we were off.

"Don't start with me, Michael. I'm not in the best frame of mind."

"Well, you should at least tell someone where you are going. It would have saved a lot of time."

"I'm sorry if I squandered your time."

He threw me a quick glance of annoyance. After several minutes of silence, he spoke. "I'm sure you are aware that the false cover over the mine shaft was constructed by human hands. Someone meant for you to fall in."

"How would anyone know I was going to Botallack?"

"Perhaps you mentioned it, or someone could have followed you?"

"I'm quite sure I didn't mention it to anyone."

"The only other explanation is vandals. I hope we're not going to be plagued with vandals. I'll have to send a couple of men to fix that hole right away."

"What makes you think it was vandals?"

"One man couldn't have lifted that cement stone alone."

"Did anyone at the house express concern about my absence?"

"I hate to bruise your ego, but to be truthful, the Lamberts, with the exception of Binky, appeared more relaxed, almost jovial. The Melvilles were too wrapped up in themselves to think about anyone else."

259

"What about Jason?" I saw a vein throb at his temple. His jaw twitched as though he were grinding his teeth.

"He's been around."

Everyone was gathered in the front parlor waiting for lunch. Evidently someone had invited Jason to stay for the noonday meal.

An expression of utter shock registered on everyone's face. Even Aunt Lydia's and Amanda's eyes widened under arched eyebrows. Whether they were surprised to see I was still alive, or appalled at my wretched condition, I couldn't tell. Jason was the first to approach me. He took my bandaged hands in his, and held me at arm's length while he surveyed me.

"What ever happened, Jennifer? We were so worried about you. At least you seem to be in one piece, thank God."

"I'll explain everything at lunch." I pulled my hands away and turned to Michael. "You will stay, won't you, Michael?"

He nodded.

"Michael had me and everyone else scouring the countryside for you, Jennifer," Binky said.

"I'm sorry if I inconvenienced everyone," I said with a trace of bitterness. All of them had been living off Wyndcliffe, never doing a lick of work. They had no right to resent helping to find me.

"You are a sight, Jennifer. You don't have much time to make yourself presentable at the table. Perhaps you should have a tray in your room. Your appearance is perfectly disgusting!" Aunt Lydia exclaimed.

Dr. Marsh tossed down his sherry and came to cup my elbow. "Let's go to your rooms, Jennifer. I want to take a look at those hands."

Once upstairs, Dr. Marsh gently unwrapped my hands, then shook his head. "They're badly cut and bruised. I won't question you about it now. I suspect I'll hear all about it at lunch. Why don't you wash up and change. We'll deal with those hands later. Any other damage?"

"Some bruises, and I believe I have cut my scalp."

He examined my head. "The bleeding has stopped, but you have quite a bump there. Any headaches?"

"At first. It's gone now."

"After lunch, I'd like you to soak in a hot tub, then get ready to have a long rest. I'll tend to your hands after your tub."

"You're welcome to stay for dinner, Doctor."

"Perhaps I will, if you don't mind my staying overnight. I'm breaking in a new assistant. It will do him good to be on his own."

"You're always welcome at Wyndcliffe, Doctor. I'll see to it a room is made up for you."

He smiled and left my sitting parlor.

Edith, who was patiently waiting in my bedchamber, shook her head and crinkled her nose when she saw me. I told her what the doctor had said. She said she'd have the tub ready for me after lunch. She quickly undressed me and gave me a light wash. With my hands so sore, I felt utterly helpless. I was thankful Edith was a gentle and patient person. Dressed and a little more presentable, I went downstairs and entered the dining room as everyone was being seated.

During the meal I gave a detailed account of my misadventures and answered innumerable questions. That it was the works of mischievious vandals was the general consensus accepted by all. Directly after lunch, I went to my rooms where Edith waited.

"The doctor told me to add a goodly amount of salt to your tub, Miss Jennifer." Edith undressed me.

I slipped into the tub and gave myself up to the pure pleasure of it, even though the salt stung my hands. Edith washed my hair, taking great care around the lump on my head. I had to admit the salted water seemed to absorb the aches from my body. When the water lost its warmth, I got out of the tub.

Dressed in my long-sleeved, high-necked, flannel nightdress, I sent Edith to fetch Dr. Marsh.

He came bustling into my bedchamber, black bag in hand. "I don't know how you stand it, Jennifer."

"I'm fairly used to aches and pains."

"No, no, no. Downstairs, I mean. The squabbling that is going on between the Lamberts and the Melvilles. I daresay Lord Fox seems to be enjoying the scene."

"What about Michael?"

"He left shortly after you came upstairs. Now, let's see those hands."

I held them out. He took them in his hands and peered at them for several seconds. He opened his bag, took out a tin of salve, and spread the greasy ointment over my hands, then bandaged them.

"There . . . that should do it for now. I would suggest you wear a pair of gloves to keep the bandages in place while you rest."

"Thank you, Dr. Marsh."

He grinned impishly. "Don't thank me until you've seen my bill."

"What were they quarreling about this time?"

He snapped his bag shut and sat down. "Mrs. Melville insists on hiring men to police and guard Wyndcliffe Manor. Mrs. Lambert called her sister a senile old woman. And said that no one was going to murder her in her sleep. Mrs. Melville called her sister a name, and back and forth it went. Soon Annabel and Amanda were at each other's throats. But I daresay you've heard it all before."

"What about Binky? Did he join in?"

"No." He smoothed down the sides of his wiry gray hair. "Strange young man."

"Why do you say that?"

"Something about that young man strikes me as odd. He seems aloof from the world around him. He looks at his mother, father, and sister as though they were strangers. Haven't you noticed, Jennifer?"

"I can't say that I have. He's always been pleasant to me."

"Maybe I'm getting too critical in my old age. I know the lad drinks too much. Perhaps that accounts for his seeming aloofness."

"Oh, Binky's all right. I suspect he's not very happy here. He'd much rather lead the life of Lord Fox. Tramping about the Continent. Socializing in London," I said, trying to make excuses for Binky's peculiarities.

Dr. Marsh put his hands on the arms of the chair and pushed himself out of it, then stooped to retrieve his bag. "Well, I'll see you at dinner, Jennifer."

"Did Jerome show you to your room?"

"Yes, he did. I'll have a look at those hands again in the morning before I leave. Continue with the hot, salted baths until you feel fit, Jennifer."

"I feel fit now."

He smiled. "You won't in the morning. I daresay you'll find your body stiff and still sore. I'll see you later, Jennifer."

After dinner that night, I went into my parlor and retrieved the book I was reading. I fluffed my pillows up, got into bed, then rested the book on my propped-up knees. The last thing I remember was slipping down in the bed, my legs straightening.

Somewhere in the mindlessness of sleep, distorted,

eerie images crept into my mind, as if the mind becomes empty of reality so the unreal can capture it.

I heard wails from my grandfather's bedchamber. I floated toward his rooms, doors opening on their own as I approached. When I floated into his bedchamber, all was quiet. He lay peacefully in bed, a red gash across his throat. I smiled benevolently at him and he sprang into a sitting position, his eyes wide with terror. He croaked the name Michael. As he did, a fresh gush of blood burst from the wound in his neck.

I was so startled, I dropped to the floor, my head hitting the fender of the fireplace. I wasn't knocked out, but I could neither move nor speak. Grandfather left his bed. With each step he took, blood exuded from his throat. I wasn't afraid, because I knew he was coming to help me.

Suddenly, another figure was in the room. A giant of a man whose body was covered like a feral beast with long, fine hair. At first his physical appearance didn't alarm me. But the fact he had no face began to frighten me. When I saw the butcher knife in his upraised hand, I became terrified as he came toward me.

I tried to move, to run, to flee, but my body wasn't responding to the signals from my brain. The beast came closer and knelt down on one knee beside my body, the knife about to strike.

Grandfather hurled himself at the hairy figure, but he was no match for the quick slashing of the butcher knife. The beast stood, the knife flashed, and one of Grandfather's hands floated up through the open ceiling. The scene changed to the promontory at Botallack.

As I lay immobile, I watched the hand disappear into a clear blue sky. Another flash of the knife. Another hand floated skyward. Soon a large wave crashed as high as the promontory, its mist enveloping Grandfather. The beast turned to me, the bloodied knife firm in his hand. He sank to his knees beside me. As the knife began its downward plunge, I started to roll faster and faster, until I rolled off the edge of the high promontory. An inky blackness consumed me, as I began to fall to the jagged rocks below.

Before my body hit the rocks, I woke up.

The room was dark. I lighted the oil lamp beside my bed and took it to the ormulu clock on the mantle; it was a little past midnight.

I put the lamp back on the nighttable, picked up the book which had fallen to the floor, and got back into bed. I tried to read, but the dream haunted me. I remembered old Zoe saying all dreams have a meaning. If one could perceive the meaning of dreams, one would be wiser about oneself and the world in general.

I thought long and hard about my dream, but could make no sense of it, never mind discern the meaning of it. The only easy part was my falling off the cliff. I suspected it was related to my falling down the mine shaft. But my grandfather without hands? A faceless beast? I could fathom none of it. I pondered on about the dream until I fell into a restful sleep.

Shafts of light pierced my eyelids. I knew Edith had pulled the drapes open. It had become a ritual. What wasn't part of the ritual was the loud scream that issued from Edith's mouth.

Twenty-One

I peered at her through sleepy eyes. "What's the matter, Edith? Isn't it a little early for screaming?"

She covered her mouth with one hand. With her other hand, she pointed to the foot of my bed. The doctor was right. My body was stiff and sore as I struggled to sit up. When I did, and looked at the foot of the bed, I rubbed my eyes with the back of my gloved hands. I stared at the object in a mixture of horror and awe.

Stretched out on the coverlet was the kitten from the Botallack mine, its slit throat staining the coverlet with its blood. My first impulse was to cry for the animal's demise. Then reason gave birth to fear. Someone had come into my room at night and placed the animal there. Whoever it was could have just as easily slit *my* throat. Compassion turned to anger.

"Get me a fresh pillowcase, Edith."

She nodded, her hand still over her mouth as she scurried out. When she returned with the pillow case, I put the mutilated creature in it and placed it on the floor.

"Edith, I don't want you mentioning a word of this to anyone, not Cook, not Jerome, especially not any

266

of the maids. If you do, I'll dismiss you. Understand me?"

"Yes, Miss Jennifer." Terror was still in her eyes, but she seemed to be returning to normal now that the kitten was out of sight.

"Wash the coverlet yourself, Edith."

"They'll ask me why I'm going the laundry, Miss."

"Tell them I spilt tea or something. That the coverlet is my favorite, and I insisted you alone deal with it. If they still question you, tell them to see me."

"Yes, Miss."

I quickly donned my dark merino skirt and white shirtwaist. I tossed my cloak around my shoulders, hooked it, then picked up the pillowcase. I padded down the servants' staircase and went out the service door. Instead of walking down the driveway where I might be seen, I crossed through the evergreens to the woods, where I followed the path to Michael's cottage.

I knocked firmly on the door of the modest domicile.

A tousled, sleep-ridden Michael opened the door, clad only in breeches and knee-high boots. The sheer power of the man's physique unsettled me, especially so early in the morning. His handsome face and male potency caused me to swallow hard.

"What's wrong, Jennifer? What are you doing here so early in the morning?" The sight of me standing there must have shocked him into sudden wakefulness.

I cleared my throat. "May I come in?"

"I'm sorry." He moved aside and I stepped in. "Go in there while I make myself presentable." He waved a directional hand.

I went into what passed for a parlor. I couldn't say it was a tidy place, nor was it well kept. Sheets were carelessly tossed over armchairs and a settee. Small tables were cluttered with mugs, papers, and books. I gingerly sat on the edge of an armchair, my hand clutching the pillowcase. I stared at the ash-laden fireplace. I turned when I heard the tread of boots against the bare wooden floor. Michael had donned a black sweater.

"I apologize for the state of the cottage. I'm afraid I was never meant to be a housekeeper. Now, tell me what brings you here, Jennifer," he said, the sleep washed from his face, his dark chestnut hair neatly brushed.

I opened the pillowcase, cautiously removed the dead kitten, and placed it atop the pillowcase. Michael came over and peered down at it.

"What's this?" he asked.

"A dead kitten."

"I know it's a kitten." A trace of annoyance touched his tone. "What about it?"

"I found it at the foot of my bed this morning. This is the same kitten that lured me into that building at Botallack. As you can see, its throat has been cut. I think it might be a warning. I also believe it rules out that the trap was the work of vandals."

"Oh? What brings you to that conclusion?"

"Could I have a cup of coffee or tea?"

"Didn't you eat breakfast?"

"No. I came directly here."

"Well, come into the kitchen. I'm not a cook, but I'll do the best I can."

"What shall I do with the kitten?"

"Leave it here for now."

I rose and followed him into the kitchen. A huge open fireplace with ovens on the side dominated the kitchen. Swinging iron arms held pots and kettles. Mismatched dishes were displayed on the shelves of a doorless cupboard.

Michael stoked the fire, while I took a seat at a crude

wooden table. In a way it reminded me of Ma Boothe's kitchen, only it was far more elaborate. He swung the kettle over one section of the fire, cut some rashers off a slab of bacon, and placed them in a frying pan, which he put on a grill hovering over the fire. When the water boiled, he poured it into a teapot and set it aside to steep. When the rashers were done, he put the bread in the bacon grease to cook.

He placed breakfast on the table, sat down, and said, "Sorry I don't have any eggs for you, but I haven't picked them up yet. And you'll have to make do with tea. I don't have any coffee."

"This is fine. Do you always eat like this?"

"I deem this an occasion. The mistress of Wyndcliffe Manor having breakfast in my humble abode."

"Are you being sarcastic, Michael?"

"Not at all. I don't usually cook breakfast. At the beginning of the week I make a big pot of porridge, then heat up what I need through the week."

"Is it a question of money? I can raise your wages, Michael."

"I have enough money. No, it's a question of time and inclination. I feel it's a waste of time to cook a big breakfast for one person."

"Why haven't you married?"

"I'm waiting for the right woman. But enough of me. Tell me your theory about that flimsy cover over the mine shaft not being the work of vandals."

"As I said, this is the kitten I went to rescue when I fell into the shaft."

"How can you be sure? Most kittens look alike."

"Orange tabby cats aren't that common. What really convinces me is the kitten's back legs are broken, just like the one at the Botallack mine. That kitten was deliberately put on the other side of the shaft to lure me into the trap. Now someone has killed that kitten and put it on my bed while I was alseep, to remind me I am vulnerable and could be attacked at any time." Michael was silent for so long I began to wonder if I had made a mistake in coming to him. Perhaps *he* was the culprit, and was deciding how to handle the situation now that I had unearthed the true nature of the plot. I broke the silence. "Well, what do you think, Michael?"

He sighed heavily. "You might be right, Jennifer. I suggest you keep your doors locked in the future."

"Do you think it was the same person who killed Grandfather, that lad, and Uncle Cecil?"

"I'm inclined to think the possibility exists."

I reached for my teacup and saw my hand was trembling. Suddenly I began to shake all over, as the realization that someone had been in my bedchamber came on me with full force. I hugged myself, stood, and began to pace about the small kitchen. Michael came to me and gathered me in his arms.

"What is it, Jennifer?" His voice was soft and caressing.

"I just realized the dreadfulness of someone being in my bedchamber while I slept. Oh, Michael." I clung to him with desperation and laid my head on his shoulder.

"Don't let it get to you, Jennifer. I think someone is trying to frighten you out of your wits. Try to be strong." He stroke my hair gently, and held me tight until I had control of myself.

I tilted my head back and asked, "Do you have a spade, Michael?"

"Yes. Why?"

"I would like to bury that poor creature." He looked down at me with a strained glimmer in his eyes. He quickly released me and stepped back.

"Why not let one of the servants do it?"

"I don't want anyone to know about it. I want to appear perfectly normal. Whoever did it might give himself or herself away, if I act as though nothing happened."

Michael's smile was lopsided. "Becoming a detective, are you? I think you should show the animal to Constable Morgan. Let him make what he will of it."

"He might think I was hysterical and making up tales of fancy. No. I want to do this my way."

"Why did you come to me with this, Jennifer? Why not Binky? Or Lord Fox?"

"I trust you," was all I could say.

"Under the circumstances, you should be wary of whom you trust. I might be the villain trying to scare you away from Wyndcliffe Manor. Have you ever thought about that?"

"Yes. But I couldn't see any reason for you to scare me away from Wyndcliffe. It would gain you nothing."

He ran a splayed hand through his thick hair. "I'll bury the animal for you. What are you going to do now?"

"Go back to the house. Dr. Marsh wants to look at my hands."

"How are you feeling otherwise?"

"A little stiff and sore. Otherwise I'm fine."

"I have some business to take care of this morning. Would you care to take that trip to Land's End this afternoon?"

"I'd like that."

"We'll take the trap. I don't think you're up to riding."

"I don't think so either."

I waited in the rear parlor while Dr. Marsh finished

his breakfast. I sat and stared out the French doors. Was I the next intended victim of the throat-slashing fiend? If so, why didn't he do it when placing the kitten on my bed? The perfect opportunity was there. Why postpone the deed?

"You look pensive, my dear. Still plagued by the aftereffects of your fall?" Dr. Marsh strolled into the parlor looking jovial.

I managed a smile despite my dire thoughts. "Not really."

"Well, let's have a look at those hands." He proceeded to unbandage my hands after I removed my gloves. "Ah youth! The young can heal themselves quicker than any medicine. Your hands are coming along nicely. I'll leave a tin of salve for you. After your salted bath tonight, slather your hands with the salve, rebandage them, and put the gloves back on."

"All right."

"Well, my dear, I must leave now. My surgery awaits. I dare not leave my young apprentice on his own for too long. Many thanks for your hospitality."

Shortly after he departed, Jason came into the parlor. His dapper and fashionable attire accentuated his good looks.

"How's the patient this morning?" he asked, cheerfully taking a seat across from me.

"You stayed the night?"

"Amanda entertained us until quite late. I hope you don't mind."

I shook my head absently.

"I say, you look a bit peaked, Jennifer. Why don't you come with me to Foxhill, and let me give you the grand tour? It'll be a pleasant diversion for you. I'm sure Annabel and her mother won't mind if you join us."

"Not this time, Jason. Thank you for the offer, but I'm really not up to it." Actually I wasn't up to Aunt Joyce's moaning about the loss of her husband, and Annabel's cloying manner toward Jason. Besides, I was looking forward to the trip to Land's End.

"I daresay you're doing everything you can to avoid me, Jennifer. Why? Do you find me repulsive?"

"Of course not, Jason. You're a very handsome man."

"Then why don't you favor me more?"

"I don't want to encourage any hopes of marriage you might be entertaining."

"Really, Jennifer. Your experience at the Botallack mine should be proof you need a man to protect you. It wouldn't have happened if you were my wife, and you know it."

"Perhaps not, Jason. But I don't love you."

"What has love got to do with marriage?"

Startled, I gazed at him in wonder. "Everything."

"That's a childish attitude, Jennifer. As time passes, you'll see things differently. One outgrows romanticism."

I smiled, knowing I could never marry someone as jaded and cynical as Jason. I suspected he loved himself too much to ever love anyone else.

"We're ready, Jason," came Annabel's squeaky voice, as she and her mother came into the parlor.

"I really shouldn't be travelling about in my bereavement. I suppose Cecil would want me to carry on," Aunt Joyce whined.

Jason stood and flashed them his best smile. He extended both his arms for them to take. "I've been looking forward to playing host to such lovely ladies. I promise you an excellent tea at noon. Shall we go?"

When I was sure they had left, I padded down the

273

corridor to the foyer leading up to the library. Instead of turning right, I turned left toward the chapel. Once I entered the chapel, a peace settled on me. I sat down in the first pew and gazed at the small altar. I closed my eyes with the intention of reliving the events at Botallack. Perhaps there was a clue that I had overlooked.

Different images played across my mind. A beautiful woman with golden red hair was reading stories to a little girl perched in bed. I saw her clearly and knew she was my mother. More images came flooding in. My father and grandfather teaching a little redheaded girl to ride her new pony.

I remembered one day when the house was full with guests. I was sent outside to play with the other children, who were a little older than me. At first I didn't recognize the images of Annabel and Amanda, but I couldn't mistake that wiry, carrot-colored hair of Binky. With a slight breeze blowing, his hair stood out straight in all directions. I remember laughing about it.

"What's so funny, Jennifer Hardwicke?" Binky asked.

"Your hair. It looks like a witch's broom."

"You'll be sorry you said that, Jennifer Hardwicke. You're always poking fun at me, and someday I'll get even," he warned.

I remember sobering instantly. "I'm sorry, Binky."

"Go tell Grandfather, Binky." The golden curls of Annabel bounced as she jumped up and down.

"Grandfather would take her side. He likes her more than he does us," Amanda said, her expression darkly somber.

"Then why don't we throw mud on her dress?" Annabel suggested.

"Why are you so mean to me, Cousin Annabel?" I

274

remembered asking.

"You're the one who is mean, Cousin Jennifer. Whenever we come here, all you do is show off your fancy new clothes and new toys," Annabel declared.

"You always ask to see them," I defended.

"Show us your new pony, Cousin Jennifer," Binky said.

The four of us trotted off to the stables. I had the head groom bring out my new pony. I took the reins and paraded her around.

"Let me ride her. It's the least you can do after laughing at me."

I handed Binky the reins, watched him mount, then take off toward the fields.

"If my brother gets hurt, it'll be your fault, Cousin Jennifer," Amanda said.

I was very uneasy when Binky and my pony were gone so long. When he finally pulled into the stableyard, my uneasiness turned to rage. My pony's legs were cut and bleeding from being ridden through briars and thickets. Binky dismounted with an air of triumph.

The minute the groom took the pony away, I dashed at Binky, pushing him to the ground. I sat on him and began punching him around the shoulders and face. Amanda frantically tried to pull me off, while Annabel stood there giggling. I took a handful of horse manure and pushed it into Binky's face. Amanda began to scream, which brought out the grooms and stable boys.

With Binky crying, we were ushered back into the house. Before I had a chance to explain, Aunt Lydia began hurling vindictives at me. When my mother defended me, Aunt Lydia turned on her. A full-fledged family argument was underway when we children were sent to our rooms.

"I'll get you for this, Cousin Jennifer," Binky whispered to me, before we were led away to our separate wings.

The Melvilles and Lamberts left the next day. The parting was bitter. A few weeks later I was on my way north with my parents. I still couldn't remember the actual accident. Perhaps it was best I didn't.

I opened my eyes and gazed at the altar once again, thankful that pieces of my memory were starting to return. I couldn't help but wonder if Binky had held a grudge all these years. No. We were adults now. I couldn't believe Binky would exert that much energy, preparing a trap for me at the Botallack mine. I went to the library to make up pay packets for the staff.

The wind whipped my hair as we stood on the rocky promontory of Land's End. The smell of the sea was strong. Gulls circled above us with their strident cries, as though we were invading Vikings.

Though not really jolly, Michael seemed to be in an expansive mood.

"You're in luck, Jennifer. The day is clear enough for you to see Wolf Rock and the Isles of Scilly."

"Where?"

"To your left. About twenty-eight miles to the southeast of here. They claim those outcroppings are all that remain of the legendary land of Lyonnesse."

"Why is it legendary?"

"Surely you've heard the ancient Celtic legend of Tristram and Iseult?"

I shook my head. "I don't think so. But then, my memory isn't as crystal clear as it should be."

"Don't you remember anything?"

"Bits and pieces. I do believe it is starting to come back to me though. Tell me about Tristram and Iseult."

"The earliest known story was told by twelfth-century Anglo-Norman poets. It seems Tristram was the nephew of King Mark of Cornwall and resided with him at Tintagel, even though his homeland was Lyonnesse. King Mark sent Tristram to Ireland to fetch his future bride, Iseult. On the boat back, the two young people drank a love potion, which bound them in a fatal passion.

"After Iseult's marriage to King Mark, she continued to meet Tristram. King Mark discovers their continued affair and sends Tristram to Brittany, while keeping Iseult at Tintagel. In Brittany Tristram marries another princess, called Iseult the Blonde. Still he languishes for his Irish Iseult.

"When he is wounded in battle, Tristram believes he can only be cured by Iseult of Tintagel. He sends for her, telling the captain of the ship to raise white sails if she is aboard, black if she is not. He has his wife watch for the ship. But she is a jealous woman and tells Tristram the sails are black, when, in reality, they are white.

"Tristram dies of despair. When Iseult of Tintagel arrives and learns he is dead, she falls lifeless on his body. There have been many versions and additions to the tale. Back in the fifteenth century, Sir Thomas Malory makes Tristram a knight in King Arthur's court."

"I wonder if the tragic tale is true? It sounds like Shakespeare's Romeo and Juliet."

"Shakespeare had a tendency to borrow a lot from other tales and legends."

"Is there really a Tintagel?"

"The ruins of the great castle are still to be seen at

Tintagel on the north coast of Cornwall."

"I'd love to see it."

"It's a long ride. Some sixty miles northwest of here."

"Still, someday I shall go."

The wind picked up and I gave an involuntary shiver. Michael came closer and put his arm around me. As the warmth of his body surged through mine, I felt as though I had been struck by lightning.

"We'd better head back. Clouds are beginning to obscure the sun. It can get cold up here fast, especially when the wind starts blowing more strongly," Michael said.

The ride back to Wyndcliffe was leisurely, as Michael related more stories about King Arthur.

When he left after escorting me into the stableyard, it seemed that nothing could spoil the elation I felt after so marvelous an afternoon. Or so I thought.

Even in the foyer, I could hear Aunt Lydia upbraiding Amanda for not including herself in the little party Jason took to Foxhill Grange. Unashamedly, I stood there and listened while I took off my gloves. I also began to unwrap the bandages from my hands, stuffing the cloth into my skirt pockets.

"What's the matter with you, Amanda? I didn't raise you to be bashful. Letting that mealy-mouthed, feather-headed Annabel go off practically alone to Foxhill with Lord Fox, is the stupidest thing you've ever done. I want you to be Lady Fox, but I need your help! I can't do it all alone. Annabel is out there right now strolling with Jason, and they're unchaperoned. Now get yourself out there, Amanda."

"Can I help you with something, Miss Jennifer?"

Jerome had come into the foyer so quietly, I was startled and spun around.

"No, thank you, Jerome. Are Mrs. Melville and

Annabel back from Foxhill already?"

"Yes, Miss. It seems Mrs. Melville felt ill, and had forgotten to bring her medicine. They were only gone for a little under two hours."

"I see."

"I understand Lord Fox will be staying to dinner, Miss."

"Oh? At whose request?"

"Mrs. Melville's. She felt she owed him a treat for disrupting their excursion to Foxhill. It seemed to mollify Lord Fox, Miss."

"Mollify him? Why should he be upset over such a trifling matter, Jerome?"

"He wasn't at first, Miss. When he learned you had gone to Land's End with Mr. Savage, his mood turned sour. Forgive me for telling tales, Miss Jennifer. It is not my habit to indulge in relating household events. In this case, I thought you should know. I hoped I haven't overstepped my bounds, Miss."

"Not at all, Jerome. I appreciate your telling me."

I ascended the stairs and was beginning to head down the corridor toward the West Wing, when a piercing scream issued from my rooms. I stood still for a minute, to see if the cry was repeated. When it wasn't, I lifted my skirts and increased my pace. I was halfway down when Jerome appeared at my side.

"What happened, Miss Jennifer?" he asked.

"I don't know, but we'd better hurry and see."

Jerome flung the door to my bedchamber open and stood aside for me to enter. Edith was sitting on the edge of my bed, holding her index finger and crying.

"Whatever is wrong, Edith?" I asked.

"I burned meself," she replied between sobs.

"Let me look at it," Jerome ordered. He took her finger and studied it.

"As long as it isn't a major catastrophe, I'll wash my hands and face, then change for dinner." I proceeded to the lavatory where the washstand was situated.

I poured water into the basin from the pitcher. I cupped my hands and was about to lower them into the basin to splash some water onto my face, when suddenly Jerome flew at me!

The force of his body against mine knocked me to the floor. I looked at his face—which was contorted in frenzy—and thought his mind had snapped. Was Jerome the madman behind the murders at Wyndcliffe?

Twenty-Two

Jerome stood, offered me his hand, and said, "Sorry, Miss Jennifer."

I took his hand and got to my feet. "What got into you, Jerome?"

"I had to stop you from putting your hands into that basin, never mind putting any of that water on your face. Knocking you asunder was the quickest way I could think of. Come see Edith's finger, Miss Jennifer."

I padded back into my bedchamber.

"Show Miss Jennifer your finger, Edith," Jerome said. "Then tell her what happened."

I looked at Edith's finger to find the tip of it red and beginning to blister. It looked terrible. "Perhaps we should send for Dr. Marsh."

"Oh, no, miss. Cook has some salve that will be fixing it," Edith said.

"How did it happen, Edith?" I tried to keep my voice quiet and soothing.

"Well, I knew you had returned, so I thought I should test the water in the pitcher to make sure it hadn't chilled. I stuck the tip of my finger into it. That's when it burned me! I never heard of water burning," she told me.

"When did you fill the pitcher?" I asked.

"I put fresh water in it when you finished washing after lunch. I went to eat, then busied meself with me afternoon chores. I never touched the pitcher again, Miss Jennifer." A plea coated her words.

"I believe you, Edith. You'd better go downstairs and have Cook tend to your finger."

"Aye, Miss." Holding her finger in the air, Edith quickly departed.

"May I demonstrate a point for you, Miss Jennifer?"

"Certainly, Jerome."

"A piece of paper, if I may."

I went into my parlor and retrieved a piece of paper from my escritoire. I went back to the bedchamber and handed the paper to Jerome, a quizzical frown on my face. I trailed him into the lavatory, where he dropped the paper into the washbasin.

A hiss was immediately followed by a white, misty steam rising from the basin. When the steam had evaporated in the air, no trace of paper remained. I looked at Jerome expectantly.

"Acid, Miss Jennifer. Someone must have replaced the water in your pitcher with acid. That's why I couldn't let you dip your hands into it."

The grisly results began to sink in slowly. If I had dipped my hands in quickly and splashed my face . . . the horror of it made me tremble!

"Shall I get you a brandy, Miss Jennifer? You don't look too well, if I may say."

"I'll be all right, Jerome. The nastiness of the deed just came to me."

"It is a horror, Miss. Shall I get rid of it for you?"

"Please do, Jerome. Both the basin and the pitcher. Please replace them with new ones."

"Yes, Miss." He gathered up the items and departed. I went to the window and watched the misty fog roll

282

in from the sea, as the sun lowered in the sky. *Who is doing this to me?* If someone wanted me out of the way, why not slit my throat and be done with it? The thought made me shiver. Perhaps a brandy wasn't such a bad idea.

The outside mists undulated, swirling until they began to form into an ethereal shape. I wasn't afraid. In fact, I welcomed the configuration of my grandfather. I wanted to dash out and embrace the image, as though I would find everlasting protection in his arms. I raised the window, stuck my head out, and breathed the damp air as though the mist would fortify me.

The gauzy mouth began to move, but I could hear no words. I strained to listen. I was rewarded, not with answers to my many questions, but with another warning.

"Jennifer . . . beware All Hallow's Eve . . . beware All Hallow's Eve . . ."

The misty form began to disintegrate, its damp particles spreading out in the fog. I closed the window, went down to the library, and had that brandy.

Jason gallantly offered his arms to Amanda and Annabel, as we began the parade to the dining room. As always Aunt Lydia was on Uncle Nigel's arm. I suspect Binky was ordered to escort Aunt Joyce into the dining room. His expression clearly registered his distaste for the chore. I felt uncommonly lonely as I walked by myself into the dining room. I dearly wished Michael had never moved out of Wyndcliffe.

While Jason confidently entertained Amanda and Annabel, Binky kept looking at me with blatant curiosity, until I couldn't stand it.

"Whatever are you looking at, Binky? Has my hair turned green?"

"I'm sorry, Jennifer. But there's something different about you, and I can't put my finger on it."

I wondered if his stare was not one of curiosity, but rather one of amazement that my hands and face weren't burned with acid. The more I thought about everything, the more suspect Binky became.

"Now I know what it is," Binky declared. "You don't have your bandages on. Are your hands all healed?"

I held my palms up for him to see. Cuts, bruises, and raw skin were still in evidence. "I thought the air would do them more good. I'll put the salve and bandages back on before I go to bed."

Laughter interrupted my tête-à-tête with Binky. Uncle Nigel looked up startled, while Binky and I looked down the table at Annabel and Jason. Amanda relented and let a slight smile curve her lips.

"What did I miss?" Binky asked.

"Oh, Mother. Jason has decided to make his All Hallow's Eve soiree a masquerade ball. Isn't that delightful?" Annabel gushed.

"Yes, dear," Aunt Joyce absently replied.

"What's so funny about that?" Binky asked grumpily.

"Jason said he is going to dress as Little Bo Peep. He said Amanda, Jennifer, and me should dress as sheep, so he can gather us up. Isn't that wickedly amusing?" Annabel clapped her hands.

"Yes, dear." Aunt Joyce's tone lacked enthusiasm.

"I don't think it's the least bit funny," Binky remarked. "I hope you weren't serious, Jason."

"I'm deadly serious about it being a masquerade ball. But I was teasing Annabel about Bo Peep and the sheep. Don't you think a masquerade ball is most appropriate for All Hallow's Eve, Binky?" When Binky shrugged, Jason asked, "What about you, Jennifer? Who would you come as?"

"I haven't thought about it."

"She'll probably come as a coal mine pit girl," Aunt Lydia offered with a sneer.

Though Aunt Lydia's suggestion was less than friendly, it gave me the idea to go as a Gypsy. But I didn't say anything.

"What about you, Amanda?" Jason asked.

"Oh, she'll probably come as a wicked witch," Annabel replied for Amanda.

"I wouldn't dream of wearing the same costume as you, Annabel," Amanda hurled back at her.

"No one would ever believe I could possibly be a witch. But your personality suits the character perfectly, Amanda." Annabel gave her head a haughty toss. "I'll probably come as a medieval princess."

"Then I shall assume the role of a knight errant, and come to your aid when you are in peril," Jason said, his smile gallant and beguiling.

"Stuff and nonsense," Uncle Nigel grumbled.

"Don't be stodgy, Father," Binky said. "A masquerade ball may prove amusing at that. Life around here has been much too dull of late."

Dull? Three murders, falling down a mine shaft, a mutilated kitten, and acid. I certainly wouldn't have called life at Wyndcliffe dull.

The conversation turned back to costumes and engendered an argument between Amanda and Annabel. Binky and his father hotly debated the merits of a masquerade ball. I was glad when dinner was over, and I could retreat to my hot bath.

After describing what I wanted in the way of a blouse and jewelry, I sent Edith to Penzance. I ate a solitary breakfast, then went to the library to peruse the bills that had come in during the last two weeks. As I began to write out checks, I was diverted by male voices in the foyer. At first I couldn't make out what they were saying. But the voices soon became strident. I was about to leave the library to see what the disturbance was. I opened the library door and almost walked straight into Michael. I immediately stepped back.

"What was going on in the foyer, Michael?" I asked, then resumed my seat behind the desk.

"I had a slight altercation with Lord Fox," Michael answered, as he strode into the room and took a chair in front of the desk.

"About what?"

"Nothing of any importance."

"I could hear you in here. I'm sure all the servants heard. I'd like to hear it from you, Michael, rather than hear gossip from the servants."

"He mentioned something about a masquerade ball. I said something about it being a stupid idea. I'm afraid the conversation got out of hand."

"What else, Michael?"

"If you must know, I asked him if he had taken up permanent residence here. One thing led to another, and I warned him about poaching on the Wyndcliffe estate. He flew into a rage and bitter words were bandied about."

"Poaching? Why would Jason poach our lands? What would he poach?" Amusement sparkled in my eyes.

"A milch cow here and there. Sheep."

"Really, Michael. His lordship has no need of our animals. He has enough of his own."

"Have you seen his estate?"

"No."

"Then don't jump to conclusions, Jennifer."

"Jason is seldom on his estate. He's usually abroad looking for racehorses. Perhaps, unknown to him, one

286

of his men might be poaching. For that matter the poacher might be a complete stranger. The idea is so ridiculous, I see no need to continue this line of conversation."

"I should have known you would take his side," Michael said bitterly.

"Oh, Michael." I shook my head wearily and changed the subject. "What brings you to Wyndcliffe?"

"The harvest is in. I brought you the figures on the size of the various crops." He took the folio he was holding, leaned forward, and placed it on the desk. "Are you going to Jason's ball?"

"I expect so."

"The Lamberts and Melvilles, too?"

"I'm quite sure they are."

"I thought everyone here was in mourning, including you."

"Since coming to Wyndcliffe, I've found mostly sorrow. I don't think Grandfather would mind if I had one night that might possibly be enjoyable. Besides, Jason mentioned he was asking a number of other estate holders. It presents a good opportunity for me to meet my neighbors. I might learn a few things. What about you? Are you going, Michael?"

"I wasn't asked, but I'm going anyway, especially if you're going to be there."

"I'm flattered."

"Don't be. I'm going to spite Jason. For some reason, it rankles him to see us together."

Any merriment that might have momentarily claimed me vanished. I was hurt to think Michael was using me as an instrument to get back at Jason. I felt a need to hurt Michael as much as he hurt me.

"I'm sure Jason's ball will be a jolly success. I don't doubt the ladies will be in a row to dance with him."

"Including you, I suppose."

"Definitely. After all, he is quite handsome and a peer of the land. Being a bachelor makes him all the more attractive. Did you know he wants to court me?"

"I suspected as much. His fawning over certain people is obvious. I never thought you that naive, Jennifer. I was under the assumption that you could see through his pretensions. I see I was wrong. You're just another silly young girl." He abruptly stood, turned, and headed for the door.

I jumped up from my chair. "I haven't dismissed you, Michael."

He turned and gave me a sardonic smile. "Is the Gypsy girl aching to become a peeress of the land?"

"Perhaps. What difference does it make to you?"

"None. Goodbye, Jennifer."

"I still haven't said you could go."

"You can't order me about like some field hand." His voice was hard and cold.

"I can as long as you're in my employ."

"Then consider me in your employ no longer." He swung the door open, went through, then slammed it shut behind him.

I slumped back in the chair, my body quivering with an impotent rage which soon gave way to tears. Some time passed before I regained my composure.

I made a pretense of studying the facts and figures Michael had brought me. But my brain comprehended none of it. For two reasons I couldn't bear the thought of losing Michael. I could never operate the mines and farms by myself. And I loved the man. Why did I let pride overcome my better judgment? Michael was right. I was a silly young girl. I should have been able to handle the situation as a mature adult, and not let anger color my words.

I got up and peered around the room, trying to think of a way to mend matters. When I tried to think of a way to preserve my pride, I realized there was none. Michael was too stubborn to come to me. I would have to go to him and apologize. But I would not humble myself. I could be stubborn, too.

Wrapping my heavy merino cloak about me, I left the manor and took the shortcut through the trees to Michael's cottage, praying he would be there. If he had gone somewhere else, time would harden the split between us. An apology must be tended quickly, before the argument became overblown in our minds.

Autumn winds scattered the colorful leaves as I walked between the trees. I mentally rehearsed what I would say to Michael. My apology wasn't shaping up the way I intended. I slowed my pace to gain more time to think.

A particularly pretty leaf caught my eye. I absently stooped to pick the leaf up. I was halfway down when I heard it. It reminded me of the sound of Rico's whip as it slashed through the air. I quickly looked up to see the point of an arrow embedded in a tree, its shaft still quivering.

I stood erect and looked around. Nothing except the trees filtering the sun's rays. I moved to view the area from a different angle. Another arrow sped my way. I suddenly realized that if it was a poacher, I was the prey.

I started to run a zigzag course through the trees toward Michael's cottage. I stopped to see if anyone was behind me. That was a mistake. An arrow cut through the right shoulder of my merino cloak. I ran with greater speed, not caring about the branches that snapped about me. Even when a bare twig caught at my hair, I kept running, as bits of my hair were plucked from my scalp.

I was relieved when Michael's cottage came into view. I sprinted toward it. Fortunately the door was unlocked. I thrust it open unceremoniously, crying, "Michael . . . Michael . . ." at the top of my lungs.

It soon became evident that no one was in the cottage. I locked the front door, then dashed to the back door and locked that. I went back into the parlor and picked up the poker resting in the fireplace. It wasn't much of a weapon, but it gave me some solace.

I huddled against the unlighted fireplace and listened. The utter stillness helped ease the tension in me. I was almost completely relaxed when I saw the front door's latch being jiggled. I clutched the poker tighter. My body stiffened when the banging on the door commenced. The din echoed through the cottage like drums of doom, shattering my nerves. When the pounding ceased, it was replaced by the pounding of my heart.

A new sound bounced into the parlor. The rattling of the back door's knob. The crashing of glass caused me to jump. I dropped the poker and darted to the front door.

My shaking hands fumbled with the lock. Finally I managed to push the key in far enough to unlock it. As I opened the door and poised to flee, a heavy hand came down on my shoulder.

Twenty-Three

I closed my eyes and swallowed hard. I took a deep breath, opened my eyes, and turned around to see a bewildered Michael standing before me. I actually threw myself into his arms.

"You're trembling, Jennifer. What happened?" he asked, holding me tightly and stroking my loose hair.

I stammered and sputtered, unable to speak coherently.

"Come. Sit down. I'll make us a pot of tea. I'm sure you could use a cup." Michael led me to the settee, then left to make tea while I removed my cloak.

I took deep breaths to calm the trembling deep within me. I chastized myself for acting like a frightened idiot. Everything was all right now that Michael was here. Or was it? Was he the one in the woods? Was he so angry with me, he wished me dead? Now I really was being an idiot. If he had wanted me dead, he never would have held me with such warm tenderness.

He returned and placed the tea service on the low table in front of the settee, then sat down beside me. I poured. After a sip or two of the hot tea, I related the events which occurred in the forest.

"Did you see who it was?" he asked.

"No."

"Perhaps it was a poacher. There's been a lot of it going on lately."

"There's no doubt in my mind that those arrows were meant for me." I reached over to the arm of the settee, where I had tossed my cloak. I shifted it around until I found the tear in the right shoulder. "See."

He ran his finger over the tear. "It could have been made by an arrow."

"What do you mean 'could have'? Don't you believe me, Michael?"

"Yes, I do, Jennifer. Why did you lock the doors? I always leave them open."

"I thought the person with the arrows was still after me. I became more frightened when you started banging on the door. Why didn't you call out?"

"I thought I might have inadvertantly locked myself out. I didn't want to appear foolish by talking to an empty house. By the way, what were you doing in the woods?"

"I was coming to see you and apologize. We both know I can't manage the estate without you."

"I'm flattered. Was there any other reason?"

"None that I can think of." Pride caused me to fib. I'd be utterly demoralized if he laughed at a declaration of my love for him.

"Finish your tea and I'll take you home," he said grimly.

I did as he requested. He helped me don my cloak and we left the cottage.

"I think it's best we take the road this time, even though it's longer," he suggested.

A strange silence hung between us as we leisurely strolled down the road toward Wyndcliffe's driveway. Michael was the first to speak.

292

"Aside from your falling down the mine shaft and this incident, has anything else unusual happened to you?"

I related the episode of the acid.

"You must realize by now that someone is trying to harm you, Jennifer."

I laughed aloud. It was a pleasant feeling to be able to laugh freely. "I would say it is pretty obvious. I even suspect it is the same person who killed Grandfather and Uncle Cecil. What I can't understand is, why I haven't been dispatched as they were. Why these piddling attempts?"

"Perhaps they don't want you dead. What you've been through would make anyone else want to get away from Wyndcliffe. It seems they want to frighten you."

"Why?"

"I wish I knew, Jennifer. I don't mean to scare you, but only your death makes any sense to me. If dead, your relatives would stand to inherit everything. Greed is a very strong reason to murder someone."

"But I'm not dead, only frightened half the time. What would my being scared gain them?"

"I don't know."

"Perhaps there is an alternative motive." I told him the story of what I had done to Binky when we were children.

He laughed. "You were quite a terror as a child. Binky is aimless, shiftless, and not very smart. I can't see him going to the trouble of building a false cover over the mine shaft. Your Aunt Lydia is cut from another cloth. I wouldn't put anything past her, or her pasty-faced daughter."

"You don't like any of them, do you, Michael?"

"No, I don't. Leeches. All of them. I watched how they drank your grandfather's best whiskey and brandy, order and eat the richest of foods. Never once did any of them offer to pay for a thing, or lift a finger to help with the work. Your grandfather should have made them stand on their own two feet a long time ago. He was too softhearted for his own good."

"You liked Grandfather, didn't you, Michael?"

"Yes, I did, in spite of everything."

"In spite of what? Did he mistreat you?"

"Oh, no. He treated and trusted me like a son. My father was bitter about our family's loss of Wyndcliffe. He instilled that bitterness in me when I was young. It soon dissipated when I went to work for your grandfather and came to know him. Besides, too much time has passed to keep kindling resentment."

"I agree with you for a change."

He smiled down at me. "I'm pleased to know we can agree on occasion."

"There was a time I felt quite bitter toward Frank Boothe, for taking me into his house without contacting the police or trying to find my relatives. That man used me cruelly. But being with the Gypsies changed my mood, temper, and general outlook on life."

"Don't tell me you don't harbor a trace of resentment toward the man." A sly smile crept across Michael's face.

"I don't. I realize that Frank Boothe was a man who worked hard all his life, and all he had to show for it was ignorance and poverty. He had nothing to look forward to except more drudgery. He was more to be pitied than hated."

We chatted amiably, neither mentioning the earlier argument, and it was assumed Michael would still manage the estate. During our walk I was bathed in happiness. Michael seemed to be the man I had first met.

*   *   *

All Hallow's Eve had arrived. My hands had healed quite nicely, and I was thankful. Edith had procured my blouse from the seamstress and the gold bracelets from the jeweler in Penzance.

After a hot bath scented with lemon verbana, I insisted on dressing myself. I donned my chemise and six petticoats, then tossed the white cotton blouse over my head. The blouse was a perfect replica of a Gypsy's—off the shoulder with short, puffed sleeves. I tucked the blouse into my dark merino skirt. Edith brushed my coppery hair until it shone, then tied it back with a ribbon. While she did the clasp of my locket, I put my golden-hooped earrings on. I divided the bracelets between my wrists, then stuck my feet into dancing slippers.

"How do I look, Edith?" I asked, as I twirled about the bedchamber.

"Like the day you first came here, Miss Jennifer, only your skin is much whiter now."

"Good."

Everyone was waiting in the foyer for me. Binky was dressed as a pirate, replete with black patch over one lens of his eyeglasses. A shiny sword hung from his waistband. Aunt Lydia wore a chambermaid's outfit. I couldn't understand why she chose that particular costume, except that it was mostly black. It seemed she had a proclivity for dark clothes.

Uncle Nigel wore his black evening dress with a blue satin slash diagonally placed over his white shirt, a few medals were pinned on the sash. He looked the picture of a proper English diplomat.

Amanda and Annabel were decked out in what might pass for elaborate gowns of princesses. Amanda's gown was a subdued pink. She had pearls around her neck and dangling from her ears. Her hair was piled atop her head with a coronet of artificial flowers circling her dark brown hair. I thought she looked quite fetching.

Aunt Joyce and Annabel almost looked like cartoons from *Punch*. Annabel's princessy gown was a garish yellow. She was ladened with all sorts of sparkling jewelry, including a tiara on her head. I thought she looked comic, but Amanda kept tossing her glances of envy mingled with anger.

I suppose Aunt Joyce wanted to be thought of as a fairy queen. The gauzy material of her gown and the wand in her hand brought me to that conclusion. I couldn't help but wonder what the servants thought of our motley group.

I rode in the carriage with Aunt Joyce and Annabel. Aunt Joyce rattled on about her various ailments, while Annabel wondered aloud who would be there and how she hoped Jason would find her delectable. All I worried about was Michael showing up. I would find the ball dull indeed if he wasn't there.

Through the quickening darkness, we could see Foxhill Grange loom before us. A giant building was silhouetted against a charcoal and pale pink sky. A shudder ran through me, as I recalled Michael's warning about All Hallow's Eve.

The ground floor was ablaze with light. Carriages lined the driveway. The three of us put our eyemasks on. Mine was dark green, Annabel's yellow, and Aunt Joyce's white.

Jason, costumed as a harlequin, was in the foyer greeting his guests when we entered.

"You look exquisite, Annabel," Jason said, taking her hands in his.

"Do I really?" Annabel gushed.

"Decidedly." He turned to me. "No matter what you wear, Jennifer, you are a most beautiful young woman."

296

"Thank you, Jason."

"I do hope you'll do us the honor of dancing for us. I made sure the violinist knew some Gypsy airs."

"How did you know I would come as a Gypsy, Jason?"

"Gossip between servants. You will dance, won't you?"

"I'd be delighted." Already my eyes were straying to the great ballroom in search of Michael. I was relieved when the Lamberts arrived and occupied Jason's attention.

I padded around the ballroom and quickly came to the conclusion that Michael wasn't there. Unobtrusively, I strolled across the foyer to the dining room, where a large buffet held an assortment of various delectable foodstuffs. Liquid refreshment flowed copiously. Waiters were carrying trays of champagne into the ballroom.

I filled a small plate and nibbled while studying the various characters in the dining room. Some of the costumes were ingenious. My heart tripped when I saw *him*. No one could mistake the potent, masculine figure of Michael Savage. He wore a white shirt open at the neck, with billowy sleeves so characteristic of Lord Byron, the poet. His tight black breeches were tucked into polished knee-high boots. A black mask was over his eyes, but his ebony eyes were unmistakable. When he spied me, he came my way.

"Now you are the Jennifer I remember best, or should I call you Esmeralda?"

"Esmeralda for tonight only."

"Can I get you something to drink?"

"I'd love a cup of strong coffee, but I guess I'll have to settle for punch."

"There's champagne," Michael said.

I shook my head. "Nothing strong."

297

He returned with my punch. "Have you seen his lordship?"

"Yes. He's the harlequin." I put my empty plate on a side table and took the proffered glass of punch.

"A perfect costume for a buffoon," he commented. "I hope you will do me the honor of the first dance this evening, Esmeralda."

"Of course, Michael. Do you know any of the people here?"

"I have a good idea who most of them are. Would you care to meet some of them?"

I nodded and drained my glass, then put the empty glass on my plate. We ambled around the dining room, as Michael introduced me to several people. Most were surprised finding one so young the owner of the Wyndcliffe estates. We moved on to the ballroom, Michael cupping my arm possessively.

We were discussing the crops with an elderly and corpulent gentleman when the music started. Michael excused us and swept me onto the floor to the lilting strains of a waltz. He was a masterful dancer and, even though I had never waltzed before, I had no trouble following his lead.

As he whirled me around the floor, I knew what heaven must be like. His eyes were filled with warmth as he smiled down at me. Michael was wrong. All Hallow's Eve was going to be splendid, without any reason to be wary.

Annabel, in Jason's arms, twirled by us. Jason smiled and nodded to us. Annabel only had eyes for Jason, a supercilious smile on her face.

I would have been content to dance with Michael all night, but propriety demanded a number of dancing partners. I consoled myself with the knowledge that I would dance the last dance of the evening with Michael.

Binky insisted I do the scottish with him. He was a vigorous, if not light-footed, dancer.

"Let's get something to drink," Binky suggested when the dance was over.

We repaired to the dining room, where I got a glass of punch and Binky opted for champagne.

"Quite a spread," he said, waving a hand over the long buffet. "I wonder what all this cost Jason. I daresay a pretty penny."

"Your sister looks lovely tonight," I commented.

"Amanda can look presentable if she wants to. Unfortunately, she seldom wants to," Binky said languidly. "Well, it will soon be the new year, and we'll be out on our arses. I wonder what Father will do. He had hoped to marry Amanda off to Jason, assuring all of us a home and income for life."

"What makes you think he won't get his wish, Binky?"

"Look over there." He nodded.

Jason and Annabel, balancing plates of food in their laps, were having a tête-à-tête. Jason seemed to be doing most of the talking, as Annabel offered squeaky giggles at certain intervals.

"That doesn't mean he is going to marry her, Binky."

"He's getting close to asking. I've seen the signs before."

"What will you do, Binky?"

"When?"

"When you have to leave Wyndcliffe."

"Aren't you going to be magnanimous, Jennifer, and let us live out our lives at Wyndcliffe?" Though he tried to make light of the suggestion, his eyes reflected a seriousness that was almost deadly.

"I don't think that would be wise, Binky. And it's not what Grandfather wished. I'm sure the solicitor will make sure the will is carried out. Besides, I might marry one day and have a family of my own to fill Wyndcliffe."

"Why don't you marry me? That would solve all our problems."

"The offer flatters me, but I respectfully turn it down."

"Then I shall have to continue my quest."

"What quest?" A smile formed on my lips and laughter glinted in my eyes.

"The quest for a rich young lady. Or old. Or widowed. I've been scanning the prospects here and have come up with a possibility. She's very rich, but oh so ugly."

"There is another alternative."

"What?"

"Take a position."

"How droll! I have no conception of how to work for a living. There's even another alternative.

"Do away with you, my dear cousin. As the will states, if you went on to that grandest of rewards, the estate would come to us."

I kept the smile on my face, but my innards quaked. My death would solve any and all problems the Lamberts and Melvilles might have. Was Binky the one shooting arrows at me in the woods? I was about to ask him about his prowess with bow and arrow, when he drained his champagne and spoke.

"Well, I'd better go and find Miss Ugly. As they say 'a bird in the hand is worth two in the bush.' I suppose I can always stare at her hands. Ta-ta, Jennifer."

I was so immersed in the thought that the Lamberts or Melvilles might do away with me, that when a hand rested on the small of my back, I jumped.

"Forgive me, Jennifer. I didn't mean to startle you," Jason said with a smile.

"My mind was elsewhere, I'm afraid. I thought you

were with Annabel."

"I was. She deserted me to refresh herself. Are you prepared to dance your Gypsy dance?"

"Of course."

"Good. I've been boasting to everyone how I've secured a Gypsy to dance for us."

His offered me his crooked arm. I took it, and he led me into the ballroom and left me in the middle of the cleared floor. He signaled the violinist, who left the dias and joined me. He commenced a popularized version of Gypsy music. It was quite danceable. I untied my ribbon and boldly tossed it to a male bystander. Once I began the wild dance, I became lost in the spirit of it. I imagined I was back at the Gypsy camp, with Carla and Zorina clapping for me. As usual Rico was staring at me moodily.

When I finished, the applause was gratifying. The men stared at me lustily. I looked for the one face whose expression I most wanted to see.

Michael was standing alone at the entrance to the ballroom. To my dismay, his arms were folded across his chest, his hands not clapping. He bore the same moody expression that Rico had always given me.

"Encore!" someone shouted.

I shook my head and padded off the dance floor, where Aunt Lydia accosted me.

"How disgraceful, Jennifer Hardwicke! How dare you shame us all like that! If Wyndcliffe Manor were mine—as it should have been—I would send you packing at once. To think my daughter lives under the same roof as a hoyden like you."

"It won't be for much longer, Aunt Lydia. I believe you're due to leave at the beginning of the new year." I was tired of her holier-than-thou attitude. I neither wanted nor needed someone upbraiding me for everything I did.

"Well, I never! No snip of a girl is going to sass me, young lady. It's time you were taught some manners."

"By who?" I felt rebellious. Aunt Lydia had a way of riling me. Perhaps I was upset because Michael didn't show enthusiasm for my dancing. I started to walk away, but Aunt Lydia grabbed my arm. "Let go of me."

"Don't you ever turn your back on me, Jennifer Hardwicke, or I'll—"

"You'll what?" I interrupted, and yanked my arm free just as Uncle Nigel joined us.

"Nigel, this snip is being most disrespectful to me, because I spoke my mind about that horrible dance of hers," Aunt Lydia complained.

"Horrible? It was positively scandalous! She had the men leering at her in a most suggestive manner. Annabel is in tears, because Jason couldn't take his eyes off Jennifer." He turned to me. "We'll have to do something about you, Jennifer, before we become the laughingstock of Cornwall."

"As you soon will be leaving Cornwall, I am not your concern." I lifted my chin in defiance.

"How could you, Jennifer?" Annabel strutted up to us, dabbing a lace-edged handkerchief at the corners of her eyes. "I think Jason was going to ask me to marry him tonight. Now all he talks about is you. You're a dreadful, dreadful person, Jennifer. I hate you. Your coming back to Wyndcliffe has spoiled everything for all of us. I wish you were dead!"

"I don't think you're the only one," I said dryly. Aunt Lydia glared at me with icy eyes. "This is ridiculous," I said aloud, then marched away.

I intended to look for Michael and ask him to take me home. On second thought, why should I leave? I was not ashamed of the way I danced. I thought I was rather good. No. I would stay and enjoy what was left of the evening. Besides, I looked forward to having the last dance with Michael.

But I did need to refresh myself first. I went into the foyer and headed for the wide staircase. I was stopped by a liveried servant who I presumed was Jason's butler.

"Can I help you, Miss?" he asked.

"I was going upstairs to refresh myself."

"We have prepared a room downstairs for that purpose, Miss. I'll show you the way."

"I'd prefer to go upstairs." I wanted some privacy to collect myself. I was sure the one downstairs would be crowded.

"I'm sorry, Miss. No one is allowed upstairs."

I let him show me the way to the room downstairs, wondering why no one was allowed upstairs. The more I thought about it, the more curiosity nagged at me.

When I finished, I didn't return to the foyer. Instead, I investigated the rear quarters of Foxhill Grange. Everything seemed in order. Most of the doors were locked. Only the library door was open.

I went back into the corridor and shrugged. I tried to tell myself I shouldn't be nosing around Jason's house. On the other hand, Jason made free use of Wyndcliffe Manor. Why shouldn't I explore Foxhill Grange a little? He was always bragging about it, and stressing how he wanted me to see it. What was upstairs that Jason didn't want anyone to see? I asked myself, then answered my own question. Jason probably didn't want a lot of people tramping about up there, perhaps breaking priceless objects. Some of the gentlemen were becoming quite tipsy.

I was about to rejoin the other guests, when I spied a dark, narrow staircase, which I presumed was for the servants. All was dark in that section of the corridor, and the staircase would have been missed if one wasn't studying the surroundings as closely as I was. I padded

303

toward the staircase like a naughty child about to stick her finger into a plum pudding.

With no one around, I lifted my skirts and slowly proceeded up the staircase toward a dim, flickering light. At the top of the stairs an oil lamp sat on a crude wooden table. The flame sputtered erractically. I turned the wick up and was rewarded with a good steady light.

The corridor was narrow, with doors which I soon discovered were linen closets. Once away from the service area, the corridor widened. I couldn't understand why all was in darkness. At least one or two small wall lamps should have provided some light. Even a dim light would be better than none. How did the servants find their way around?

Coming to a large door, I cast my gaze to the area between the bottom of the door and the floor. No light, not even a faint one. I took a deep breath and slowly opened the door. I stepped in, holding the oil lamp high above me.

My mouth fell agape. The room was empty! Totally devoid of furniture. Not even a drape or a curtain at the windows. Dust and cobwebs were everywhere. I examined two other rooms, only to find them in the same condition as the first one.

As my investigations led me down the corridor, I came to a turn from which quivered a hazy light. I poked my head around the corner and the bright light dazzled me. Once my vision adjusted to the sudden light, I could see I was on the verge of entering a long hall, which served as a landing for the staircase and overlooked the foyer. I slipped to the other side, so I could peer down at the foyer. I had to see the other side of the manor house. Perhaps Jason cut off one wing and used the other wing for living purposes. After all, why should an entire floor be maintained, when only

Jason inhabited Foxhill, especially as he was away most of the time.

People were milling about the foyer, some going to the dining room, some to the ballroom. I looked longingly at the other side, where more darkness prevailed. I had to find a way to cross the landing without being seen. I had a feeling that the butler wouldn't hesitate to come after me and bodily drag me down the stairs in full view of everyone. That would really set Aunt Lydia's teeth to grinding.

Suddenly my sojourns with Carla came to mind. With a smile, I remembered how we used to sneak up on a farmer's vegetable garden.

Placing the oil lamp in front of me on the floor, I got down on my hands and knees. I began to inch my way across the landing, gently pushing the oil lamp in front of me. Ages seemed to pass as I crawled. My heart thumped loudly, as I expected someone to see me at any minute. But I made it across without mishap.

The corridor was as dark as the other one, not even a glimmer of light. Surely Jason's living quarters and bedchamber were in this section. Perhaps every lamp had been put to use for the ball.

I began opening doors. Nothing but dismal and empty rooms. I frowned. Why was this entire floor so desolate and barren? I didn't dare stand there and ponder the question. I had been gone quite a while, and soon someone would wonder where I was.

I assumed one side of the house was like the other, and began to seek out the servant's staircase. Once on the ground floor, I could always claim I had lost my way and no one would suspect I had been upstairs. At least I hoped they wouldn't.

As expected there was a servant's staircase. At the top where I stood was a similar wooden table. I set the oil lamp down on it and quietly made my way down to the bottom, where I found myself in a quandry. I was facing two doors. I opened one to reveal a staircase leading down belowground. I certainly didn't want to go any farther down. The obvious choice was the other door, even though I had no idea where it led.

My hand was trembling as I reached for the knob. A sense of dread came over me. For a moment I thought it might be best if I went back upstairs and returned the way I came. But I was leery about being caught on the landing this time. I didn't want to press my luck. I turned the knob and opened the door.

Light from the ballroom skimmed vaguely over a rectangular and open area, causing shadows to eerily dance over what appeared to be a courtyard, much like a Roman atrium. A strange aura cloaked the court. A stench of rot and decay assailed my sense of smell. What once must have been a beautiful courtyard with numerous flower beds and marble statues was now overgrown with noxious weeds. The statues were chipped and begrimed. Confined to the ground floor, one would never know the horrid neglect of Foxhill Grange.

Thoroughly shaken, all I wanted was to get back into the well-lighted rooms and be surrounded by people. I spied a door directly across the courtyard. Judging from its position, I was sure it opened underneath the main staircase in the foyer. Perfect, I thought. I started across the courtyard, whose stone paths were covered with lichen, moss, and fungus.

I heard my grandfather's voice ringing in my ears and saying, "Run . . . run . . . run." I stopped and shook my head to clear it.

When I looked up, I saw the glint of a butcher knife over my head. I was about to scream, when a hand clamped firmly over my mouth.

Twenty-Four

There was no sense in trying to kick my assailant or stomp on his foot. With only my dancing slippers on, I would hurt myself more than him. But Gypsy life had prepared me for any contingency.

Simultaneously, I bit down hard on the hand over my mouth and thrust my elbow into the ribs of my attacker. I heard the knife clatter to the ground and started to run toward the door. My assailant was swifter. He grabbed my arm and spun me around with such force, I stumbled to the ground.

He looked down at me, a diabolical smile on his face. As I started to get to my feet, he reached down and grabbed a fistful of my loose hair. He pushed me back down and started to drag me by the hair. I had to use both hands to hold the hair between my scalp and where he had hold of it, to ease the pain. I tried to impede his progress by dragging my feet, but with dancing slippers on, I couldn't dig my heels in anywhere.

He was dragging me to the center of the courtyard, I began screaming, hoping someone would hear me. He stopped for a second to kick me in the head. The point of his toe caught me in the temple, dazing me. I didn't dare risk another scream, lest he kick me harder and cause me to pass out. I needed my wits about me. As long as there was life left in me, I had a chance to save myself.

"Why are you doing this to me?" I asked hoarsely, as we reached the center of the courtyard.

"You have spoiled everything. All my hopes. All my plans. Once you're dead, I can start to live again."

"Is it money you want? I'll give you money."

"Stand up."

"No."

"You want your head kicked in? Perhaps that would suit you better."

He twisted my hair more tightly around his hand. I saw his foot move back for a swift kick. "No," I cried. "I'll get up." I moved slowly, my mind desperately seeking a solution to my predicament.

I was in front of an old fountain. The water in it was coated with green slime, and looked thick with algae.

"Perhaps this is the better solution. No blood." He began to force my head into the rank water.

I braced my hands on the edge of the fountain and resisted with every ounce of strength in me. But he was stronger. I thought my neck would snap under the strain. With his sudden shove of brute strength, my elbows buckled and the tip of my nose touched the fetid water.

Seeing his goal almost accomplished renewed his strength. An intensely powerful shove put my head under the water. I fought with vehement desperation. My arms thrashed about, trying to claw at his hands. I couldn't hold my breath much longer.

"Grandfather . . . Grandfather . . ." I repeatedly screamed in my head, as though I could conjure up his presence by wishing it.

The pain in my lungs was becoming unendurable. My mind was dimming. I could no longer think. When I felt all was at an end, the hands holding my head under the water were gone, and my head was swiftly pulled from the water.

With hands resting on the rim of the fountain, my hair and face dripping with slimy water, I took in great gulps of air until my head cleared.

Finally I turned to see what had happened. With his mask off, Michael extended his arms and I rushed into them.

"Are you all right, Jennifer?" he asked softly.

"I am now. Oh, Michael, get me out of here and take me home."

"I will shortly. I've sent for the constable. We must wait until he gets here."

"Out here? With *him?*"

"I'm afraid so. You can go back in if you wish."

"Like this? No. Besides, I feel safer out here with you, Michael. What if he wakes up before the constable gets here?"

"I doubt if he will. I hit him quite hard."

"How did you find me?"

"I started looking for you when they commenced the last dance of the evening. I searched the entire ground floor. I tried to search upstairs, but was told no one was allowed up there. I was about to go anyway, but was impeded by the butler and three brawny men. It came to me that you might have decided to go outside for some air. I looked out the front door, but you were nowhere in sight. Then I remembered that there was a courtyard at Foxhill. After a short search, I found the door under the staircase. The dim light couldn't mask the gaudy costume of the harlequin. I pulled your head out of the water, and pulled him off you at the same time."

"Fortunately, just in time. Oh, Michael, what is happening?"

"I suspect we'll soon find out. What were you doing out here?"

"Jason was always talking about showing me Foxhill Grange. When the butler wouldn't let me upstairs, I thought it strange and became curious." I went on to tell Michael of the desolation I found upstairs.

"Indeed, that is strange. This is the first time I've been to Foxhill Grange since I was a lad, when Jason's parents were still alive. My mother collected old clothes for the church. I remember Lady Fox, Jason's mother, taking us upstairs, where she went through her closets. To make a long story short, I was dazzled by the opulence we saw. I assumed it was still the same."

"Well, it's not. It has been stripped bare." I pushed my wet hair away from my cheek. "Michael, I really must wash my face and hands. I feel all sticky and slimy."

"There's a washroom down the corridor on your right. I best stay here until the constable comes."

I went through the door I originally was headed for. It did open under the staircase. Down the corridor a little way was the room converted to a lavatory. I looked in the mirror and almost frightened myself. I looked like an ogre out of a fairy tale.

I washed my hands and face, then did what I could with my hair, finishing by pouring the rest of the water over it. I dried my face, then rubbed my hair with one of the large towels until it was dampish. When I left, Michael was waiting for me outside the lavatory door.

"I can hardly wait until I get home and have a proper bath," I said. "I look a fright."

"You look fine to me. The constable, Sergeant Thompson, and two uniformed policemen have ar

rived. They are in the library and sent me to fetch you."
He cupped my elbow and steered me toward the
library.

Lord Jason Fox sat in a straight-backed chair
looking dazed. Constable Morgan was puffing on his
pipe, while Thompson had his notebook and pencil at
the ready.

"Ah! You've found her, Mr. Savage. Miss Hardwicke, I thought you would wish to hear what this
scoundrel has to say, so I deferred the questioning until
you were present."

"Thank you, Constable. I am most anxious to hear
his explanations."

"We have already ascertained that he killed your
grandfather, the young lad, and Cecil Melville. Now
for the reasons behind all this murderous mayhem."
The constable turned to face Jason. "Now, Lord Fox,
would you care to tell us why you murdered all these
people? And why you attempted to kill Miss Hardwicke this evening?"

"I would not." Jason glared at me, hatred spewing
from his eyes. "I want my solicitor here."

I slumped in an armchair. Michael perched on one
of its arms.

"I can understand your position, Lord Fox. But as
you have already admitted to the murders, and Mr.
Savage having caught you in the act, so to speak, I
think it is to your advantage to tell us everything now,"
the constable urged.

"I didn't know what I was saying earlier. I was in a
daze from the beating that brute inflicted on me."
Jason nodded in Michael's direction.

"Come, come, Lord Fox. The more you delay, the
harder it will be for you once we have you down at the
station. We have a cell down there where the men—
who have been waiting for a solicitor and a trial date—

haven't seen a woman in some time. They are rather brutish men. I'm sure they would welcome a handsome young man such as yourself." The constable gave Jason a wicked smile.

Jason paled, his ashen lips twitching. "You wouldn't. I'm a peer of this land."

"I'm a very perverse man when I don't get my way, Lord Fox. I might be inclined to deem it the only cell available. On the other hand, if you cooperate, I might find we have a single cell for you. Do you wish to enlighten us now?"

Jason's lower lips trembled. He stared blankly at some unseen object. He had to clear his throat twice before he began.

"Mr. Hardwicke had found out I was forging his name on checks from his checkbook, and he threatened to expose me. Things were bad enough. I couldn't afford a scandal."

"You had access to his checkbook?" The constable's eyebrows shot up.

"Everyone had access to that checkbook. He never locked it away. At first he thought it was Nigel Lambert. But then he caught me tearing a check out. Before he had a chance to contact the authorities, Jennifer arrived. He told me he was going to postpone the disclosure for a few days, while he enjoyed the return of his granddaughter. Then he would see I was punished to the full extent of the law."

"What were you doing at Wyndcliffe that fateful day?"

"I was about to start courting Miss Annabel Melville. When Jennifer arrived, I knew the old man would make a new will. Killing him would prevent any new will, and would also keep him from exposing me. I expected him to send for his solicitor, not make out the new will on the day Jennifer arrived."

"I'm surprised Mr. Hardwicke let you into his rooms. How did you manage that?"

"I told him I wanted to make restitution for the forged checks."

"Why didn't you, instead of committing murder?"

"I didn't have any money."

"You could have sold the grange."

"Foxhill Grange was heavily mortgaged. My father was a poor estate manager, and my mother had a penchant for spending. When they died the debts were enormous. I had to mortgage the place to pay off all their debts, with enough left over to continue my way of life." The bitterness in Jason's voice was almost palpable.

"And the young lad?"

"I heard Jennifer was nosing about the checks. Sooner or later she would find the lad, and he'd tell her I was the one sending him to the vendors to cash the checks. He'd tell her everything for half a crown. I had to stop him."

"And Cecil Melville?" the constable continued.

"He caught me dumping the lad's body and started blackmailing me. I was in no position to keep paying him. By then, it was getting easier to solve my problems by murder."

Constable Morgan went to the desk and tapped his pipe on an ashtray, the ashes of tobacco gently falling out. "Why Miss Hardwicke? She was no threat to you."

"When I heard the contents of the new will, I decided to court her instead of Annabel Melville. She was more desirable than either of the other young women. Though I have a persuasive way with the ladies, I couldn't get through to Jennifer. She was having none of me. When I caught the way she gazed at Savage, I knew I would never conquer her. I was in a quandry, when Mrs. Joyce Melville suggested that if Jennifer

313

was out of the way, all her problems would be solved. It put an idea into my head. With Jennifer dead, the Melvilles would have half the estate. Mrs. Melville also assured me she would put no obstacles in my way if I were to marry Annabel. The notion germinated in my head until it became the only possible solution."

"May I ask a question, Constable Morgan?" I was stunned by Jason's confession.

"Certainly, Miss Hardwicke."

"Why the open mine shaft at Botallack? Why the cat? Why the acid and arrows in the woods, Jason?"

He wouldn't or couldn't look at me. He continued to stare straight ahead.

"I wanted to frighten you into believing you needed a husband to protect you. I hoped that you would turn to me."

"How did you manage that heavy cover over the mine shaft by yourself?" Michael interjected.

"A simple task of leverage and the brute strength of a sturdy horse." Bitterness tinged Jason's voice.

"I could have been killed, Jason," I said.

He turned and stared out the window without comment.

"You are a ghoulish piece of humanity, Lord Fox," the constable said, shaking his tonsured head. "Take him away, men, before I change my mind about a private cell." He addressed me next. "You'll be available for the trial, won't you, Miss Hardwicke?"

"Of course."

"Mr. Savage?"

Michael nodded.

I got up from the chair. "Is it all right if I leave now, Constable Morgan?"

"Yes. You must be anxious to get home after tonight's experience."

"I am."

314

Once in the foyer, Michael said, "I'm afraid everyone has left. I have a carriage. I'll take you home."

"Thank you." We remained buried in our own musing for the greater part of the drive back to Wyndcliffe. I had a thought and voiced it aloud. "I wonder if the constable is going to do anything about Aunt Joyce. After all, she was the one who put the thought into Jason's head and practically urged him on."

"I don't think he'll charge her formally. Even Jason didn't accuse her of being involved. She only voiced her thoughts aloud. She certainly had nothing to do with the other murders. We'll have to wait and see what happens at the trial. Good night, Jennifer," Michael said, as the driver brought the carriage to a halt before the entrance to Wyndcliffe Manor.

"Good night, Michael." Jerome came out of the house and helped me down from the carriage. He let me precede him inside.

"Has something transpired, Miss Jennifer?"

"Why do you ask, Jerome?"

"Everyone was unduly excited when they came back from the All Hallow's Eve ball."

"It was an exceptional evening, Jerome. You'll hear all about it sooner or later, so I may as well tell you now. I'd rather you hear the truth than innuendos and half-truths."

As I related the events, Jerome's expression hardened but he didn't say a word. I had my hot bath and felt infinitely better. But nightmares peppered my sleep, nightmares of drowning in slimy water.

I awoke late. Late for me, that is. I entered the dining room shortly before ten in the morning. I was surprised to see Uncle Nigel and Binky there. Even more

315

surprised to see Jerome just laying out the breakfast buffet.

Seeing the look on my face, Binky said, "With everyone coming home so late, Jerome didn't start the buffet until we came down. Quite a night, wasn't it, Jennifer? We wormed the whole story out of Jerome."

"Didn't Michael tell you?"

"All Michael said was 'Ride hard and fast for the constable, Binky.' The look on his face told me to do it right away and ask no questions."

"I'm grateful you did. Michael saved my life last night."

"Who'd ever think Jason was a beast at heart. Shocking!" We repaired to the buffet and secured our breakfast. After returning to the table with our ladened plates, Binky said, "Though your night was a horror, Jennifer, I did rather well."

"What do you mean, Binky?"

"Remember me telling you about Miss Ugly?"

I nodded, even though it wasn't my clearest recollection of the evening.

"I spoke to her father, and received his enthusiastic consent to court his only child. With all that money, I don't care how she looks. Besides, I spent quite a bit of time with her last night, and she is rather sweet. I have to admit she has a comely figure. You won't be seeing much of me, I'm afraid. I'll be too busy courting her."

Uncle Nigel cleared his throat. "You won't be seeing us at all, Jennifer."

My eyebrows arched. "Oh?"

"I've taken a position with Holden and Sons, as a representative for their china and crystal in America."

"Are Aunt Lydia and Amanda saddened at leaving?" I asked.

"On the contrary, they're anxious to leave. Lydia is appalled at her sister's involvement in this matter, even

316

though it is slight. She and Annabel can hardly wait to leave here."

"When will you be leaving, Uncle Nigel?"

"In two weeks. Travel arrangements are being made now. Holden and Sons will house us in a New York hotel until we find a place to live."

"Amanda is as excited as she ever gets. She heard there are more single men than women in America," Binky added, then stood, "I must be off a-wooing."

"I must leave for London. So many details to attend to, you know." Uncle Nigel wiped the corners of his mouth on a napkin, then stood.

I finished my breakfast alone. When Jerome came to clear the table, I asked, "Where are the Melvilles, Jerome? They should be down by now."

"Mrs. Melville and her daughter left quite early this morning, Miss Jennifer."

"Left? Where did they go?"

"They didn't say. One of the maids said the Continent was mentioned, and that Miss Annabel kept talking about Paris. I do know they kept three maids busy packing all their belongings, Miss."

"I see. What time did they leave?" I wondered if I should tell the constable.

"Quite early, Miss. The driver has already returned with the carriage. He said they just made the seven o'clock train from Penzance to London."

"Thank you, Jerome." I drained my coffee, then went into the library.

Sitting at the desk, I decided not to notify the constable about Aunt Joyce. If the trains were on time and they made prompt connections, they'd be well on their way to London by now. I strongly doubted if I would ever see them again. With the Lamberts leaving for America, Binky possibly marrying before the end of the year, and the Melvilles no longer at Wyndcliffe, I

317

wondered what I would do with this great big house with only me living in it. I had to think and plan my life. What better place to meditate than Botallack?

I didn't bother to change into a riding habit or don a hat. I put on my cloak and went to the stables, where I pulled my skirt between my legs in the Gypsy manner. The men at the stables were used to my odd behavior and paid no attention.

At Botallack I tethered my mare to a piling and walked to the edge of the promontory. The wind was brisk, causing my reddish gold hair to fan out behind me like a bright banner. I tried to conjure up the spirit of Grandfather, with the hope he would advise me on how to spend my days. But the sea mist remained nothing more than mist. In my heart I knew he was at rest and would never come to me again.

I turned and was about to go back to my horse, when I saw a rider coming fast toward me. With his thick chestnut hair storming about his head, I couldn't mistake Michael Savage. He tethered his horse next to mine and strode toward me.

"When Jerome told me you went riding, I thought you might come here," he said.

"Did you hear about Binky, Uncle Nigel, and the Melvilles?"

"Jerome brought me up to date on everything. Now you'll have some peace at the dinner table."

"I wonder if the bickering might be better than absolute solitude at the dinner table." I turned and gazed at the thundering sea. Michael stood behind me and rested his hands on my shoulders.

"I'll still be around, Jenny."

When he said Jenny, all lost memories came flooding back. My prince was never in a picture book. Michael himself had been the prince of my childhood. He was the one who had rescued me when I got in trouble with

318

the other children. He was the one who had picked me up when I stumbled and fell. He always seemed to be on hand when I needed him. I turned to face him, my eyes brimming with love.

"Michael, will you come back to Wyndcliffe Manor to live?"

"It wouldn't be proper, Jenny. Even Binky is going to find another residence when his family leaves."

My heart beat rapidly as I contemplated a bold, unladylike, and risky move. I gazed up at him and, with trembling hope, asked, "It would be proper if there was a legal bond between us."

He smiled broadly and his hands tightened on my shoulders. "Jennifer Hardwicke, are you suggesting marriage?"

I swallowed hard. "Of course, it would be a marriage of convenience. I wouldn't interfere in your private life. We'd have separate quarters and . . ."

He put a staying finger over my lips, then threw his head back and laughed. "My dear, sweet, little Jenny. I've wanted you for my wife ever since I saw you as a Gypsy, valiantly fighting off those villagers. I fell irrevocably in love with you then, and decided to court you the minute you woke up."

"Oh, Michael, why didn't you tell me sooner?"

"When Dr. Marsh told me you were James Hardwicke's granddaughter, I thought it best to wait and see how things went. When you became sole heiress to the Wyndcliffe estate and Lord Fox entered the picture, I lost hope. I had no title to offer you. Besides, I was afraid you'd think I wanted to marry you to regain the estate. I couldn't bear the thought of you thinking I was a mere fortune hunter. I love you too much for that."

"I've loved you all my life, Michael. I never noticed Jason when you were around."

319

He pushed aside a stray tendril which the wind had blown across my cheek, then pulled me into his arms, his mouth coming down on mine in a searing, probing kiss. As we clung to each other as one, and the kiss became one of urgent desire, I knew ours would never be a marriage of convenience.